Th

XIIIth

Parable

And other Stories

Andrew FM Wilson

This paperback edition published 2021 by Jasami Publishing Ltd
an imprint of Jasami Publishing Ltd
Glasgow, Scotland
https,//jasamipublishingltd.com

ISBN 978-1-913798-45-1

Dedication

For all who inspired these, and many other stories, and of course - for my family.

Jasami Acknowledgements

The Jasami team is integral to the production of all of our titles, as they are talented, creative and hardworking.

Executive Editor
May Winton

Editors
Rafe Petersen
Emma Toft

Marketing - Social Media
Rafe Petersen

Table of Contents

Flipside

Danny

Danny Gilmour sat nervously in the chair and tried his best to look confident and arrogant. The oppressive nature of the office in which he sat made this impossible. He fidgeted again, resisting the impulse to turn round. Where the hell was he?

Brent Thomas, Assistant Director of First National Bank! Yeah, great idea, go ask that pompous fucking prick! thought Danny. He felt rage and humiliation threaten to overwhelm him. He gripped the edges of his chair tightly and felt the wood bite into his hands, the pain helped a bit. He took a sip from the vile coffee that some stiff lipped, pointy chest bitch had brought him. "Hi Mr Gilmour, I'm Simone, if you need anything please let me know."

He remembered something an old friend had said, "Bank's coffee is dependent on your bank account! Overdrawn or low income and you get the machine shit, one of their VIPS and you get the full Italian percolated good stuff!"

Danny smiled to himself, and it diffused his anger somewhat. Another sip and he smiled ruefully. Machine shit, he said to himself. Poetic justice! His business in tatters, wife away with some banker, his house a signature away from repossession and his beloved club depending on this Brent Thomas and his oily, slimy fucking backroom deals!

How did it ever come to this? He angrily slammed the coffee cup back onto the polished mahogany desk just as the glass ornate glass door opened and Brent Thomas strode in with his thousand-pound tailored suit and polished high grade leather shoes. All in all, he was exactly the kind of person Danny hated! He put down his resentment with some difficulty.

"The coffee ok, Danny?" said Thomas with a sickly smile.

Danny returned the smile. Your name in a bank is also determined by your income, No money and it was first name basis, money in the bank and it was all "sir" and "Mr." Danny shook his head to clear it as Thomas sat in his black shiny leather seat, his feet pressing into the luxurious soft pile carpet. He picked up a folder, opened it and took out a single document. With another sickly flash of his whitened teeth to Danny, he began to read it. With furtive looks, occasional sighs and one solemn tut, he finally finished reading. With careful precision and a look of practiced finesse, he placed the paper purposefully on his desk.

Danny stared at him, holding his resentment in check, his hands biting into the wooden arms of the chair

"Mr Gilmour."

Sudden Surname use equals bad news, more corporate parlance! Thought Danny.

"Let me be blunt and to the point, a valued customer such as yourself deserves no less," said Thomas sardonically. "The answer is no."

Danny fell back in his chair, the urge to smack Brent Thomas right on the jaw was intoxicating. "No?" he said softly. "After all the money I made you, all the business I sent your way, and you say no!"

"Danny," began Brent.

"Save it, Brent!" spat Danny. "I've heard it all before! All the bullshit, all the promises, and all your condescending, offending fucking crap!"

"If it wasn't for the Inland Revenue's investigation things may have been different." If Thomas was intimidated, he didn't show it.

"Inland Revenue? After everything that's happened, you bring it all down to the god damn taxman? If anything, it's you and this bank that should be under investigation! I've seen your client list, your associates! I've brought millions of pounds through your door over the years, and you took it all, you blood sucking leech! And now, when I need you, the answer's no? You aspire to be a legitimate and honest business, all the while sullying yourself in the underhanded, backdoor shit you claim to loathe!" Danny jumped to his feet.

"Sit down, Danny!" said Brent forcefully," and stop acting like a schoolboy bully! There are always ways around this!"

"What ways? I need two hundred grand by the end of the month, or you and your god damn bankers take my club! You won't lend me any money and you won't let me access my other funds! Are you totally deluded or what?"

"When I sold you that club, I warned you there could be serious repercussions. Besides, there are other ways to access money." Thomas leaned back in his seat and cleared his throat. With a covert glance he smiled. "You've heard of Karl Ellis I presume?"

Danny looked at him in disbelief. "Karl Ellis? Of course, I have! His brother works for me!"

Brent smiled. "I had heard that didn't believe it myself. Considering Reice's, shall we say 'indiscretion', I didn't think anyone would touch him. Karl's made it quite clear that anyone who works with his brother could consider him an enemy."

"Yeah, well, I figured the chance of me meeting, let alone working with Karl was so remote. And besides, Reice has his uses."

Brent nodded and flashed his overly white teeth. "Well, no matter. Just so happens that Karl Ellis is looking for someone with special connections here in Glasgow. It's for a limited period, a high risk, high reward job. He's been a very close associate of this bank and I personally, have close ties with him."

He smiled a bit too smugly for Danny, who couldn't resist adding, "Like I said, it's you who should be under investigation."

Brent's sardonic smile quickly vanished. "Facetiousness will get us nowhere, Mr Gilmour," he said vehemently. "I have suggested you for Karl's operation and he is very interested in working with you. I have taken the liberty of agreeing your fee of three hundred thousand pounds. That would more than cover the outstanding debt on your precious club and would go somewhat to clearing the arrears on your house. Karl would also arrange for the Inland Revenue investigation to simply 'disappear'."

"You accepted this for me?" said Danny in disbelief. "Where do you get off, Thomas? Jesus Christ! Karl Ellis? What were you thinking?"

"I was thinking you would much rather involve yourself in a short-term, questionable venture than lose your home, your club and, most likely, any chance of ever again sipping that famed wine you are so renowned for. You still have a bottle of Château Moulton-Rothschild 1945 in storage here, I believe."

Danny fell back in his chair and shook his head. "When is this going down and what am I supposed to do?" He sighed deeply. It had come down to this, had it? How had he fallen so far? A name that once opened doors and struck fear throughout the Glasgow Underworld reduced to consorting with London gangster scum; accepting jobs from lurid bankers and political puppets! He felt sick. He felt used and helpless, locked in someone else's game!

Brent Thomas smiled and nodded, accepting his victory. He opened the top drawer of his desk and took out a large brown envelope. He pompously and theatrically slid it over to Danny, who looked at it with scorn.

Well, so be it! He would play their game! Sometimes you have to sow some manure to grow tulips! Someone had said it to him long ago. He couldn't remember who.

Grabbing the envelope from the table, he stared long and hard at Brent Thomas who held onto his sickly smug attitude. Danny felt his resentment grow as he stared. Brent Thomas, Assistant Director, political wannabe, tied to countless politicians, both in Edinburgh and Westminster. Face of charities, of fundraising, of good clean business. If only the people knew the truth.

Yes, he would do it. He would get himself out the shit he had fallen into, he would take Ellis' money and clear this stupid debt with the bank, get the fucking taxman off his back and regain his empire! And then?

Then Brent Thomas, Karl Ellis, and anyone else who thought him the idiot, would pay! They would pay dear, and they would pay long! Danny Gilmour would once again be up there with the elite. He would once more be feared and respected.

Brent Thomas saw only the acceptance in Danny's eyes and he nodded, saying, "Very good, Danny. I'll contact Karl and tell him to expect your call. We'll have this unfortunate business cleared up soon." He stood and extended his hand.

Danny stood and drew himself to his full height. He stared with obvious anger at the expectant hand of Brent Thomas. "My name is Mr Gilmour! Call me Danny once more, you arrogant piece of shit, and I'll rip that handmade silk tie off your neck and hang you with it! I'll not forget this, Thomas! I'll not forget the way you and your fucking associates have treated me! We'll talk real soon, Brent, just the two of us!"

He turned, slammed his chair back under the table and walked to the door, deriving much satisfaction at the look of shock and fear apparent in Brent Thomas' eyes.

Thomas tried to smile as he smoothed his tie and jacket. He sat down in his chair and tried his level best to remain the haughty executive he had been only moments ago. Yet the look in his eyes, the agitated way he tried to sit and, above all, the layer of sweat that began to form on his brow all conspired to reveal the fact that he was not. He cleared his throat and picked up his phone. "It's me. Gilmour's in, I've got them all now. He's desperate and needs this, so it won't be a problem." He laughed then, though there was still the residue of fear apparent in his voice. "The puppets are all in place now. It's only a matter of time."

Danny Gilmour, in contrast, was no longer the worried man he had been. Yes, he would do this job and people would once again fear him. They would remember him, and people would pay!

And you, Brent Thomas! You will pay most of all, you stuck up, pompous, arrogant, cheap bastard!

He clutched the envelope that promised his freedom as he walked from that office a far taller, far wealthier man than the one who had entered it. Passing by the clerk's desk he paused and strolled over to the thin, angular stuffy looking clerk. "Gilmour," he said arrogantly dropping a small envelope on the desk. "Get me my security box."

The clerk hurried from the desk and returned a few moments later. Danny thrust his key in and opened the box. He ignored the many varied items – remnants of his past life, and took from it a bottle of wine carefully wrapped in a red velvet cloth. He removed the cloth and held up the bottle to the surprised clerk. "Ever seen a bottle like that?" he asked.

The clerk shook his head.

"Well, this bottle is worth more than your house, your car and worth more money than you will ever see in your entire miserable career!" He gently placed the bottle back into the box, took out another box, which he opened to reveal a Glock 18 pistol and four magazines. This he kept before he closed the box and thrust in back to the shocked clerk. "Ain't life fucking sweet!" he yelled. With a near frenzied laugh, Danny Gilmour walked from the building without a care in the world.

Reice

The door closed with a slam. Reice Ellis jumped up, fists ready. She stood there, dressed to kill.

"What the fuck?" said Reice, aghast.

She raised a finger to her bright red lips. "Shhh," she said seductively, before pushing him back and then violently shoving him onto the bed.

"Do you have any idea what my fucking psycho of a brother would do to us both?"

She giggled and ripped his shirt open.

Reice threw a hand to his forehead as she began nibbling at his chest. "He'd cut my fucking balls off!" He tried to push her back, but she grabbed his hand and shoved it back against the pillow.

"Jesus fucking Christ!" said Reice. "And as for you… he'd fucking rip your head off!"

He moaned as she pulled at his trousers, smiling seductively He sighed deeply and lost himself in the moment.

Afterwards, she lay on her side, away from him, breathing heavily. Reice on the other hand lay on his back, the worries of the world apparent on his face. His hands were behind his head as he stared at the ceiling. He sighed deeply. His brother's wife? The one woman whom he should never have looked at, and yet he could not ignore the electric pull between them. Others had noticed, of course. Some had laughed at the very suggestion of her and Reice, convinced that even he wouldn't be that stupid. He'd laughed with them. Of course not! All the while it grew stronger between them, more alluring and harder to resist. The casual meetings, the accidental touches, the furtive glances at her, only to discover she was looking at him! It all was too much, it all was too insane and should never, ever have happened!

"I'm a fucking dead man!" he said. She, of course, ignored him or didn't even hear him.

Suddenly the phone rang. Reice aged ten years while she moaned slightly before turning over.

"Hello?" said Reice tentatively. He jumped bolt upright and pathetically tried to pull the covers over himself. "Yeah, I'm here," he said quietly. "What? No… I'm on me fucking own here! Yeah, had a late night, so what?"

Sweat formed on his brow as he looked more and more like a rabbit caught in the headlights. He subconsciously covered her bare shoulder with the duvet. "Yeah, mate. I'll be right there. Give me a fucking minute for fuck's sake, yeah?"

He slammed the phone down and gave her a shove. "Get up! Jesus! I'm a fucking dead man!"

He staggered from the bed and grabbed his trousers, he failed in the first attempt at pulling them over his left leg. She still had not stirred and, in anger, he grabbed a cushion from the chair and threw it at her.

She stirred long enough to throw it back at him.

Reice staggered and then fell into the chair with a look of incomprehension. He ran his fingers through his hair and rubbed his eyes, his heart pounding in his chest as he looked at her lying there. She had turned over onto her front and her naked buttocks glistened with light sweat. She opened her legs slightly and he stared.

His erection was swift and almost painful as he stood and, as though powerless to stop, he made his way over to her. He straddled her and she moaned slightly as he entered her once more. Her hand grasping his thigh as her head turned exposing her velvet soft neck. He kissed her ever so softly. "I love you, Reice" she whispered.

Reice groaned. Why her? Why did it have to be her? "Don't say that! Just..."

"Love, love, love! I love you!"

He thrust in harder as she pulled on his thigh. His orgasm approached and he gasped loudly as she yelled "Yes!"

He fell from her and collapsed on the bed, throwing his hands to his face. "I'm fucking dead!"

Brooks

Steven Brooks sat alone in the small anteroom, waiting. He was trying his level best to remain calm, but his hands sweated so much and his legs trembled. His breathing, when it came, was quick and shaky. His eyes darted left and right, up and down. He rubbed his hands together for the hundredth time.

You're losing it! The voice in his head continued on, mocking him. Look at you! One minute in there and they're all gonna know, Officer!

Brooks clutched at his head, not caring what it revealed. He knew he had fallen, and it was only a matter of time before they realised it. His head hurt from facts, figures, acquaintances, operations and, most of all, from the things they made him do! He had tried for months, years even, to convince himself it was all for the greater good! He was going to show them! He was going to do what no one else had been able to do! So what if he had to skirt close to breaking a few regulations! They would understand in the end! They would realise everything had been necessary. Sure, some people were hurt, but they deserved it (he told himself). They had it coming and had chosen their own destiny.

What about the murders? Are they justified too?

Shut up! Shut up! He yelled inside. I never killed anyone!

Wrong! You never pulled the trigger, never struck with the knife, never gave the mortal blow, but you were there! You never stopped that madman from killing! Where was the police sense of duty there?

Brooks closed his eyes tightly. I had no choice! I had to go along with it, or they would've rumbled me and it would all have been for nothing!

Wrong again! You were scared, Officer! Terrified at what he'd do to you, your moral high ground has nothing to do with this! Besides, you loved it! You were addicted to the highs he gave you!

Addicted to the highs? Me? Brooks jerked involuntarily in his chair. I never once enjoyed what I did! It was pure and simple necessity! The laughter in his head was vicious and long.

And the heroin, the cocaine? Where in your precious Regs does that come into play? You're going to fail their drugs test today and what then? There's no way you can talk yourself out of that one! Line of duty? They'll not hesitate to kick you right out that door and you'll be lucky if they don't convict you right alongside your good friend Ellis!

Brooks groaned softly. The cocaine! Even now it was calling to him! He wanted a hit so much! One more hit, just to get me through this bullshit, then I will quit! I will quit! I will quit! They had to understand! How could he be expected to get through all this without it? The pressure was so intense! It was killing him. He needed a way to get through it and cocaine was it. Temporarily of course, it also served to convince Reice Ellis that he wasn't a cop, that he was really... was really what?

He couldn't even remember his own name! Steven Brooks! A ridiculous made-up down and out computer hacker, a once proud top-level programmer working with the best indicted for cyber fraud and jailed for two years, a cover story that had now become the reality.

Broke, addicted to cocaine and lucky enough to "stumble" upon the recently outcast Reice Ellis, who needed someone of his skills for a number of jobs and to help keep his money moving around the world, and out of the hands of the law. That was how it started, a simple enough undercover job. Then came the insidious aspects, the women, the flash cars, the money, and the highs. All in the line of duty though, that became his way out, what he told himself when his wife began to lose faith and the lines of reality blurred.

"It's only temporary", he told her when he awoke in a strange bed with a strange woman feeling hungover, drugged up and completely wasted. It would only be for a short while, and then he would renew the wedding vows, would arrange a second honeymoon in Florida where she had originally wanted to go.

The pain when it came didn't hurt as much as expected. Was it the drugs, the drink or had he just fallen so far by then that it never really mattered? There were no tears, just deafening silence as she packed her bags and politely asked him which of their shared belongings he wanted to keep. None, he told her. Watching her solemnly pack her clothes and pick up stuff he had bought her and pack it all neatly into boxes, it finally started to hurt. He had kissed her passionately then, more passionately than he had in years. The glass ornament bought for them by her terminally ill mother fell from her hands then shattered on the dark laminate flooring in the living room of their perfect home.

Tears cascaded down her face as her mask slipped. She had tried to grab him to her but, with self-loathing and anger strong in his mind, he had pushed her away, told her to keep the house, keep everything before turning and walking out of her life forever. He barely heard her collapse to the floor in uncontrollable pain and anguish as he shut the door on his home and on his life.

Yet, he felt little. No regret, no love, no fear. There was only duty, only the assignment which must be seen through to the end.

Now, sitting alone after all this time in the police interview room, his life once more hanging in the balance, he began to regret so many of the choices that once had seemed so noble and important to the job. A great sob took him, which he desperately tried to cover up. The tears were frustrating and so inappropriate!

All in the line of duty, said the voice in his head. How hollow are those words now!

A door opened and a tall, uniformed police officer entered. She stood above him. "Officer Wilton? They're ready for you now."

Painfully, Brooks got to his feet. Wilton? Wilton? Who the hell was Officer Wilton? Stephen Wilton no longer existed, perhaps never existed. There was only Steven Brooks, and he had a job to do! Bring it on! He said to himself as he arrogantly walked into the room and faced the four members of his execution squad. Amazing how quickly he could assume the Brooks persona. It was so easy and enticing to be that in control! He shook his head sadly as he read their faces. They had already tried and convicted him.

"Have a seat, Officer Wilton," said one solemn member of the squad that would effectively end his career. A big fat bloater with five chins and pompous eyes. "We have some questions."

The female officer nodded once to the assembled commission before closing the door promptly behind her. Once outside, she smiled ruefully. So long, Wilton, she thought to herself.

Karl

There was near frenzied activity in the house that was used to the most manic comings and goings, and out of which more than one body had been carried and more than a handful of people had left with less limbs or digits than they had entered with. Today was, by normal standards, even more shocking than usual.

It was a notorious house, on the outskirts of Elderslie, Paisley, and belonging as it did to Karl Ellis. One of the most sought-after London underground figures who had latterly made his name north of the border. Despite being linked to some of the most well-known and highly publicised crimes, the Police had never been able to make anything stick to Karl Ellis and he remained a very large and very prominent thorn in the sides of both The Metropolitan and Strathclyde Police forces.

It was nearly two thirty in the morning, and even for this house, there was a large number of vehicles parked outside the main gates, and many more people than normal were scurrying around the house, a few nosy locals who happened to "pass by" were quickly moved on.

A large black series seven BMW slowly pulled up to the main gate, its occupant was hurriedly passed through the increased security and headed toward the front of the house. The driver quickly exited the vehicle and opened the rear passenger door. A very large, very overweight important type got out the car without looking at the driver. He straightened the front of his suit and finished his phone call. One of the armed men from inside the house ran to greet him.

"He's upstairs, Mr Jacob."

Mr Jacob favoured him with a sideways glance and simply said, "Humph." Once inside he began the climb the stairs. Near the top he paused to catch his breath and wiped the sweat from his brow. Mr Jacob, attorney at law, currently charged over one thousand pounds an hour and had never had to move fast in his life, he saw no reason to begin now. Eventually, he resumed his climb.

The door to the master bedroom was open and its occupant could be seen slumped in a chair, his shirt collar wrenched open, his dress trousers were blood stained and dirty, and he clutched a bottle of vodka in his left hand. The knuckles on his right hand were bleeding, the blood dripping onto the white woolen carpet. He stared at the body of a young woman lying on the floor. The belt that he had strangled her with lay across her naked chest, the white pants she had on were speckled with blood. Her eyes were open and staring at the ceiling. Blood encrusted her mouth and at least one of her perfect teeth was missing.

People were running back and forth in obvious shock at the recent chain of events. Most people here had at one time or another been called on to remove, among other things, the occasional young girl, but nothing of this magnitude. The wife of Karl Ellis, dead by his own hands!

Karl grew aware of the hugely obese man blocking his doorway and breathing asthmatically. He grimaced and looked away.

Jacob looked at a chair which was quickly brought to him by a house aide. It creaked and groaned, threatening to give way as it accepted his bulbous bulk. He sighed deeply as he took out a small Dictaphone and began reciting. Karl watched him silently, refusing all attempts at communication.

"I will need something to go on, Mr Ellis," said Jacob willfully, the jowls on his red cheeks wobbling incessantly. "This is not some minor indiscretion easily brushed aside."

Karl smiled weakly.

"Did anyone actually see anything?" he asked aloud.

In a room full of career criminals, it was perhaps the most ridiculous question ever asked.

Karl began speaking then, so quietly that Jacob was forced to lean in to hear. "I gave her everything. I trusted her more than anyone I ever knew." He bowed his head in grief. "She was everything to me! Everything! I never saw it coming."

"Mr Ellis. We need to move fast. People are bound to be talking already. Several of your neighbours have been seen near the house. I believe it is only a matter of time before the police come asking questions," said Jacob solemnly.

Karl drank heavily from the vodka. "Then deal with this fuck up, Jacob. That's what I pay you for!" Karl sniffed and wrinkled his nose. "You stink, do you know that? I can smell the pork fat oozing from your skin, you fat pompous prick!"

Jacob's cheeks reddened further. "Mr Ellis, I..."

A commotion began in the hallway, shouting and the noise of a fight. Karl recognised a voice in the fray.

"Let me in, you bastard!" More yelling and more shoving and a moment later he stood in door.

Reice Ellis surveyed the carnage, his eyes widened in shock as he saw the corpse. He turned and met the burning stare of his brother. "Karl..."

Karl threw the bottle of vodka at Reice who nimbly ducked, it sailed on into the hallway, shattering against the wall. Karl was on his feet aiming a punch at Reice's jaw. It connected and sent Reice crashing into the hall. With a cry of rage Karl grabbed a gun from the table beside his chair. He fired twice just above Reice's head. He stared in shock at his brother.

"Mr Ellis!" yelled Jacob in shock gasping for breath. "Let us not commit a second murder when the first has yet to be dealt with!"

Karl stood over his shocked brother. "Of all the people it could've been, it just had to be you!"

"Karl..."

"Shut the fuck up, brother!"

Karl appeared to be wrestling with his rage, the gun, tightly gripped, wavered in his hand as he aimed directly at Reice.

After what seemed like an eternity, Karl threw the gun behind him onto the bed. It was clear he was fighting hard to regain his composure. He cleared his throat several times before he could speak, when he did it was pained and husky.

"Get out of here, Reice. You and I... we're finished. Get out of here, get out of my life. If I ever see you again, I will kill you. That is a promise, brother mine!" He raised a steady hand to silence Reice. "Don't open your lying, treacherous mouth. I mean it. There is nothing left between us. You've killed me, Reice. You took from me the one thing that truly mattered. Whether she came to you, or you went to her is irrelevant. What's done is done and this can never, ever be repaired."

Reice made to speak again, but the venomous stare in his brother's eyes and the surrounding henchmen stayed his tongue. He scrambled to his feet and inched closer to Karl in a last gasp attempt at unity.

Karl recoiled a full two steps, he turned to the man at his side. "Tony, if he is still in this house in three minutes time... kill him. In fact, five grand to whoever garrotes my brother!"

Reice turned, grief obvious on his face as he ran down the stairs for the last time. As he neared the door, he heard Karl yell one last time, "You are dead to me, Reice! Don't come back here! Don't ever try to make contact again! You hear me Reice? Reice! You are a dead man!" Karl screamed long, painfully and with unbridled rage as Reice began his flight into obscurity. Torrential rain soaked him to his skin as he ran shivering and alone into the night, her voice still ringing in his head.

"I love you, Reice. Don't worry, everything will be ok."

The Job

The table was long and scattered across it were various plans and schemes... all had been rejected. The three men sat drinking heavily. There was a mixture of drinks, beer, spirits, and an almost empty pot of coffee that had centre place on the table before them. Each man looked increasingly tired and not even the music in the background helped to calm the strained nerves of those occupying the chairs The choking stench of cigar smoke from one of the men hung low in the air.

"We have been over your plan about a million times already, and it won't work," said the man near the top of the table. He shook his head and scowled deeply as he blew yet more vapid smoke into the already claustrophobic air. Reice was perhaps the most vicious one of the group, he was a killer and everyone knew it. "How many more times do you want to go over the same ideas, Danny?"

The man seated at the head of the table looked at Reice in disgust and it was obvious that he was the leader. "Until we either find a way to make it work, or until we find a plan that will work!"

Danny faced him and Reice edged backwards from the table, poised for violence.

It never came, Danny smiled. "Okay, let's hear your plan!"

"You already have, and it's been rejected like all the others." Reice took a long drink of his beer and yawned deeply. "I need a rest, let's break and come at it fresh in the morning. I've sat in this shithole for ten straight hours!"

A small, thin, nervous man at the end of the table, Brooks, shook his head. "You go if you want, I'll stay and work on these."

Reice shrugged and made to stand. "Okay."

Danny's hand on his arm stopped him. "No one leaves until we sort this out, you hear? I told Karl that we'd be ready with a plan in the morning."

"Come on, Danny!" said Reice. "We need more time! Two days to plan this entire job from start to finish! It's practically impossible. A week... maybe."

"We don't have a week," said Danny. "In case you've forgotten, the cops grabbed our courier and our goddamn package! He's been in that cop shop for close to twenty-four hours now. God only knows what he's told them! As soon as the cops figure out what he's carrying there's no way we'll get anywhere near that bank!"

"No one will be able to crack the code," ventured Brooks.

"You prepared to take that chance?" asked Danny. "I'm not, and neither is Karl. We need to get this down tonight! Understood? No one leaves." He stared at the assembled group, just waiting for an objection, when there were none, he continued, "Right, Brooks, about the optic security measures, can we bypass them?"

Brooks shook his head and handed Danny a schematic. "No way, one wrong retinal scan and the doors close on both sides, locking us in. It's no use. I must admit, it's some system they have, top of the line," he said in admiration.

"Okay, what ways around this do we have?"

"None!" said Reice, "take a look, Danny! It's a waste of time, tell Karl we need another target, this one's just become unbreakable. Fucking dick head courier! You should've let me pick it up!"

Danny shook his head. "No one tells your brother anything! You of all people ought to know that! He gave me this job."

"Your cock-sucking pal Thomas 'gave you this job'," spat Reice.

"At Karl's request, Reice! Of all the people he could have trusted with this, he picked me! This is my one big chance to get out of this shit-hole city and onto what's owed me! Do you think I'd be happy just running my club forever? Eh? Holding fucking retirement parties for fat bald pricks or hosting fucking bingo nights for purple headed old women? We're going in, if Karl wants this, then he gets this," he said slamming a finger into the building layout. "And no stupid security measure's gonna stop either him... or me. Is that understood?" He climbed to his feet. "Does everyone understand?"

Brooks nodded firmly, while Reice nodded, almost bored.

"Gemma!" he yelled. A waitress came running in.

"Yes, Mr Gilmour?" she said.

"Another round of drinks, sweetheart."

She nodded and began clearing all the empties away.

Danny, all the while staring at her said to Brooks, "If we can't decide on an actual plan, then let's discuss the basics, Getting in."

Both Reice and Brooks cast sideways suspicious looks at the waitress.

"You can talk in front of her," said Danny. He grabbed her by the waist, forcing her to fall onto his lap. "You won't say anything about what you hear, will you?"

Struggling to get up, Gemma shook her head, "Of course not, Mr Gilmour."

Reice nodded in apparent submission, said, "All taken care of, Danny. At that time of night there shouldn't be that many guards, not enough to cause us big problems anyway."

Danny smiled and let Gemma go. She immediately grabbed the empties and hurried from the room. "Okay, we appear to have somewhere to start, we'll go over Reice's part."

Reice grabbed hold of the drawings he had made. "Brooks will be positioned in the van when we go in, he'll need to move pretty quickly. We already know when the last pick up of the night will be, I've arranged for a small accident to occur to that van and I'll be going in in their place, that'll give me the element of surprise, but once I take out the first couple of guards, whoever's inside the booth will trip the alarm, that's when I need Brooks. When the alarm goes, we'll have about ten seconds to cut in and override it. After that, the place will be shut tighter than a duck's arse in winter waters."

"What about the phones?" Danny asked.

"I'll be scrambling any mobile signal and taking out the land lines… piece of cake!" said Brooks. "The main alarm line will be going nowhere either."

Danny nodded. "Okay, where does that leave Karl and me?"

Brooks jerked his attention from the schematic. "Is Karl coming with us?"

"'Course he's coming, Brooks! Since that idiot courier got grabbed by the coppers last night and lost the original do you honestly think Karl would take a chance on this happening twice?" He turned back to Reice. "Go on."

"Well, this is the part we're stuck at! We need to figure out some way to access their systems, if we can do that, as well as dummy up the CCTV link so no smart security prick catches on, we're in," Reice leaned back, "and that's where my part ends. I get us in, provide a little back-up, the rest will be up to you."

Danny smiled. "I know my part, Reice."

Reice drew his lips to a tight smile. "Just how involved will Karl be?"

"As involved as the rest of us, seems he's getting tired of everyone calling him yellow, that small incident back in London last month convinced him that some people think he's going soft."

Reice shook his head. "No one ever dared say that when I was with him."

"Yeah? Well, you ain't with him anymore, Reice. You blew it! Just remember, you wouldn't be here if it weren't for me. Your loyalty is to me now, not your brother. You just remember that when the shit hits the fan out there," said Danny.

"Don't tell me where my loyalties should lie!" spat Reice, "I know my part in this, I'm paying for my mistakes!"

"Just make sure we don't pay with you."

Reice and Danny faced off for a few seconds before Reice angrily grabbed his sheets. "Once we're inside you and now Karl will basically just be bystanders, I'll be faking the hit on the vault and leaving a mess for the cops. Brooks will have all the real fun inside. We'll be covering him, but of course should you decide to really go for the vault instead of ..."

"Not a chance!" snapped Danny, "we already talked about that! We're in for the one thing only. Once Brooks here finds a way to hack into the bank's system, we get what we're after, enter the virus to wipe our tracks and get out. I'm sure that Karl will see you get your just rewards. Anyway, your debts don't concern me, Reice. Go for a bank job on your own time!"

"I always said that you and Las Vegas don't mix," said Brooks softly. "Besides, the vault's run on a different system to our target. I'd have to completely redefine…"

"There's no point in talking about this, I've made my decision." Danny leaned back to show that the conversation was over.

Reice looked at his watch and sighed. "Look at the time, will ya? We've been at this for hours and still we're no closer to a solution!"

Just then the door opened, and Gemma returned with the drinks. She placed them down, ignoring Danny's attempt at eye contact. She left too quickly.

Reice stared at the door. "Why don't you just go fuck her, Danny? Then I can get some sleep for two or three minutes."

Brooks laughed, Danny turned scarlet. "Fuck you, Reice! If we weren't short on time you'd be out on your arse! Christ only knows why I ever took you on!"

Reice shrugged.

"You're the one who's tired and wanting this over with. Well, wake up and start taking things seriously! All it takes is a little time! This is doable! Do you think I'd risk my neck if I didn't think we could do it? And Karl, you think he'd get personally involved if he thought otherwise?" Danny sighed deeply. "Do you all see my point? Reice, you and I go back a long time. This could really clear things up between you and Karl. If he sees that you can pull this off, you never know…" he shrugged his shoulders.

Reice nodded gently. He was about to speak when the phone rang.

Danny picked it up. "What?" he said in annoyance. "I said we weren't to be..."

Suddenly his face changed, his eyes widened in horror. "When?" he said quietly, then said, "Okay."

He replaced the receiver and faced the group and when he spoke, it was very quiet. "Karl is on his way in."

Brooks recoiled in shock and even Reice looked terrified. "He's on his way up and we don't have things ready..."

"I know, I know," said Danny. "Shut up and let me think!"

After a few seconds he turned to Reice, said, "That's it then. We go with your plan."

"What?" said Brooks, "Danny, are you crazy!? We'll never make it, and you know it! We need a Trojan Horse to hack into the security system, not a fucking ram raid through the front door. I can't do it in time!"

"Shut up!" bellowed Danny, "we can make it."

At that point the doors were thrown open and a short man entered. He was dressed in a black suit and dark grey trench coat, his hands were covered by black leather gloves and his eyes were hidden behind dark designer glasses. His posture was cold and calculating. It was clear he was in charge and knew it.

He paused, took in the room and its contents. In contrast to the nervous tension in the room he was a picture of serenity. He sighed deeply and said, "Evening."

"Karl," said Danny standing up, he motioned for Karl to sit.

Karl ignored him and stood where he was. "You have everything in order." It was not a question.

Danny stumbled over his words. "We're uh... having a few logistical problems, last minute things, you know, nothing to worry about."

Karl brought his dark glasses to bear on him. "Sit."

Danny fell into the chair, fearful, Karl's dark eyes upon him. "I take it then everything will be completed before tomorrow?"

"Of course, Karl, no problem!"

Karl smiled marginally. "I don't need a 'yes man', Danny. I don't need someone who makes unfulfilled promises."

"We're ready, Karl," said Danny, conveying more confidence than he actually felt.

"You came very highly recommended via mutual associates," said Karl. "Let us hope this transaction goes as smoothly as detail would suggest."

Just then Gemma came in and motioned to Karl.

"Whisky. Neat."

She nodded and turned away, a strange look of anger and adrenaline rippled across her features, unseen in the room, given the uneven tensions.

"Karl," said Reice, venturing forward. "This really isn't the best possible target. I mean, we've spent most of the evening going over the security systems, and frankly they're damn near impossible."

Karl stared impassively, not looking at Reice. "Nothing is impossible. You were quick to assure Danny here that your friend Mr Brooks could handle it. Are you now going to tell me, brother, that you have made yet another mistake?"

Reice's face flushed. "No, Karl… it's not that… it's just… if we had more time."

"We all knew there would be difficulties in this assignment. Nothing that's worth this much should be easy." He moved closer to Reice and, still not looking at him, said, "You want to leave?"

"No, no," Reice stated quickly. "I'm in."

"Until I say otherwise," he returned his attentions to Brooks. "Well?"

Brooks tried to hold a stare, failed, and instead looked down. "I'm sorry, Karl. I've tried, but I can't find any possible way to access the system. As Reice says, perhaps with more time…"

"We'll be ready," said Danny with more confidence than he could ever feel.

"Really?" Karl turned to look at Danny, shook his head. "Your Systems Analyst tells me that you cannot get in. I don't need empty promises, Danny. I have had enough of them from elsewhere," he turned his head a fraction to indicate Reice. "You know the opportunity I have given you. There are at least ten other crews who would jump at this."

"I know, Karl," said Danny quickly, "and I know how much faith you've put in me…"

Karl laughed. "Sit down, Danny before you strain something. I never expected you to be able to do it. You were right, of course, Mr Brooks. The system is literally unbreakable." He turned back to Danny, said, "I only gave you this assignment because you'd taken my brother in."

Reice looked up with a glint of hope.

Karl removed his mirrored glasses and stared directly at Reice. "I just wanted to see you fail one last time, brother!"

"You fucking…."

"Sit down!" barked Karl with such intensity it defused Reice, who fell into his chair, covering his face with his hand.

Karl shook his head. He pulled a memory stick from his pocket and dropped it on the table.

All eyes looked at it.

"There's your bypass, Mr Brooks, with that you ought to be able to get into the system. It will also subvert all the security cameras," Karl said with a slight smile.

Brooks stared, wide eyed at it. "How?"

"I have my sources. Let's just say it was very, very costly and I expect some return on my investment." He turned to face the door. "Danny, where's that stupid bitch with my drink?"

Reice stood up. "I'll go see."

Danny stopped him. "No, I'll go," he said, he quickly stood and pulling at his tie as though it was suddenly choking him, left the room.

Brooks picked up the stick, inserted it into his laptop and busied himself at the screen. Karl stared hard at Reice, who stared back with obvious anger in his eyes.

"So," said Karl in a tone filled with mock sincerity. "How's my brother getting along these days?"

Reice smiled, a hint of rebellion in his eyes. "Not too bad, considering what happened."

"Don't give me the sob story, Reice! It's been five years and you're still playing the poor little me. I was the victim, not you! I was the one who was betrayed!"

Reice shook his head sadly. "Never in my whole life have I ever betrayed you. We're brothers, Karl. I didn't know how you really felt about…"

"So I always thought," replied Karl sadly. He took a cloth from his jacket and began cleaning his sunglasses. "I should have killed you, Reice. My one regret is that I didn't."

"Why?" asked Reice.

"Why didn't I kill you?" asked Karl and when Reice nodded, he shrugged. "I really don't know. Consider it the last remnant of my sentimentality."

Reice sighed. "Karl...."

Karl raised a hand. "I've said all I intend to say. We'll leave it at that."

Reice nodded in submission. "Can things ever get back to the way they were?"

"No." Karl stood up. "Where's my damn drink?"

At that moment there was a loud bang in the other room.

Reice leapt to his feet. "Gunshot!" he yelled as he grabbed his gun from the table.

Suddenly Danny came into the room, a strange look of confusion on his face.

"Danny?" said Reice uncertainly.

"I… I went in there," he said, motioning to the adjoining room, "Gemma was on the phone. I… she was... she's a fucking cop, Karl, was telling them you're here!"

Brooks winced and turned towards the other room.

Karl scowled deeply, a momentary look of surprise taking him. "So you killed the bitch."

Danny shook his head. "No, Karl." he said with a grimace.

Both Karl and Reice instinctively looked down at Danny's chest. As he pulled his hand away, his suit jacket fell open to reveal a deep red blossom spreading across his abdomen, the blossom smelled of death.

Danny leaned heavily against the doorway and coughed, breathing hard.

Reice cursed and made to move.

"Drop the gun, Reice!" The voice came from behind Danny.

Reice looked up and saw Gemma standing there, pistol pointed right at him. He dropped the gun on the table.

"Brooks!" yelled Reice.

With lightning speed, Brooks pulled his gun and trained it on Gemma.

Unexpectedly, Karl began to laugh. A slow belly laugh that gradually got louder. "Well done, sweetheart, well done. You've got a gun in my face," he raised his hands in a mock surrender, "but what is you think you've got on me?"

"Everything, Karl, this entire place has been under surveillance for a long, long time. Mr Gilmour isn't as smart or as careful as he likes to think. We've been onto him for months. He should really have been more careful about who he lets into his club." Gemma smiled, her eyes glittering.

Behind her, Danny groaned. She ignored him. "I've got all these conversations recorded. Danny seems to be your greatest admirer, he's talked about lots of things we could never prove before. The recordings are remarkably clear."

Gemma moved the aim of her gun to encompass Karl.

His face registered a range of emotions. He remained silent for a few moments before shaking his head. "No cop has ever gotten under my skin before, I spotted them all." He laughed again, "Strange that, don't you think, Reice? Once more you're the thorn in my side; the fucking rotten apple!"

"Fuck off! What's that supposed to mean??"

"What you used to always say, how you could spot a fake a mile off? Well, I guess there'll always be the one that gets past you."

Reice scowled. "Not in the old days."

"The old days!" said Karl mockingly. "Why do you always cling to the ancient past? Sure, they were good times, and we were unstoppable, right up until you betrayed me!"

"I never betrayed you!" Reice said explosively. "That shouldn't have happened, I know, but I wasn't solely to blame, if you'd been there a bit more, paid more attention…"

"It's not that I'm bothered about! But the fact that it just had to be you!" yelled Karl, "anyone else, I'd have killed them where they stood and forgot about it. You betrayed me, Reice! The one place I never expected it to come from! I was always there for you!"

Reice laughed. "There for me? When were you ever there? You were always away on "official business" leaving me to tidy up the rough edges, always leaving me to clear up the mess you made while you were off playing with the big guys! Fucking golf clubs and fancy restaurants, thousand quid-a-ticket dinners! Why was that, Karl? Why was it always you?"

Karl slammed a fist into the table. "We both know what I did was for our collective good." Karl changed his voice, his appearance and looked grief stricken. "I never cut you out of anything, you were the one; you were the equal I couldn't admit to."

"Equal?" spat Reice. "Your own damn brother and you would never admit that! What chance did I have to be accepted as an equal?"

"I did it for you, for us! One of us had to be the public face, and we both know that wasn't you! You were the one everyone feared! That was your talent, you kept the others at bay. I was the brains, you were the brawn!"

"Yeah? Well maybe I wanted more! I was never seen in the same league as you! It was always 'where's Karl? Ask Karl! Check with Karl' ever since The Rooftops and the time with Blake it was always the same, I was sick of that shit!"

"Stop with the melodrama, Reice!" yelled Karl. "There was no other choice!"

"Enough!" yelled Gemma, who had stood watching the scene with mild amusement that had quickly turned to hate. Danny still hung onto life against the door but had given way to a drooping slump. "As interesting as it is, this behind the scenes look at the Ellis brothers, I still have a job to do!"

Karl turned to look at Gemma, "Do you know, in all the excitement I'd forgotten about you." He smiled. "Brooks, shoot that bitch!"

When nothing happened, Karl turned. "I said…" his sentence trailed off as he realised Brooks had aimed his gun at him.

"I don't fucking believe this!" yelled Karl, "what, you a cop too?"

Brooks turned to look at Gemma, his face deadly serious. "I'm Detective Inspector Wilton of Serious Crime Squad," he said. "That gives me jurisdiction. Do you understand? We don't have time for me to prove it just now. I need a leap of faith, Officer. Can you do that?"

Suddenly, without warning, Reice lunged at Brooks. He caught him on the chin and Brooks fell into a chair, his gun falling to the floor. "Mother fucker!" he yelled as he continued raining blows onto Brooks.

"Leave him alone, Reice!" yelled Gemma, she knew now where her loyalties lay. "Get back or I swear I'll kill you where you stand!"

As Reice turned to look at her, Brooks punched him hard in the groin. He fell back, Brooks retrieved his gun and brought it to bear on Reice's face. He rubbed his jaw. "Ok, Reice. You earned that but try it again and I swear I'll blow your fucking balls off!"

Reice coughed. "Hardly a Cop technique, is it?"

"You ok?" asked Gemma.

Brooks nodded and it was only then that he realised she was sweating, her heart racing. She turned and stared at Karl, again the look of hatred and rage filled her eyes.

"You a bit out of your depth, huh, you need to sit down?" He laughed. "Pathetic! How'd you ever get your claws into old Danny here?" He turned and looked at Danny, who had collapsed and was leaning against the wall.

"I need a doctor!" moaned Danny. "I'm fucking dying here!"

"Shut up, you prick!" yelled Gemma, "months I've taken your cheap tricks - grabbing my arse and fondling me at every turn! I had to endure your lecherous shit! So just sit there and shut up for once!"

"Well put," said Karl. "You must be thinking all your birthdays have come at once with all of us here, eh, and for what? For Officer Brooks to take away your catch, bet that burns! Chance to make your career and it's stolen away!"

"Up yours, Karl, just to see you rot in hell is enough for me!"

Karl shook his head. "You seem to be taking this very personal. Why is that? What did I ever do to deserve such venom?"

Gemma moved forward, her mouth set in a grimace. "What did you do? What did you do? You remember Duncan Blake, don't you?"

Karl smiled. "I take it he was someone special?"

"He was my husband, you bastard!" She yelled. "And he was your partner! He looked up to you, trusted you and you cut him out and killed him!"

Karl shook his head. "It was just business. He..."

"You shot him five times, you sick son of a bitch!" Tears burned in her eyes.

Karl shrugged. "He came after me! It was self defence."

"Don't… don't try and justify it!" She sobbed as she pushed the gun into his forehead.

Karl took two steps back and tried to be haughty, yet it was obvious this ghost from his past had rattled him. "So how come I never heard of you, eh? All the dinners, the parties, the late ones with Blake, I never once saw you."

"Duncan wanted us kept away from all of you, he didn't want us caught up in that part of his life."

Karl smirked. "Yeah, and those skirts he had hanging off his arm wouldn't take to you too well. Maybe he didn't love you like you think, huh? Maybe you were just a convenient bunk up on the nights he wasn't out fucking the staff."

Gemma grimaced and her fingers tightened on the trigger. "How little you know of him! He knew you though, Karl. He knew exactly what kind of man you were."

"Gemma," said Brooks softly. "We want him alive."

She looked at him, her eyes burning. "I'm not going to shoot him, that'd be too easy."

Karl smirked. "So... What's your story, Officer Brooks or Wilton? How long have you been sniffing at my arse?"

"I've been on you for seven years."

"Seven years?" said Karl incredulously. "How the hell did you hold a case that long? Huh? I'm no Copper, and I admit that puts me in the fucking minority around here, but even I know that there's no way you'd be allowed to run with this without bringing them anything! And you didn't have anything until fucking Miss Marple here handed it to you! You sure you're still a cop, Brooks? Or could it be you were drummed out because you couldn't produce the goods?"

"Don't start with me, Karl! I lost everything because of you! My wife, my kids, any chance of a normal life because I wanted to be the one! I wanted to be the one who nailed you!"

"I'll say this for you," said Karl, "when you set your mind to it, you're pretty determined!"

Brooks levelled the gun at Karl. "I don't find that particularly funny."

Karl turned to Reice, How long have you known DI Wilton, Reice?"

Reice scowled. "Over three years, right after…."

"And you said you can spot a cop." Karl laughed. "Now do you see what I mean? A cop on both sides of you and still you sit here playing with your balls! You're a liability, Reice! A fucking waste of time! Three years this prick's been at your side, and you couldn't even see it!"

Reice lowered his eyes.

"So, what now, Officer Brooks, I take it you'll be taking me in, poor little Gemma gets nothing."

"Taking you down is the important part. Who gets to do what is irrelevant."

"And then what?" asked Karl.

"What?" asked Brooks, a look of surprise on his face.

"What do you do now? Seven years, Brooks. What can you do now? Have you even thought of one single possibility after this moment?"

"Get a life! That's what I'm going to do!"

"Oh, come on! I'm your god damned life! Without me or my brother you're nothing. Admit it -you've got a taste for the life now!" He flicked a glance at Reice. "Am I right?"

Reice nodded, his fists clenched in silent rage. "Yeah," was all he could manage.

Brooks remained silent.

"Well?" asked Karl. "Right, ain't I? What are you going to do once I'm out of the picture? Go sit on a beach, paint, maybe try Speed Dating? Face it! You're used to this. The money, the cars, the respect! We gave you all that! It's who you are now!"

"I'm warning you… shut up!" Brooks thought for a moment. "Why are you here, Karl?"

"What?"

"What brought you here? Years I've waited for you to make contact with your brother, and now suddenly here you stand. Why is that? If I didn't know better, I'd think you were running from something."

"He is."

It was Gemma. She was staring at the floor as though deep in thought. "Now it makes sense! We heard that he was selling up a lot of his assets in London and Glasgow for short end money too, thousands under the asking price. We could never figure out what it was."

Karl looked at her with murder in his eyes.

"Is this true?" asked Reice. "What the fuck is going on? What are you… what are we into?"

"Fuck off, the lot of you! I don't answer to you! You've still got nothing, Brooks! Look at you! If I picked you up and shook you, you'd rattle! There's nothing inside you! I bet every time you look in a mirror you see me! You're not a cop! Yeah, I'm sure you were at one time. That look in your eyes, I've seen it a hundred times. Where do you jack up?"

Brooks paled. "What?"

"Your arm? No, that'd be too easy to spot. The old in between the toes trick? Hurts like fuck, doesn't it?" Karl laughed. "Or maybe you're onto your balls now, that it, Brooks? You inject that skunk into your sack?"

"Fuck you, Karl!" spat Brooks.

"There's no way you could pass a medical! Your habit stands out a mile! You're a used-up junkie, Brooks!"

"You finished, Ellis? Yeah, I'm a junkie, so what? I did what I had to do to get inside, and those starched collared, narrow-minded idiots couldn't see that! Sitting in their ivory towers surrounded by procedures and operational guidelines! Make me go for counselling? Take me off 'active assignment', but hey, guess what? None of that matters now! I'm taking you in and everything gets wiped clean!"

"Like I said, Brooks, I am your life!"

"You're not that important, Karl!" spat Brooks.

Karl laughed. "No? Seven years important, dick head! I bet that..."

"Karl," said Reice and there was venom in his voice. "What is going on?"

"What does it matter? You got what you wanted. We're back together. All is forgiven. Once we get out of this fucked up mess. I'll see you all right."

"And me?" said Danny, coughing. "What was to happen to me? Did you fuck us over, Karl?"

Karl looked between the two, saw his support weaken. "Reice?"

"Tell me, Karl? What are you in to?"

Karl looked almost in a rage, it quickly subsided, and he suddenly looked like a man desperate. "Okay, okay! I fucked up. Is that what you want to hear?"

"Go on," said Reice.

"This job, we were never keeping what we took."

Danny let out a hollow laugh. "So, there was no fucking money, you bastard!"

"We'll all get paid, I'll see to that! Truth is I'm in so much fucking shit and to cut a long story short..." Karl cleared his throat and swallowed nervously, his gaze shifting over all the faces staring at him. His voice dropped to barely a whisper, "Brent Thomas offered me a way out."

Reice winced and looked at him incredulously. "We're working for that fucked up political puppet?"

"I had no choice!" When everyone remained silent, he continued. "I needed money fast, truth is I'm well and truly fucked. Thomas was going to take the heat and get me out of this mess!"

"Then we caught your courier," said Gemma.

"That's right!" said Karl, looking like a caged animal, "and screwed everything up. That's why I had to push the deadline for this job."

Reice shook his head. "Why us, why me?"

Brooks looked thoughtful. "Because he needed someone who wouldn't ask too many questions, would go on trust. Since you wanted back, you'd have taken any job Karl offered because you thought it would clear you."

Behind them Danny groaned. "And I wanted to save my ass and move up! I knew in my guts what a mistake it was dealing with Thomas! What a fucking mess!"

"It's all true," said Brooks in disbelief. "You're finished, on the run? I don't believe it! All these years I've tried to bring you down, and here you go and do it all on your own!"

"How did things get so fucked up, Karl?" asked Reice and there was genuine grief in his voice. "We had it all, just the two of us. How did we lose so much?"

Karl lowered his head.

At that moment, Danny let out a moan and collapsed to the ground. All eyes turned to look at him as he fell.

Karl pulled a gun from a pocket in his coat, Reice grabbed his from the table. All of a sudden, they found themselves in a standoff.

Karl aimed directly at Brooks, who aimed back. Reice, who was aiming at Brooks, turned to point directly at Gemma, who showed her uncertainty by aiming back and forth between the two brothers.

"Come on, Karl!" said Brooks. "It's over! Gemma's no doubt called for back-up."

Gemma looked at Brooks in surprise, shot Karl a quick look before nodding. "Uh, yeah," she lied.

Brooks smiled. "There's no way out. It's over."

Karl laughed. "Over?" He shook his head. He had again regained his air of command. "Do you know the reason why I've always won, why I'll continue to win and yet your kind never do?"

"Tell me."

"I understand the meaning of sacrifice. I understand the intricacies involved. I know what I want, and nothing can ever get in my way. You want to know the secret? Let no one inside. Arm's length, no closer!

"I lost my wife too, Brooks, but not through anything as inane as a divorce. She learned too much about me, too many questions, assumptions and I remedied the situation. I understand how to survive."

He turned and looked at Reice who had a mixture of grief and rage on his face. "Besides, I don't like tainted goods! And I always cover my back, copper. Leave no witnesses, let no one get too close." His eyes glazed over, and he took a deep breath, "and finally, don't let any idiot brother bring you down, or fuck you over!"

In sudden realisation of what was happening, Reice swung his gun towards Karl, yelling, "Jesus! No!"

Karl fired directly into Reice's chest. He fell like an oak, his eyes betraying total shock.

Gemma let out a scream and fired, the bullet hit Karl between the eyes, his face registering shock as he fell.

In a reflex action, betraying how far he had really fallen, Brooks fired at Gemma, hitting her twice in the chest. She looked at him in disbelief, her eyes searching him for some clue. She gasped once, then fell, dead before she hit the ground.

Brooks fell back two steps, realising what he had done. He dropped his hand to his side, still with his finger on the trigger. He surveyed the carnage around him while gasping for breath. No need to check for pulses. He aimed his gun at the door, ready for any would-be hero to come in. It seemed like an eternity, any second now three or four armed men would come running in, take one look at the bloodbath and he would fall in a hail of bullets, one more body in the mass.

They never came. The thump-thump of the music had most likely drowned out the massacre.

With a shaky breath, Brooks wiped his mouth. He picked up a glass of vodka and downed it in one gulp. Placing the glass on the table, he reached over and pulled the memory stick that Karl had brought from his laptop, stared at it intently for a moment, before dropping it into his pocket. Closing the laptop, he placed it inside his case and slung it over his shoulder. He pulled his mobile phone from his pocket, scanned the numbers and hit dial. He cleared his throat and tried his best to sound calm. "It's me. We really, really need to talk." He swallowed hard. "No, it has to be tonight. You know where. Half an hour and if you're late I'm not waiting. There'll be no second chance." He cut the call and dropped the phone and his gun in his jacket pocket and with a final look at the bodies and the mess, he left the room and headed off into the night.

Gemma

Gemma Blake sat alone on the park bench staring. A cold wind had blown in across the river, but she barely noticed it. She still wore the black dress she had worn hours before at the funeral. Evening had settled in with a promise of rain and her feet were cold from the slushy remains of last night's snow. Her stare had settled on a passing boat as it meandered down the river Clyde. Her mobile phone rang once more but she ignored it as she had all previous calls. Her flight from the post funeral soirée had caused a stir and no doubt her family some concern, though she didn't care. She had to be alone, had to get away from all the kind words of comfort and the constant sickly sympathetic cuddles, looks, and pats on the back.

"You'll be fine!" How many times had she heard that or "We're sorry for your loss, he was a wonderful man." It got to her after a while. Wonderful man, yeah sure! He could be kind, loving, generous, and warm. But he was stubborn, he was jealous, he was arrogant, he was naive, he was...

He was dead! That was what he was, her husband. How did things ever get to this? From the day their eyes met across the crowded stage of The Rooftops bar she knew that they were destined to be together forever.

"One day, I'm going to be someone here! I'm going to own this club, then this city!" And he did, for a while, until the drugs, and the life, and the power took him away, leaving in his place a hollow, twisted caricature of the man she fell in love with.

"They will all remember me!" It became his own personal rhetoric and she had to watch him slip away one piece, one line of cocaine, one drink, one late night at a time until she couldn't stand it anymore. The pregnancy, even that wasn't enough to bring him back. He went further down a road she couldn't follow as he tried to be in what he called "the company of kings."

Gemma sobbed uncontrollably in the twilight drizzle. What was left in life now? What did she have?

Revenge! That was what remained, what drove her. Karl Ellis! The devil himself who had reached out and taken everything she ever had. She would get him if it took fifty years and soon she would begin, soon she would start. Everything was in place and it had taken some doing! Duncan Blake's father, the Assistant Chief Constable, had used his authority to push and pull things around, arranging for her to be involved in the operation to bring Karl Ellis down. It had almost cost him his career arranging her entry into the huge undercover operation. But Gemma had been impressive in her meetings with the C.I.D squad responsible. She had passed the psycho analysis tests, the board of enquiry, she had passed her meeting with the Detective Chief Inspector. All that remained was the extensive training. It had all moved so quickly after Duncan's murder less than a month ago.

"We have an inside source in the banking industry," said Peter Blake. They had been in his study at his spacious home in the outskirts of Bearsden, near the town of Milngavie. Just the two of them, the mother-in-law from hell was busying herself in the kitchen as usual and Peter had demanded she leave them alone. In contrast to the sharply dressed and smart gentleman she was used to seeing, Peter was unkempt and looked nothing like the imposing father-in-law she was used to. His neat, grey hair was messy and at least a week's worth of stubble graced his chin. News of his son's death had literally knocked the wind out of him. He sipped at the large whisky he had poured himself moments before. Gemma's vodka lay untouched on the large table. He closed his eyes and sighed painfully. "He's just set up a big money job between Karl Ellis and a low-life called Danny Gilmour." Another long drink and he had drained the glass, which he quickly refilled. "My DCI has suggested a job in Gilmour's club. He's just fired a couple of waitresses amid a flurry of euphemisms and sinister threats. Gilmour is fond of young girls and, as such, they either leave disgusted or he fires them for not succumbing to his charms." Peter winced and looked painfully at Gemma. "Strathclyde Police have a D.S. undercover who works with the type Gilmour is looking for. Gemma, you are a beautiful young woman whom my Duncan loved dearly." He swallowed with a dry throat and shook his head. "You are exactly the type Gilmour would go for in his club. If you could stand the perversion of that man, then we... you would..."

Gemma stood, crossed over and embraced Peter Blake who sobbed as he grabbed her tightly.

"I loved your son more than life, Peter," she said softly. "I would go to hell and back for him. I failed him once when I took Paul and walked away from him. I thought it would bring him to his senses…"

Peter sobbed. "You didn't fail him, Gemma. I knew you couldn't stay. You had to protect my grandson. My son.. When he allied himself with the Ellis brothers, he wasn't the same person he had been…"

Gemma embraced him softly. "None the less, I did fail him, and I will never forgive myself and if putting up with that animal Gilmour will get me nearer to Ellis then I will do it gladly and with a smile on my face! There's nothing he can do to me that I can't handle in order to bring him down!" She smiled sadly at him, and he looked away. It was too much!

"He loved you more than you ever know, Gemma. You were the one for him. No doubt of that! When you left, he knew the price. He never stopped loving you. I thought the birth of your son would have been enough to change him, to have brought him back, I know that..." He swallowed painfully. "I know Duncan and I never saw eye to eye, that he had fallen so far into a life of crime and that left me with no option but to turn away." As Gemma looked away, he took it as rejection. "I had to, Gemma! Not just because of my job but because his mother and I... we couldn't bear to watch. I spent too long trying to protect him from behind the scenes and risking everything because he was my son. No one knows the depths of the things I did to protect my boy, not even Duncan was aware."

They had talked long into the night planning, scheming and preparing and it was decided that after a short and intense training session in London, Gemma would head back to Glasgow and find her way into the employ of Danny Gilmour. Then she would be that much nearer to Ellis! She marvelled at Peter's directness and authoritative stance on the telephone as he arranged her meeting with the contact from Strathclyde Police.

Her phone began ringing again and broke her reverie. This time Gemma took it from her pocket. She absently pressed the answer button and was only vaguely aware of the voice on the other end.

"Gemma, Gemma?" said the worried voice. "It's mum, Gemma, talk to me. Are you ok? Where are you, sweetheart? Daniel, I don't think she can hear me." There was some indistinguishable noise then a male voice appeared, "Gemma. It's dad. Come on, pet. Tell me where you are. I'll come get you. Come back, we're all worried about you."

As though aware of the call for the first time, Gemma lifted the phone to her ear, "I'm going to get him, Dad. I'm going to kill Karl Ellis."

"Gemma, no one's killing anyone. The police will get him, and they'll arrest him. He'll pay for what he's done. We'll talk about that some other time. Where are you? We're worried sick! I'm coming to get you."

She shook her head. "I'm fine, dad. I don't want to grieve anymore. No more talking, no more crying, no more yelling, I'm going to get Ellis, I'm going to get him for Duncan. No more talking, dad." She cut the call off and dropped the phone into her pocket before walking off toward the river.

I loved you, Duncan. More than you can ever know. I'll get him for you. What happens to me after this doesn't matter, he'll pay for what he did to you. I swear that with all my heart!

What Lies Beneath?

Where to begin? I must confess that the question has plagued my mind for hours now, ever since I was talked into writing this down. How to tell you; how to explain both to you and to myself, because though it happened long ago, I still cannot wrap my mind around the concept; I cannot face up to it. At this point in time I do not believe I shall ever be able to explain. As for the nightmares, my doctor says I can expect them to decrease with time, though he was somewhat less than co-operative when asked if they would disappear entirely.

In order to write this account, I am forced to carry my little typewriter around, as my hands still shake so much that I'm afraid whatever I write will be illegible anyway. I warn you now, that once my account has been written and read by you, I am confident that we shall be joined in our terror. Therefore should you be of a nervous disposition, I recommend reading this only during the day, no doubt several of you thrill seekers will insist on reading a page or two at midnight.

I will be asking several things of you over the next few pages as I invite you to read my tale, to recollect with me the night of terror that I experienced, I would ask that you suspend all disbelief. Ignore what you have been told of the occult and witchcraft. I myself was once an opposing speaker on such matters. If you feel able to do this, then by all means, read on....

My tale begins at around eight am, several days into a holiday which I had imposed upon me. A large stone cracking from my bedroom window rudely awakened me; I jumped up and ran to the window, expecting to see some local village idiot run away laughing. Instead, to my surprise I saw my college friend and coworker Ian Kelly.

"Kelly? What the hell are you doing? Trying to break my window?" I raged. I confess to being somewhat of a tyrant when wakened. This particular method had left me even grouchier.

Kelly ignored my outbursts and only then did I see that he was dancing and jumping around. Obviously something had taken him. "Duncan, you've got to come quick, Brian's called me, and they've found it!"

Now if I may digress here, my name is Dr Alexander Jeffries, and the Brian in question was my immediate supervisor at

Strathclyde museum, located on the outskirts of Glasgow, Dr Brian Reid. I was by trade an archaeologist, specialising in ancient lore. We had been friends since the late fifties, and I had begun working for him about four years ago, nineteen sixty five to be exact. I was working on a long term assignment searching for proof of certain historical legends, as I said earlier, I had no belief in the occult as such, but was intrigued by the facts behind the legends, and one such tale really appealed to me. I had stumbled upon it almost by accident and with characteristic determination and zeal, had hounded my superior into opening up a very small fund and allowing me to busy myself with looking into this intrigue. I was almost immediately struck at the complete lack of information, but as you will see, it proved not to be an issue. It haunted my dreams and occupied my thoughts for years and years and now suddenly, I was on the cusp of achieving it all. I had worked myself almost into a form of mania when, concerned at my mental attitude, I was barred from working and sent home and into that imposed holiday of which I have already mentioned. Now here was Dr Kelly telling me that I was, as I had always known, not quite mad.

My tiredness and foul mood fell from me like a blanket. All the months of work, the late nights, the content trips to the library and of long days scrolling through the tedium of microfiche and foreign correspondence. In my excitement I almost jumped from my window. "Wait there!" I yelled and in record time was dressed and had washed.

I ran from my home pulling my coat on. "We'll take your car," I said to Kelly and without waiting for an answer I jumped into the passenger side of the vehicle.

Now, Kelly, usually very conservative about petrol and the use of his motor car did not even utter a grievance, instead he gunned the car to life and sped down my driveway at incredible speed.

"I was just sitting in the lab, cleaning the upper condyle of a middle-aged Cro-Magnon femur we have recently taken possession of," he said, sounding more and more like a little boy who'd just seen Santa, "when the phone rang; took me about an hour to get the story from Brian, all I could hear was the sound of heavy machinery and him laughing." Kelly hit the brakes hard, almost forcing me through the windscreen; the other driver signaled his annoyance with a resounding blast from his horn.

"A lot of good it will do if you kill us!" I snorted.

Again, Kelly ignored me. "It was right where you said it would be; you were right to suggest the higher altitude."

I accepted what would be my only compliment with an air of indifference. I had been snubbed by these two doctors enough times in the past, and admit to a small half smile at seeing the never-wrong Dr Kelly give me my due.

"Anyway, we've got to be there by nine tonight. I've chartered a small plane that'll take us direct from Prestwick, so we need to head straight there." He fumbled in the glove box and pulled my passport from it. "I grabbed it from your locker to save time," he said with a grin.

"Now hang on," I said, looking down at my very inappropriate attire. "You didn't say we were going! I thought we were off to the museum. Look at me! Where the hell am I to get some proper clothing?"

Kelly cast a sideways look at my corduroy trousers and short sleeved shirt. "Don't worry, we'll send for some things, you can borrow some of mine."

I looked at his expanding waist and rolled my eyes.

And that was that, only an hour ago I had been sound asleep dreaming peacefully about my three-week vacation. Here I was now, on my way to some far off land - no luggage, and with nothing except a lunatic driver at my side.

I knew then that this was going to be one hell of a trip, I realise now just how much of an understatement that really was.

After a horrendous flight from Prestwick Airport and a stopover in god knows where, meaning of course he lied about the direct flight - Brian know how much I hate flying, we arrived in the small Serbian village of Kisiljavo, and eventually made our way to the operation centre only a half hour late, the rain was as thick as I had imagined on the way up. Arriving at the camp I was pleasantly surprised to learn that the weather front had moved downward, the earth was sodden, though, and a mild breeze had settled in threatening to chill us to the bones, however, I expected a warm welcome from my colleague, though to look at Brian you'd think we were a week late.

He stormed up to the helicopter before the rotors had even slowed, yanked the door open and pulled poor Kelly right from his seat.

"Christ! What kept you? You know what's going on here!"

My explanation about the air traffic controllers' strike and the terrible weather proved to be no explanation at all, Brian dismissed it with a wave of his hand.

"I sent Big and Douglas on ahead - what with the time it is now it'll be dark by the time we get there!"

I resisted the urge to tell him that it would still have been dark any way had we arrived at nine.

You can imagine his response when I told him I wanted to get changed first. Let me just say it was not at all pretty, nor civil. Once again I was changed in record time and set off at a tremendous pace. Ten minutes later poor Kelly was panting heavily. A suggestion that we slow down earned me several curses and unwelcome suggestions from the good Dr Brian Reid.

Once he had decided we were making good time after all Brian seemed to calm down, becoming his usual boisterous, happy self.

"We were digging on the second sight when young McAllister suddenly hit something; we scrabbled around in the dirt and uncovered what appears to be an old oaken roof. So far we've uncovered about twelve square feet, the roof itself is in remarkable condition, and I'd have thought it would have at least buckled under the weight of the dirt."

I felt my excitement match Brian's. Kelly for his part was silent; eyes wide open as he hung on for Brian's every word.

"Has anyone ventured inside?" I asked.

Brian shook his head vigorously. "No, there isn't an obvious entry point, and we daren't risk opening our own. I thought it better to wait for you." he grinned then. "That's what I pay you for anyway."

For good measure I threw in a comment about how seriously underpaid I was for a man of my expertise. - This was, of course, ignored.

After a further quarter of an hour I saw lights in the distance, the familiar lights of an excavation site.

"Ah, good old Douglas got the lights on," said Brian cheerfully.

Eventually we reached the sight, all I had hoped for, all I had prayed for lay before me as I looked down the excavated hole and saw what had got Brian so excited, what had earned me a rude awakening that morning, it was the top of a ruined castle.

Not so ruined if the rest was in as good condition as this tower roof was. Aside from the dirt there was not a sign that this was anything other than a perfectly good local building.

Except that we were very far up a mountain and it was buried beneath several tonnes of mountain.

"Give me a flashlight," I called. A second later young Nathan Big handed me the required instrument. I shone it down along the smooth roof. I could only imagine how deep this castle extended into the dirt.

I lay down to get a better look at the design. When my hand touched the surface my heart grew cold.

"It's warm," I said, barely a whisper.

Young Kelly gasped, Brian changed colour in a second and young Big merely nodded.

I looked at the latter.

"I didn't want to say anything, you know; in case you thought I was uh, mad."

I moved my hand further down and sure enough it was definitely warm.

"Probably the warmth from the lighting," said Brian, indicating our equipment.

I moved my hand to the dirt above the tiles, closer to the light: Cold. Stone cold, the warmth definitely had to be coming from inside, but how? The level of dirt and the analysis so far conducted pointed to the fact that this building, whatever it was, had lain covered with at least three centuries of dirt, silt and rubble. Could something still burn deep inside?

We retired for a debate that lasted for the best part of an hour. Should we blast a hole? Would the structure survive? Should we do an ultrasound, and what of the heat generating within?

It was eventually decided that I should cut open a small area enough to admit myself. So, I set to work and a while later I had cut a through most of the toughened, old wood, and only a piece of hard board remained.

The feeling of heat was still very much apparent, so much so that I worked up a sweat despite the cool wind of the night.

Brian handed me my requested saw and I cut straight. The wood fell through; followed by a pressure adjustment and the foul smell of air, long stale and dormant assailed us.

"Smell that?" said Dobson from behind me. "Putrid!"

I shone the light through the hole I had made. It appeared to be a small chamber, not dissimilar to the tower like rooms in fairy tales, though much more foreboding. There was no furniture. I couldn't tell at that stage if there was a carpet or not because the entire floor was covered in layers of dust, it reflected, casting eerie patterns in the light of my torch.

"What do you see?" Why Kelly was whispering, I do not know. I guess it just seemed the proper response. Every ounce of my body yelled caution.

"I'm going in," unconsciously mimicking Kelly's whisper.

I lowered myself into the tower and dropped onto the floor, my landing echoed deep into the belly of this building, seeming to go on forever.

"Duncan," hissed Kelly. "You okay?"

I looked up through the opening and grinned. "Guess that woke the dead."

Young Kelly's eyes widened and Brian shook his head. "Not funny."

"Is it safe for us to come down?" asked Kelly.

I explained that I'd rather go alone; too many people walking around on this floor could be dangerous as I hadn't really inspected it, and besides, I was the only one really qualified for this. Too many people and priceless artefacts could be broken or passed by. No, I was convinced it was much better to go alone.

So, with my team waiting for me at the opening, I proceeded to make a further inspection of what we had discovered. I had a small tape recorder with me which recorded the entire venture, though I lost that and subsequently must recall all the events from memory. The exact manner of how I lost the instrument will be explained later.

After a thorough search of the room, I located a large wooden door, which to my delight was unlocked. I informed Brian and the others about my intentions and proceeded out of the initial room.

Now, if I may backtrack a little. As to the warmth I had noticed earlier there was still no explanation for it. There was indeed warmth to the place not unlike a hotel corridor. None the less, I was still shivering, whether with adrenaline or fear I still cannot say.

The next half-hour I discovered nothing much of interest except drawing to the conclusion that this place was in fact vast, definitely a castle of sorts. I encountered a great number of bedrooms, all with sheets on the bed and a great deal of dust confirming for my overwrought imagination that no one had entered any of these rooms for a long time. Still, seeing all the beds made up like this was a little disconcerting to say the least.

I believe it was around that time that I heard a loud banging noise, annoyed to think that Brian or Kelly had ignored my advice and entered the place. Though there was no further activity, I put it down to structural disturbance. We had, after all, disturbed the pressure on this ancient thing quite recently and there was bound to be an adjusting period.

After going down a few floors I began to notice a change in the rooms, they became more state like, more like guest areas than anything else. I encountered a very large ballroom, complete with dinner plates and a rather antiquated piano, which to my delight was still tuned perfectly.

I played a small tune, cruel in my belief that if he were able to hear it young Kelly would have been off down that mountain screaming bloody murder. After a few minutes my joke was over and I again resumed my exploration.

I eventually moved into an area that resembled living quarters, the rooms took on a more intimate look, the pictures on the walls were more akin to individual tastes as opposed to the room decor look the other bedrooms had. It was upon close inspection of one of these quarters that I made contact with my first disturbing find. I entered a room that in contrast to the others was very untidy, signs of a struggle were apparent in the way the table was overturned, with plates and the like smashed on the floor. I had turned to leave when my eyes fell upon the bed.

There lay the exposed figure of a corpse. I took a moment to recover from the shock and made a closer inspection. This man had not died of natural causes, the eyes were thrown open in terror and the jaw was locked in a scream. I then noticed the bindings on wrists and feet. One hand was free of the bindings though with considerable tissue damage, the flesh, which was by now dry and withered, was torn from the wrist; he had obviously pulled his arm free at considerable cost.

Judging from the taunt skin and the general look of the cadaver, I'd say it had been there a long time. I ran from the room, feeling my first sense of fear since entering this tomb. A further search of the surrounding rooms uncovered twelve more bodies, bringing the total so far to thirteen. Not being a superstitious type I did not bother trying to relate the figure to any kind of sick ritual. What I did notice, however, was that all appeared to have been murdered. A knife or some other sharp object had been carefully shoved up through the underside of the jaw, straight into the brain. Death would have been instantaneous. Others appeared burned, others had strange markings etched on them, all written in a language I had never seen before. There were also identical and inexplicable wounds on the chests of each victim at the approximate position of the heart. My best attempt to describe these wounds would be as though done by an animal like a large dog or the like.

With a feeling of intense trepidation I continued along the corridor, my imagination must have come too at that point for I remember hearing all sorts of noises and seeing all kinds of shadows move. These shadows were most often seen, however fleetingly, from the farthest point of my peripheral vision, almost at the point of there/not there. It was disconcerting at best and only added to my unease.

I admit I wanted to flee, to go to a tavern and recount my tale with my friends, have a laugh over my piano joke. But I was curious; it was also my job. How many different ruins had I explored? I stopped dead in my tracks at that point as I suddenly realised that there was the exact root of the problem which had, until now eluded me: Ruins! This was hardly a ruin. A good housekeeping job and this place could open for business.

Relentlessly I continued my voyage of discovery. Each room had within it a myriad of treasures - from art, to plate, to antiquities of all kinds, and not only that, they were not from one specific area.

There were items from ancient China; Greece; Afghanistan; Egypt, I even spotted many differing items from late in the Byzantium Empire. Although by now I was not at my best professionally and failed in my job terribly.

To whom did this castle belong? Why and how had it been buried this way, not even a slightest hint of collapse was apparent anywhere. And still, all around this place hung the air of death, a stale musty odour that seemed to cling to every wall, to every door, to every curtain and cling to my throat in the most unsettling way. By now I had long since given up opening curtains; all I ever saw was the most unnatural darkness caused, in fact from dirt, piled up beyond the windows, just as it should be given that I was by now many metres underground. The fact

Brian had had to dig so deep to even find the top of the tower told me, logically, that I would see only blackness from the windows. I discouraged myself from thinking just how deep I was inside the castle, how much dirt was above me. I had long since told myself not to think of structural collapse, if it happened I was helpless, destined to become another relic in this place which would become my sepulchre.

I tried to calm myself by attempting to become once more a doctor of archaeology and gently remind myself that my being here was the culmination of a lot of work. I was, after all, the one who had insisted on this venture. Uncovering allusions to a castle no one had ever heard of, finding obscure references in documents of the time and even interviewing the local people who had insisted they had seen light coming from up in the mountain after unusually strong autumnal or seasonal storms. Then there were the drawings in the library of a large, monstrous place. So many things pointed to an undiscovered castle, some rogue warlord from the crusades? Many, like Brian believed it a royal family, exiled from their homeland. To me it didn't matter, the thought of such a treasure just begging discovery was too good an opportunity to pass up. So I had convinced Brian to give me the funding and to hire locals to begin an investigation. Then, once I had worked myself to exhaustion I had been ordered to take a vacation. What happened then? Just after my leave started Brian found the bloody thing!

So here I was. Deep inside this castle, surrounded by murdered bodies and enviable treasure and the find of a life time, and right now I would have traded it all to be home in my bed having been wrong about the existence of this mysterious and terrifying conundrum.

It was after I had searched the fifth floor that things really started to scare me. The noises grew more apparent, coming from inside, and definitely not structural. There was also a terrible smell, like some rotting vegetation that sometimes preceded me in a room or had suddenly appeared outside of a room I was exiting, and there were the sightings.

Every so often I would catch a glimpse of something just pulling round a corner, yet when I got there, nothing. Was I going out of my mind? Was the air so bad in here I had started to hallucinate?

There was one other worrying thing, the one thing that made me realise I was still quite sane: Fresh footprints. They were as clear as day just before me. With my heart in my mouth I carried on, more cautious now. I came eventually to a large iron door; the footprints lead me straight here. The smell was strongest here, like death itself; I tore a strip from my tunic and wrapped it round my face, desperate to rid myself of the smell that was now tearing at my very senses.

With terror engulfing me I shoved the door. Locked. I pulled and pushed but it would not open. With what I could only describe as a sense of relief I walked away from the door. I had tried, after all. At least I could say that.

I had gone less than twenty feet when I heard the most awful noise, like rusted metal being moved after so long. I grew cold, realising where the noise had originated. I withdrew my small revolver and returned to the large iron door.

I was not surprised to find it ajar, with the coldest black I had ever bore witness to permeating from within. I shone my torch through the opening and saw my light swallowed whole. It would not penetrate onto that awful blackness more than a few feet.

As I approached the door I wretched, even through my face cloth I could smell it. Death, decay and what I could only call pure evil. Powerless to prevent myself from resisting, I entered the blackness.

After taking several steps inside the room panic threatened to engulf me, I struggled to breath and my chest was pounding terribly. Several times I nearly dropped by revolver and torch due to the slick perspiration which was now emanating from me. What had caused this change in my fear response? I suddenly realised what was wrong: I was not alone. I heard the sound of strained breathing, ever so slightly from within the room. With my hand shaking, I lifted my gun. "Who's there?" I demanded, surprising myself with the authority in my voice.

I heard it then, a voice, a voice speaking again after a long silence; I strained to hear it.

"So, you have found me!" The voice was cold, making my hairs stand up even further. It radiated hatred and sounded as though... well, as though it had not spoken for a long time, as if every word was forced through old and unused vocal chords.

Terror hung at my back; I wanted to turn, to run but was paralysed on the spot. "Who's there?" I yelled again.

There followed a loud moan that seemed to tear at my thundering heart.

"Show yourself?"

"But I have no light," whispered the voice. Its next statement chilled me to my very soul. "Can you not see? I see you clearly."

I managed to back away slightly.

"You would leave?" hissed the voice. "The first to see me in centuries and you would run?"

"Who are you?" I repeated.

"Who I am is not important, the fact you found me is," it replied.

I grew aware then of a kind of dragging sound, the voice becoming closer. "Ahh, youth, I know that scent anywhere. Tell me boy, how have you found what no other ever has?"

"I…I…" I lost the power of speech for a moment.

A sickening laugh followed. "No matter, boy, I am in your debt. No doubt you expect wishes, you rescue me, so I give thee three, is that not the way of it?"

A genie perhaps? I said this.

"If it makes it easier for your little mind to imagine that, then by all means, for you, boy. I'll be a genie! Shall I dance for you, play songs?" I swear then, although I cannot explain but I heard a piano play some hideous piece of old music, it was as though the piano strings were old and in need of service. It was impossible to tell from where the terrific music came from. It stopped as suddenly as it had begun.

I managed, somehow, to regain control. "Did you kill those people?"

"You found my guests! Ah! They but died of boredom, my boy. They came from all over in pursuit of a parable, for a banquet; to taste of things only the very rich and the very arrogantly bored desire. (That explained the many cultural artefacts and styles I found). They could not bear to live with what they found. A treasure chest, that's what I am. I am a purse ever full with riches never seen. They came to seek a truth they could ultimately not understand and in the end they begged me for my final gift... the gift of release until… well, perhaps it is not time to reveal the truth behind the Thirteenth Parable, not until I find it out if you are noble enough in blood."

I grew suddenly aware of breathing on my neck, the terrible smell.

"Young flesh!" he hissed. "Tell me boy, how long have you sulked upon this Earth, how long? Twenty years?"

"I'm twenty nine," I replied.

"Ah, young indeed - a fleeting moment to be sure, and in your few moments of life you found my humble home, clever of you. Tell me, what did you hope to find in this place?"

I explained that I was merely interested in the past.

The creature laughed. "What if I tell you it was all for nothing? The past is dead, boy; there's nothing there for you, would you trade the future for the past; life for death? That's a fool's errand, boy. Tell me: Why does what's gone interest you more than what has yet to come?"

I explained my interest in the past, in what I believed it taught us about what was to come.

The creature laughed a long and terrible laugh. Then fell silent. "You want to learn from me, do you?"

"Who are you?" I ventured again.

"Would you see me, Duncan?" it hissed.

I recoiled at the mention of my name. How did it know me?

As though the terrible thing could read my thoughts, he spoke. "Yes, Duncan, I know many things about you. I know the terrible fate that awaits you. What of young Mistress Victoria? Gone! She left you to your endless dreams, didn't she? Such a prize as her and you lost her to this pursuit of the past? I know all there is to know of you, Master Duncan, son of Peter and Amanda, brother to Steven and dear Elisabeth. Shall I go on? I know of the sickness forming quietly in your lungs, I know that no child of your loins will ever carry you into the next generation. Immortality through progeny is denied you, Duncan, though I offer you something greater!"

I managed to shake my head and I must have uttered something along the lines of "leave me alone!" or something as ridiculously sounding.

"Your anxious colleagues up there, shall we talk of them? Talk of how finding me has signified the end of their pathetic lives?"

Before I could reply, could regain control he spoke again. "Would you see me, boy?"

Suddenly a blinding light erupted; I threw my hands to my face. A second later I looked, seeing many candles had burst to life around the hall. Then I saw it.

The creature!

Never will I be able to fully explain what I saw. Flesh so emaciated, so decayed that logically there was no way the thing could be alive. It huddled under its broken form. Hairless save for a few long and ill-nourished strands, eyeless, bloodless, the skin so pale as to be almost green and so sunken and withered, yet unmistakably in the shape of a man. It was the undead itself; purest evil reeked from the terrible grin made from yellowed and pointed teeth. It wore around its skeletal frame a robe of the blackest black, threadbare, but suggestive of royalty.

The lifeless sockets looked up at me. A smile appeared; those vicious looking teeth flashed, the only part that looked alive.

The old tales of Dracula and the genre came to me then, I remembered all the old actors I had watched as a boy, Karloff, Price, Shreck, Lee. They did not do this thing justice. I cried aloud as I stared at the grotesque creature. The worst part of it was the familiarity – I knew I had seen this place in countless dreams, even the terrible eyes were familiar to me. As I stood there, rigid in fear and wrestling with this horrid Deja vu he advanced toward me. "Now, let us find out, Duncan, if you were worthy of my pain and sacrifice."

It screamed then, a terrible scream of anger, pain, and of rage before it lunged at me; I had never before seen such speed. He was upon me in a second. I felt hot, cold, in between; I felt the repugnant stench of decay from his very bones. My head spun, I was falling, falling, losing myself, I felt death. The foreknowledge that never again would I ever make up those hollow promises to my dear Victoria, then…

Blackness….

I awoke several hours later; I am remembering the terrible effort I exerted in attempting to rise from the cold floor. I felt weak, drained. Not realising at the time just how close to death I actually was. Now remember I said I had a tape recorder with me, I saw it broken with the tape running far down the corridor. I seemed to spend hours just trying to stand, to walk down the silent corridors.

I managed to return to my point of entry, finding no trace of my fearsome tormentor. I called out for Brian or Kelly to assist me. There was no reply. I saw the blood red of the sky above me with the first strands of dawn snaking their way through the blackness.

I recalled the creature's claims that my friends would die and my remaining blood chilled and my far for their safety helped me find within myself the strength to somehow climb up, though it took me an eternity, I finally made it up. What I saw made me fall upon my hands and knees to the earth, I may have cried aloud, I don't remember. There before me lay the prone figures of Brian Reid and young Kelly. Looking down the mountainside, I saw more bodies - all of my companions had fallen. All their bodies had been mutilated. Their faces locked in a terrible grimace of death. There had been pain, terror before the mercy of death had taken them. I was alone. The sole survivor of… of what?

So that is my tale. Somehow I was able to get myself back down the mountainside. I even saw the burned remnants of the helicopter with the remains of the pilot inside. The authorities were skeptical of my tale, no one believed it and I spent several weeks in jail before my lawyer was able to negotiate my release but I knew I could never go home, I knew I had to protect my family so I stay away.

No one found the castle, a strange quake had appeared the same day I was found at the bottom of the mountain, all traces of the castle were gone and no one was in a hurry to try and dig it out again.

What was the creature? A vampire you might say? I don't believe so, not in the traditional sense. No, for one I saw no coffins or what have you. To this day I have no idea what it was, perhaps some freak of nature, an unholy immortal. Perhaps the creature was so powerful that to him death was just another conquered foe.

What was more worrying to me was how it knew my name, how it knew so much about me. The "sickness forming quietly in my lungs" that he had mentioned turned out to be the beginnings of lung cancer, for which I am in the midst of treatment. Had this creature saved my life and if so, why? Does he have some further plans for me, plans that my death by cancer would have affected?

What if the creature had somehow influenced my mind and played me like a puppet all along, pulling me to his castle, feeding me with dreams of finding a hidden world. More terrifyingly, what if he had influenced my entire career? To this day, a year to the day since the event I have not had the same desire to return to work. All thoughts about digging in dirt are now alien to me.

And what did it mean. "So at last you've found me!" Was he merely being general in his statement, meaning me as an archaeologist or did me mean, more specifically, me? I am more inclined to believe that.

I remember long after the event walking through the town feeling eyes upon me, catching a man staring at me with a knowing smile. Was it him? Was the creature once more stalking me? I do not know, nor do I want to know, for all I know he is not yet finished with me. True he still comes to me in my dreams, laughing as he flies at me. The laugh is not a menacing one, just one of enjoyment.

So, to you reading my tale I draw your attention to one thing; just remember he is out there. I have no idea what he may look like now, for all I know he would be the man sitting next to me as I write these words. He could have been the man I accidentally nudged at the train station yesterday. I do not know. I fear I am losing my mind; I fear that this creature may yet claim me. He is out there, somewhere – this terrible creature who survived, buried underground for three hundred years, and whatever macabre or evil goal he was chasing remains unfulfilled. That leaves me terribly afraid and it should you too

I know only one thing for certain: we should all beware…

The Red Stain

Prologue

The red stain began slowly, working its way across the white shirt, contrasting with the enamel white of the garment. White upon white at first, then slowly the white retreated as the red overcame it. At first it didn't look too bad, and then gradually it was obvious: This wound was fatal.

Fatal!

That meant any chance of completing the mission was gone now; no way to finish that which he had promised, that which he had sold his very soul to complete.

This is not how I envisioned it, he thought to himself.

Death! It had such an ominous sound to it, like the slamming of a door - finality.

And wasn't pain supposed to be part of it? Yet there was no pain. He allowed himself to admit to himself that his mind probably wasn't really all that sharp.

Then he felt it; the growing feeling in his stomach, a feeling that made him want to vomit... made him want to... die! Pain! He was right pain did accompany death. Pain did block out all other thoughts and sensation.

This is it! I'm in the final throes of my life! He felt cold, so very cold.

And alone.

That was the worst feeling of all. He wasn't supposed to die like this, although at least he wouldn't have to face the others back home. Even if he could survive this would he want to? Would he want to return home? To tell them all that he had failed; tell them what he knew? Explain to them what was coming?

He shook his head, as much as he could anyway, paralysis was edging its way up his torso, how long had it been since he felt his legs, his hands? Felt… anything?

Too long! And any minute they would find him.

He grinned. No. They would not find him; they would find a useless corpse. They would still have nothing! All the searching, all the yelling and they would have nothing. They could retrieve the disc, sure. But by now it was too late.

"Do you hear me?" He yelled. "You have nothing!" He laughed then, a long and violent laugh that echoed until his very life left him, a deep cry that transformed the laugh into a howl of pain... and of rage.

The soldiers stopped again to listen to the cry; to try and place it, but by the time they had located its source they were too late.

Too late...

Six months!

He was told he would only be here six months, yet already he was half way through the ninth! He lashed out and punched the metal can that was their base.

"Hey, Jack, Take it easy, all right?"

Jack turned and saw Billy and Danny approach. Billy said: "I take it the fat bastard won't let you leave."

Jack sighed. "Billy, I'm here for another three at least. Damn him! He knows I've got a wife, and a baby daughter I ain't even seen yet. But he won't let me go! What possible use can I be to him? I've done all I can! Can't he see that?"

Billy smiled. "Apparently not. One thing about the General, seeing the obvious isn't one of his strong points." He hit Jack on the arm. "Come on, Pal. Three months, that ain't bad for a civilian like you".

"Yeah" said Danny. "Just think if you join up now you'd be here for another year, I could speak to the General for you."

Jack smiled, and gave his friend a look. "A year with you and that arse-hole? No thanks."

"Just a thought." Danny casually ran his hand down his army combat uniform and eyed Jack's shirt and denims warily. "With all the shit that's going down here wouldn't you be happier in this lot?"

Jack shook his head. "I spent five years trying to get out of that uniform and now you want to put me back in it? No thanks!" He smiled ruefully. Too many things had happened to him these past years, and the thought of returning to that uniform was enough.

He looked to Billy. "So, you do have the return readings for those soil samples yet?"

Billy shook his head. "No, the General won't release them to civilian custody yet, says he still has to clear them with ballistics first."

Jack felt the anger rising in him. "In case it's some kind of weapon, eh?"

Billy looked to the ground. "Something like that."

"I'm sick to death of these damn power-play antics of that guy!" He stormed down the corridor.

"Where you going?" yelled Billy.

"To do something I should have done a long time ago."

"Don't do anything stupid!" Warned Danny.

Too late for that!

"…And threaten him this time if you have to! I don't want their reporters in here anymore. How many times do they want me to tell them that?" General Tom Colson shook his head in anger.

The corporal before him nodded and quickly left. Colson sighed and returned to his desk. No sooner had he lifted his coffee cup to his lips when the door burst open, causing him to tip the remaining coffee down his shirt. "Jesus Christ! Who the...?" He looked up in a rage. "Oh, it's you," he said matter-of-factly. "Well, I guess you better come in."

Jack Rein stood in the doorway, his face contorted into a deep rage. "We're going to have this out once and for all!" he roared.

"Have a seat," said Colson. He rubbed the coffee from his tunic and looked up. "What're you here for."

"Cut the crap, Colson! You know damn well what I want. First you don't let me leave this damn hellhole and secondly, you won't release the soil samples and let me finish my work. Why! Why not?"

Colson stood his face livid with controlled anger. "I ought to land you on your pompous little ass right now, you civie turncoat!"

Jack stormed to the head of the table. "Any time, you bastard! It's been a long time coming!"

Colson caught himself and walked to the window. "That's in the past now. We're talking about the present."

Jack scoffed. "Since when did you know the difference?"

"Listen Dammit! I was prepared to forget what happened back then. As I recall it was you who wouldn't let it lie!" He slammed a palm on the desk. "You want to know about the soil samples, alright! They came back positive!"

Jack seemed to fall apart, as though he had been physically struck. "Positive," he whispered.

Colson softened slightly. "Yes, positive. That's why they haven't been released to you. We can't turn this over to a civilian." He raised a hand to silence Jack who was about to explode. "And it's not because of that or anything else. I have my orders, Jack."

Jack cursed loudly. "So why keep me here? You won't let me at the samples, therefore I can't do my job, but you still won't let me leave."

"Go then! Get your ass out of here, I won't argue with you anymore, if you want out, fine! You're out. Collect your things and get out. I'll have Major Gunn escort you off the base."

"Tom," said Jack quietly. "I can't leave now; I can't leave you here, especially not now."

Colson half smiled. "Jack, get out of here. This isn't the time for heroics, get out while you can. You've had limited exposure, you're clear." He turned again to the small window. "I'm sorry; I should have let you go when you wanted. I'm sorry."

"And you?"

Colson was silent for a few moments, and then finally he spoke, softly. "I've come out positive also."

"Oh Jesus, Tom!" Jack flung a hand to his forehead. "Give me access; I'll come up with a counter measure. All I need is time!"

Colson turned again. "As much as I trust you to carry out the tests I can't give you access to the data, and I can't allow you on the field. Go, Jack. Take your things and get out of here."

"Tom, I..."

"Alright! I'll send your things to you but you're going - one way or the other! I don't need you here, Jack." He grabbed his combat jacket from the stand on the wall. "I've got work to do." He walked past Jack and into the corridor without another word.

"Oh Jesus!" Shouted Jack and walked out.

"Jack! Hey Jack!" Billy Gunn yelled across the field. Jack stopped and turned as Billy approached him. "Jack, what is all this? First you tell me he won't let you leave and now I get a call from Colson telling me to escort you to the airfield, what's going on, Jack?"

Jack sighed. "I'm staying, Billy. It's fine; Colson will fill you in during the briefing." He started to walk away.

"Jack!"

"At the briefing, Billy. That's all I can tell you."

It was late at night when General Colson walked into the briefing room clutching his papers, with a look around him he noticed that all officers were present.

He approached the stand and nodded. "Okay, gentlemen, thank you for attending. I remind you that this meeting is classified. What you are about to be told is Class-One. Is that understood? Anyone who does not have that level of military clearance should leave now. No notes are to be taken and absolutely no recording equipment of any sort. There will be no discussion outside of this area. Is that understood?"

There were various nods from those assembled. "Very well." He took a long deep breath. "Eight months ago I received an order from Top Brass. All I was told is that I was to ship my men out here to this damn jungle. Now, we all heard stories about why we were being sent here. This is rumour control: We were sent here to locate a small meteorite, which crashed in this jungle. As you all know needles and haystacks don't even come close! But, after extensive searching we did find it, six weeks ago.

"Because of the strange nature of this meteorite we, the military, were sent in to keep the native population away from it, it was rumoured in the beginning that it was a UFO, but I am glad to say that there are no little green men inside."

There were various chuckles from around the room. "However, you were all aware of the civilian team we brought in, mostly containing doctors and scientists and a few others, mainly a chief meteorologist who we all know, Jack Rein. Now this team was principally here to ascertain the nature of the meteor and its composition, now I'm sure we all by now know that something is amiss."

There were a few concerned looks from those gathered.

"At first we didn't know what it was which is why we restricted access to the crash site. Unfortunately this was not enough. At oh six hundred hours this morning the two men assigned to guard the area became ill. It was noted later that these two men had guarded the site for nine hours straight. Now, no one know what happened or why, but I am afraid to say both men died earlier this evening." He stopped to allow his words to sink in.

"Sir," Danny called out.

Colson looked him out. "Yes, son?"

"Sir, what exactly is happening here?"

"At this time we are still unsure. I have orders from Washington. All non-military personnel are to be evacuated immediately, and we are to remain on site for the meantime to ensure no unauthorised access."

"What is the danger to us, sir?" asked one of the men.

"I will not lie to you. There is a risk of contamination."

"What kind of contamination?"

"I don't know. All I know is that contamination is not passed from one person to another, only direct contact with the meteor itself is dangerous."

A few men jumped up and chaos ensued.

"I was near it!"

"I touched the fucking thing!"

"Christ, I was guarding the perimeter!"

"Oh hell! I was..."

Colson banged his fist on the desk until order was restored. "Thank you," he said quietly. "Some of you are no doubt contaminated and I cannot say what will happen, we do have our best men analysing the data right now."

"It's alright for you to say that! You're not infected. We should have been told Dammit! We should have been warned!"

Colson charged from the podium and grabbed the man. "Listen you piece of shit! I am infected!" He threw man to the ground. "We're soldiers! The very thought of panicking and running should be as alien to you as that god-damned meteor outside! We are soldiers! We don't run from a damn rock! We don't...."

Jack Rein walked with his friend Danny into the small hut where the briefing was being held. "I'm sorry, Jack," he said. "I didn't know what else to do. It's a complete fuck up!"

Jack clapped him on the arm. "It's ok, pal, we've been through worse!"

Danny nodded and pulled the tent flap back and followed Jack inside.

The place was a mess. Chairs had been overturned and weapons and clothing had been dropped in what had obviously been a panic.

Tom Colson sat on the small step before the podium. He acknowledged the new arrivals with his eyes only, as though he saw them but didn't care.

"Tom, what happened?"

"Get out," said Colson weakly. "You're not authorised to be here. Sergeant, get him out of here!"

"Tom?"

Colson threw a cup at him. "Get out, I say!"

Jack grabbed him and hauled him to his feet. "Tom! What happened?"

"They left, that's what happened! I couldn't stop them, cowards the blasted lot of them. It's not like the old days, Jack. Remember? There was loyalty there, and do you know why?" He didn't wait for an answer. "Because our boys knew who they were fighting. But look here. Their only enemy is a rock. A fucking great big rock! How's a man meant to fight a rock?" He took a handgun from his side and fired a round over Jack's head. "May as well piss on the fucking thing!"

It was only then that Jack noticed he was drunk. Totally intoxicated was more like it!

"Tom, we've got to get out of here."

"What!" Tom shoved Jack back, sending him sprawling across the floor. Colson swung his pistol and aimed it at Jack. You a fucking coward too? Go then, you yellow bastard! I'll handle it!"

"Tom, put the gun down," said Jack. "Tom."

"Put it down!" A voice yelled from the doorway. Both Jack and Colson turned, saw Billy Gunn standing there, his own pistol drawn and aimed at Colson. "It's ok, Danny, I got this. You should get out of here."

Danny stood, undecided, he looked at Jack, who nodded. Danny slipped past Billy and fled the scene.

"Put the gun down, General," repeated Billy.

Colson threw his head back and laughed, looking at Billy, he spoke to Jack. "I'm not going to shoot you, Jack. I won't waste a decent bullet." He dropped the gun and sat back down.

Billy approached. "You okay, Jack?"

Jack nodded. "Fine.

Billy walked over to Colson. "Jack, we're got to get him out of here."

"We can't," said Jack. "None of us can leave now. I've got to find out more about that damn thing. There's no telling what damage it can do."

"Jack?"

"I mean it, Billy. I need to know what's causing the disease, if it's particles from the meteor we need to find out how to stop it. The wind will carry those particles for miles and who knows how many will be killed. Christ knows how many local farms have been infected already!"

Billy set his jaw into a grim line. "So what? The people here aren't our concern! My main thought is to you, and whatever's left of my unit!"

Jack turned to Billy, a pleading look in his eyes. "Billy, we can't run from this, don't you see? This thing could spread all over the planet, I know it sounds corny, but believe me we don't know the extent of this stuff!"

“What’s that I’m hearing? Rein the runner! Rein the coward wanting to stay?” Colson surged to his feet. “And you Gunn, want to run? Well, things have changed around here!”

“Tom, you’re drunk, leave off,” said Jack.

“Piss on you, you coward!”

“Tom, there’s only so much I’ll take...” warned Jack.

“And me,” said Billy. “Jack...”

Jack raised a hand. “I’ll take Tom to his bunk. Leave if you want, Billy, I’ll stay a while.”

“If you stay, I stay.” Without another word he helped Jack lift the now unconscious form of General Colson.

Major William Gunn walked into the tent bearing two cups of coffee and several charts. He dropped the charts onto the large conference table already over flowing with aerial photographs, maps sketches, and other items

Jack Rein scowled as he looked up at the latest distraction. His gaze softened as he saw Billy.

Billy smiled as he handed one cup to his friend. He took a sip from his own cup. "So, how's it going?"

Jack rubbed his eyes and sighed deeply. He slurped his coffee. "Terrible!" he replied. I've gone over everything a dozen times." He shook his head. "How's Tom?"

Billy smiled. "Sleeping like a baby."

Jack nodded. "Sure am jealous. Feels like forever since I slept! What I wouldn't give to be him about now!"

Billy smiled weakly. "Aside from the exposure."

Jack grimaced. "I know," he said softly. "What about you, Billy? Are you clean?"

Billy nodded. "Yeah, I'm clean."

Jack pulled at his lip. "Strange."

"What?"

"How you're ok and most of the unit is infected."

Billy grinned. "Because I never went near the damn thing. I stayed here where I belong. I stopped guard duty when I was a corporal."

Jack nodded absently. "Funny how Colson got infected. He made it plain from the start that he wouldn't go 'near a fucking rock' you would think he was clean too."

"You know The General, he might have ranted about it but underneath he was as curious as the rest of us."

"Yeah. All of us except for you."

Billy frowned. "What are you getting at, Jack?"

"How come you never went near it? You recommended me for this without even looking at it. My own clean health is simple enough. Colson was so into reminding me that I'm not military any more that he wouldn't let me within a mile of it. How come you never went there?"

"Because I hate all that sci-fi shit, you know that! What the hell is this all about, Jack? What are you trying to say?"

"I just find it a little odd that you asked for me without even seeing the thing. What made you think I could do anything?"

Billy stared at him for a moment before his face darkened. "You know what, Jack! Fuck you! I knew you needed the work, I thought I was helping you! Jesus, that's the last time I help you out you ungrateful son of a bitch!

"I'm here to guard a military installation not to drool over a goddamn piece of space shit!"

Jack bowed his head. "I'm sorry, Bill. I'm tired, that's all."

Billy forced a smile. "Hell, I'm sorry too. Sorry for yelling and I'm sorry for getting you involved in all this."

Jack shook his head. He took a sip of coffee. "Billy. I need go out there. I need to examine it first-hand."

Billy stared at him in disbelief. "What? Everyone who went near it is dead or dying! Are you insane? Christ, if it's a death wish you want let me get my gun it'll save you the trouble! I don't believe you, Jack!"

"Billy! There's nothing more I can do here! I need access, it's our only chance."

Billy shook his head. "Fine, but don't expect me to go there."

Jack put down a surge of anger, "I'll go alone at first light. Right now I think we should get some sleep, okay?"

Billy nodded sullenly. "Don't expect much sleep I put enough coffee in that cup to keep a rhino awake for a month."

Jack smiled as he stood to leave. "You never could make a good coffee. I don't know why I never told you that."

Tom Colson awoke with a groan. He knew he was destined for a headache but he never expected one so bad. With a cough he sat up on the floor. It wasn't hard to pretend he was drunk, his officers were well aware of his love of the booze and so his little plan worked and they had thought him incapacitated and no threat to the treason he now knew existed.

Only now he part wished that he hadn't. Reaching a hand to his skull he winced as he felt the lump underneath the dried blood. His assailant had stuck with practised ease.

Of all the people why you? He asked. He had known ever since his test came back positive that there was a traitor involved. How else had he became infected? Now that he knew the truth he wished his attacker had finished the job. He probably had intended to but why waste the energy when Colson was dead in a matter of hours anyway.

He just didn't know it yet.

With an effort he managed to stand and fight off the wave of nausea that threatened to overwhelm him. Whether it was caused by the attack or by the infection he couldn't say.

But sick or not he had to warn him. He had to!

Jack Rehn rolled over in his bunk. Desperate though he was for sleep it still would not come. He lay on his back with his hands behind his head. He felt the exhaustion in every pore of his body. Not since the war had he felt this tired. He felt sick, sick to the very marrow in his bones. Too many problems to solve; too many questions still unanswered. He felt sure he was missing something but what? His subconscious knew the answer and was trying to tell him, it wouldn't let him sleep yet it was exactly that which was preventing him from thinking straight.

The solution was also the problem. His brain was stunned; well beyond tired it had entered that state where it refused to obey orders.

So he lay there. Tired. Cold, unable to think, unable to sleep, unable to stay awake.

He began to hallucinate. He imagined the figure of Tom Colson sneaking his way up to him.

He smiled weakly. "Go away, Tom. I'm too tired for this."

His brain registered a flaw in his logic when the hallucination clamped a hand over his mouth.

"Listen to me, Jack!" hissed Colson.

Jack grew aware that he was struggling. He forced himself to calm, felt Colson withdraw his hand.

"I know what's happening; I know why we're dying! There's nothing wrong with the damn meteor. Hell, it's not even a meteor, Jack! We've been set up all along. I went to the site. It's not a meteor at all."

Is this for real? Thought Jack.

"Yes, Jack. It's real. Focus, will you?"

Jack forced himself to focus. "What is it then?" He was fascinated by a mole on Colson's chin. He couldn't take his eyes off it.

"I don't know, Jack. But it's man made, you hear me? It's man made, some kind of long range aircraft. I scanned it for radiation and it's clean!" He forced himself to take a breath. When he spoke again he sounded solemn. "I found this in my hut." He pulled a small container from his jacket.

Jack forced himself to focus on it. "What is it?"

"Some kind of airborne toxin. They're in every hut."

Jack pulled himself back, away from Colson. "So you bring it here and infect me?"

Colson lowered his gaze. "This is from under your bunk; you're already infected."

Silence hung in the air. It was several seconds before Tom spoke again. "I know who's behind this all. The meteor was a cover to protect this whole damn site. I heard them talking and I think I have this whole thing figured out! What we have is a pod from a downed space shuttle. The first shuttle to Mars, Jack. Something went wrong on their way back. They started losing it. They refused to follow orders and instead circled the Earth taking all kinds of photographs and scans then relaying them away.

"The government felt it had no choice! They had to shoot the shuttle down."

"So we're here to rescue the crew?" asked Jack in disbelief. "We've been here nearly nine months, Tom. How long does it take?"

Colson shook his head furiously. "No, Jack. We're here to find out what was in that shuttle pod! That's why you weren't allowed access to the soil samples, because they were alien!"

"Why have me here in the first place?"

"You were the alibi, Jack. By bringing you, a renowned meteorologist, they averted suspicion. People are still trying to find the missing shuttle. They don't know it's here."

"And the crew?"

"Our people had orders. We were to quarantine the crew members. But they were already dead. All of them! Jesus, you should have seen them!" He shuddered. "They were… they were horrible, Jack!"

"Then what of your unit? What killed them?"

Colson stared at him, sorrow etched on his face. "He killed them, Jack. He killed them all! He tried to make out that our people were dying from the radiation. But I found out about it. We're all dead, Jack. Expendable!" He grabbed Jack by the shoulders. "We were set up all along. I thought you would be spared, but he wants us all dead! Dammit Jack, we're already dead! There's another source at work here."

"Who set us up, Tom? Who?"

As Tom opened his mouth to speak a gunshot yelled in the night, a sudden shriek against the silence. It seemed to reverberate through the surroundings. Rolling over and over.

Jack fell back as he was sprayed with blood. He turned to look at Tom.

Tom clutched his hands to his chest where the hole was, blood fell through his fingers. His face was calm. He looked once at the wound then back to Jack. He fell forward.

Jack caught him, felt something like a data disc drop into his pocket. He made to reach for it, but Tom hissed. "No..." He coughed. "This... this is the real truth, Jack! This is the entire story! It's his logs, Jack! Get them out! Tell them, Warn them ... warn them." With that he sighed once and fell forward… silent.

Jack looked to the door. Moonlight shone onto the face of the gunman.

Jack's eyes went wide in surprise and recognition. "You!"

Danny Cain nodded. There was even a hint of sadness in his green eyes. "I had honestly wanted you to get out, Jack. You should have left here with nothing but speculations and warnings. But you had to become so fucking dedicated didn't you? When did that happen? What happened to Rein the Runner?" Danny shook his head. "You son of a bitch when did you ever give a fuck about finishing what you started?"

Jack looked once to the corpse on the floor and then back to Danny. "Why?"

Danny shook his. "There are some things, Jack that a man will sell his soul for, some things that transcend the likes of loyalty and or friendship. Some things are just too damn important." He waived his gun to indicate outside.

"The shuttle personnel brought something back with them, Jack. I saw their faces! What was in their eyes was not human. It was evil, Jack. Pure and simple!"

"So you killed them, all in the name of humanity? Without trying to understand what – its alien so kill it, that your mentality?"

"You just don't understand," said Danny sadly. "How can you have come through all we have and still be so naive? The bad guys are real. The public are weak; stupid – they need our protection. Someone has to wipe their arses."

"So that's what you do now, Danny, you clean up?"

"Sarcasm aside, Jack, you're right. I clean up the mess that our government leaves behind. But they really fucked up this time. What is it with all the romance with Mars? Christ even the Prime Minister succumbed. I blame the movies myself."

Jack stared at Danny. "All these years we served together. Did I even know you?"

"Not really, Jack. I've been the clean-up crew forever, even in the war. I had to sort things out then and sometimes that meant killing our own. But it was always for the good of the people. They are the ones who have to be protected. You, me, we're expendable! We're just the tools."

"And what are you doing now, Danny? How are you protecting them? Hardly any of us knew the truth, why kill us?"

"It's too risky, Jack. One of the shuttle crew made it all the way to the village. We had to burn the whole fucking place, kill everyone there! It's too risky. Do you know what would have happened if he had been seen? There would be a UFO sighting that we couldn't explain. Then what? I'll tell you what: Hysteria! No one would trust anyone else. Our entire way of life would be compromised! We'd die of suspicion!" He sighed. "Jack. I honestly wanted to spare you this; you going home with nothing would have secured the story that everything was all right. I could have eventually given you the fucking info to cure the locals; made you a hero, but no! You had to do it all on your own. I mean, what the fuck did you expect to find out there? I tried to get you to leave you can't imagine my surprise when Rein the Runner wanted to fight for his cause. I sure as hell fucked up there!"

Jack shook his head in disgust. "It's murder, Danny no matter how you try to justify it." An horrific thought came to him suddenly. "How many other innocent people around here are you going to kill? You're not done killing yet are you?"

Danny scowled and shook his head. "That's the problem with you isn't it? You see everything in black and white! Well I got news for you, Jack. Not everything can be broken down that simply. There are grey areas, Jack, parts you can't put into wrong and right!"

"Yeah," said Jack sarcastically, "you tell yourself whatever you need to." He began to look around, looking for anything that he could use. Danny had to be stopped! The people had to know, had to be told!

Danny droned on and on. Jack no longer listened. He had caught sight of Tom Colson's hand gun. As he had fallen, the gun had spun out of his hand.

I could reach it, thought Jack. He ignored the feeling of grief that welled up in him. This was his friend; this was Danny Cain, his friend of more than twenty years.

Jack shook his head. These thoughts would only get him killed.

"... it's time you learned the real lesson of life, Jack," Danny was saying. "And that is that sometimes you win, sometimes you don't." Danny turned, looking for a chair.

Now! thought Jack. He dived at Danny, knocking him down, at the same time his hand shot out for the gun. His fingers clasped the metal. Danny went down and, as he tried to get up, Jack brought the gun round and fired.

Click! Not the familiar roar of gunshot. Danny recoiled in surprise and looked down at his chest, saw nothing. He smiled. "Nice try, Jack. I didn't think you had it in you."

Jack lowered his head. It was then he saw the smoke from Danny's silenced gun; saw the hole in his own chest. He looked up at his friend's face, saw genuine grief there.

"Is this what you wanted?" he hissed.

Danny lowered his head, as though suddenly ashamed.

"No it's not, is it? You wanted me dead and your own hands clean." He fell backwards.

Danny remained silent, neither confirming nor denying.

Jack held his hand over his chest in a futile effort to stem the blood flow. I've got to warn these people! They must get away! He picked up his briefcase that held his lap top computer. He staggered past Danny, trying to run.

"Where are you going?" asked Danny. "You can't get out of here, Jack. This whole area is going to be sterilised!"

Jack ignored him. The extent to which Danny would go to keep this a secret both shocked and awed him. How many people were in on this? Was it Danny alone or was the entire military in on it? Did it go even further?

He half staggered, half ran trying to put as much distance between himself and Danny. He thought he heard another gunshot, turned and saw Danny stagger.

Tom? He couldn't say, and didn't want to find out. He had to get out; had to run!

At least he had the truth. He heard a lot of yelling behind him, the sounds of pursuit. He held on tightly to his lap top computer. Whatever that disc contained, he would transmit it back to his office. Jessica would find it; would know what to do with it!

He ran then, ran as far as he could, the wound was definitely a bad one and he knew he couldn't keep this up. Soon enough the bullet would do its work.

He fell into a small ditch that would obscure him for a while at least. Using what little strength remained him, he booted up his lap top, set up a data link and without even looking at the disc Tom had given him, transmitted it to Jessica's computer.

With that done, he fell back, unable to get up; unable to even move. The bullet was almost done with him.

"You have nothing!" He yelled...

Epilogue

"Over here!" The soldier yelled out.

Danny walked over, supported by a soldier. He hadn't even heard Billy Gunns sneak up behind him until the last second. His keen senses and years of training had saved his life. He dived and hit the ground hard, but wasn't fast enough to prevent the bullet from Billy's gun smashing into his shoulder.

But that didn't matter now. Billy was dead, Tom was dead, and now... Jack too.

"Sir!" One of the sergeants lifted up the lap top and pulled the disc out and handed it to Danny. "He's already transmitted the disc!"

All eyes turned to stare at Danny.

"Destination?" he whispered.

"His office. To someone named Jessica Portman."

Danny smiled. "Ah! Sweet Jessica." He turned away, satisfied. "No problem."

"Sir! This is a security breach! We'll be exposed!"

Danny turned to him. "Like I said, not a problem." He walked away from them, turned once to where the sergeant stood, "evacuate the men, the bomber will be here in less than twenty minutes." With one last glance at his dead friend he walked down the hill, away from all the hassle, from Jack, from Billy, and from Tom.

He looked at the disc in his hand, crushed it and let the pieces fall. It had been a valiant effort by Jack. But Danny knew where the disc would end up and he was man who always covered all avenues.

Always...

The Field

Prologue

The lightning flashed and forked in the rain blackened sky, followed a few seconds later by the deafening boom of thunder. The small but elegant farmhouse was virtually invisible amid the torrent of sheet rain which pounded down upon it. In the fields, the crops swayed and bowed hurled by the wind that made them unwilling dance partners.

Inside the house and huddled together in the small kitchen, a man, dripping wet from his recent nocturnal duties, had his arms thrown protectively around the woman who lay against the corner unit shivering in terror and crying in the dark. His hair was pressed to his forehead, soaked from the rain, and his clothing, soaked through, clung to him; there was a bloodied hand print on his shirt which had been exposed beneath a rent in his jacket.

"I told you… I told you," she whimpered. "He's coming!"

"Shh," he whispered, "it's done."

Back and forth she rocked, arms hugging her chest, her head shaking from side to side. "Too late… you're too late! I told you!"

He grabbed her hands and pulled them to his lips, revealing her very pregnant stomach. "I won't let anyone hurt either of you, I promise."

From amid the howling gale and the ominous thunder there came a strange mewling sound from outside in the darkness, followed by a sudden crashing of breaking wood and glass. She screamed and he gasped, his eyes widening in shock.

"Why? It's done! It's done!"

She looked up at him with such a look of sadness etched upon her terrified features. "I told you what you had to do."

He shook his head sadly. "I couldn't, I love you, but, this? …"

"And that love has damned us all!" She tore herself from his grasp, pulled the door open and ran out into the stormy darkness.

"Wait!" He cried. As he ran to the door he suddenly stopped. A sound intruded then, a strange sound - like something slithering slowly across the floor followed by a gurgling, laboured noise. He let his hand fall from the door handle and stepped slowly toward the hall, fighting a deep fear as he looked down the darkened corridor, he could see nothing but pitch black, but in the dark the strangle mewling sound continued, and it sounded closer. Suddenly, lightning flashed and for a second, illuminated the dark hallway. His eyes widened and he screamed in terror. He turned and ran into the darkness.

The rain blinded him and the freezing cold stung his exposed skin as he ran, while the ground seemed to grab hungrily at his feet as though trying to drag him down. Stumbling as he ran, he yelled her name, his voice stolen by the wind. He tried not to think of the thing back there that was probably still after him. As he ran, he was vaguely aware of an outbuilding to his left, he headed toward it, suddenly falling headfirst into the sodden earth as his head colliding sickeningly with some heavy object.

He lay there, momentarily stunned as his consciousness swam before him. Scrambling to his feet he could almost feel something grasping at his foot and that hideous unholy voice seemed to call out in rage. Onward he raced toward the outbuilding when suddenly, he slammed against it, feeling along it until his hands found the door, he ran in and pulled it closed behind him.

"Are you there?" He whispered, his voice seemed suddenly loud in the relative silence. He heard a whimper in the background and made his way toward it. Eventually he found her outstretched hand.

"I'm sorry," he said. "I'm so sorry."

"I know," she said.

"I can fix this."

She smiled lovingly at him. "It's too late, my love. Too late."

He lowered his head and gently placed a hand on her abdomen. "You're all that matters now."

As their eyes locked, she knew what he meant. A tear ran down her face. "I wish there was another way."

"Me too. I'm sorry. So, so sorry! I wish… I wish I'd been stronger." He kissed her then for the last time before standing up. He smiled with a confidence he never felt and turned back toward the door.

"I love you so much," she whispered.

"I know. Be happy, Joan, my love; for me, be happy." With that he walked outside and closed the door tightly behind him.

She lay there in the dark long after the agonized screaming had stopped; long after the tearing, ripping, and frenzied noises had died down. It wasn't until the first ray of perfect morning sunshine poured in through the gaps in the blood-splattered wooden door that she finally broke, and let the tears cascade down her swollen and grief-stricken face.

Rehab

As the certificate changed hands the applause reached fever pitch when, as one, the room thundered to their feet.

He stood there, certificate in hand and sobbed as the tears ran freely down his cheek. As he cleared his throat to speak, the applause respectfully died down.

"Wow," he began and a few laughs came from the crowd. "Never in all my years did I think I'd be the one standing here being applauded. It's usually me down there watching others passing through, feeling jealous; feeling worthless – you know how it is."

There were various nods and mumbles of agreement from the assembled crowd.

He cleared his throat and tried to form his words: "It's… it's incredibly humbling,

and it's incredible to be here."

Again the applause drowned the room.

"To Doctor Morell: I can never thank you enough," he embraced the elderly man tenderly. You've given me my life back, Doctor; you've given us both our lives back," he motioned to a young girl in the crowd who jumped up and embraced him, in her left hand she held the same certificate. "We've got news of our own," he said with a huge grin. "Two days ago, Eva became not only my saviour, but also my wife!"

Eva held up her hand to show off a sparkling wedding ring. It had been his grandmother's, so he was fond of telling her, but she loved it anyway. It seemed to sparkle with an unnatural brilliance.

The applause was louder than ever.

The doctor smiled. "I've worked in addiction for more years than I'll care to admit and I can honestly say, I have never been prouder in my life than I am of you both.

"When you came to me two years ago Eva, and you, Guy, a little over nine months, emaciated, wasted, shaking and ready to die I knew we had a long way to go and it's been a struggle, but you had fight in you and a real lust for life. Seeing you here today makes me prouder than I have ever been.

"Although you're both leaving us today, don't forget - we are always here. Be strong and above all, be happy."

The applause was still ringing in their ears as they climbed in his small beat-up black Renault Mégane coupé. As he clipped the seatbelt in place he turned to smile. "Ready?" He asked.

"More than ready," she replied. "You sure your mum won't mind me coming with you?"

"You kidding? I told her how you saved me; she's dying to see you?"

"We saved each other, babe."

He smiled and pushed the button to start the car. Offering a prayer to the patron saint of cars that it started.

His prayer was answered and he backed out from the car park and drove slowly down the long tree-lined driveway. Her hand pressed into his as they took in the bright morning sunshine, and the almost fairy-tale sounds of animals played upon their sober senses.

The drive was a relatively long one and after an hour or so the scenery changed from the hustling cityscape to a more rural setting where the countryside appeared cut nearly in uniform shapes signifying various holdings and homes. The fields were full of glorious colours, each boasting well-kept crops or animals, whilst all alluding to polite and constant rivalry as each neighbour tried to get one-up on the other.

She leaned back and sighed contently, savouring the fresh air and the scenery. Life had for too long been all about the next fix; waking up soul-sick and numb on some vomit-stained mattress, feeling like death and overcome by cravings that had led her down so many horrific roads - all stained black with memories... She shook her head to clear it and grabbed his arm, his bicep seemed so big, and so safe and nothing like the cold bony sickly arm that she used to inject into.

He turned and gave her a look that seemed to echo her own thoughts.

No, life was good now, and the past was the past – buried, gone and overcome.

Home

"How long now, honey?" she asked

For an answer, he raised a hand and pointed to a large house standing proudly on a hill before some well-trimmed hedgerows, several well-tilled fields were spread out before it. "There we are: home."

"Quite remote, eh?" Said Eva, studying the farm.

"Yup. No one for miles and miles. It's perfect."

He slowed, left the motorway, took a hard left and they were suddenly off the main road and onto one that was little more than a dirt track. The small car bounced and creaked as it made its way over and around numerous potholes. It was a long hour until they reached the open gate and pulled up in a small stone covered area in front of the house.

He barely had enough time to press the engine off button before the large white farmhouse door was thrown open and a middle-aged plump lady with white hair, pulled back, appeared, a huge smile covered the motherly face; her arms were spread wide. With a cry of happiness she raced down the small flight of stairs.

"There you are!" she cried, "I've been waiting an age to see you!"

The young man stepped from the car and embraced her warmly. "Mum!" he said with a sigh of joy.

She pulled herself from him then. "Let me look at you! Why, you look positively glowing!"

"I feel great, mum," he replied. "All thanks to Eva here," he said, pulling the reluctant girl from the car. "Mum, this is my wife, Eva; Eva, my mum, Joan."

Joan smiled warmly as she walked over, arms wide. "Eva," she said, pulling the young woman close and rubbing her arms affectionately. "I can't thank you enough for looking after my lovely boy, and for what you've done for him!"

"Honestly, it was all him," she replied lightly.

"Nonsense! I know my son, and he wouldn't have made it to where he is on his own. We've all got so much to thank you for; so much."

Eva smiled and wondered slightly if she detected a hint of sadness in the old woman's voice.

"Anyway, I've made lunch; I bet you're all starving after that drive." She took both their hands and led them into the house.

Relax

After lunch .the two young ones changed into shorts and T-shirts before heading for a long walk in the fields while the old lady insisted on clearing up by herself. "Anyway," she had said, "the last thing you two love-birds need is me and my gammy leg holding you back; go enjoy yourselves."

It was mid-afternoon when, after a walk of several miles, they came upon a large pool of water, Eva squealed in pleasure when she saw it and, taking shorts, t-shirt and shoes off, dipped her feet in the cold water. After the walk and the heat of the afternoon, the cool, fresh water was a welcome relief. "Come on, babe," she said, "come in."

He smiled and casually kicked off his trainers and shorts before wading in. "Jesus! It's freezing!"

She laughed, "Freezing? It's lovely!" She said as she swam further toward the middle.

"Careful," he warned, "there might be undercurrents or weeds there."

"I'm fine," she said. "Hurry up!"

"I'm coming," he said with a laugh. With a cautious look around him, he dropped his shorts and laughed. "Years I've lived here and I've never once went…" he trailed off mid-sentence as he realised Eva was nowhere to be seen. Frantically he ran into the freezing water! "Eva! Eva! Jesus, where are you! Eva!"

He desperately searched and felt around for her. "Christ, no!" He yelled, coughing as he swallowed some water.

A large splash appeared several metres to his right, as suddenly Eva broke through the water. "Help me!" She screamed, "Something's got my foot! Help me!"

"I'm coming!" he yelled and swam over as fast as he could, by the time he got there she had disappeared again, the water was calm, not a ripple came from it.

"Eva!" he yelled, fear echoing in his voice. "God, no! Eva!"

Suddenly, from behind him, she splashed through the water, throwing her arms around his neck; she burst out laughing. "Well, Mr; I guess you really do love me."

He pushed her away. "That's not funny, you! Not funny!"

She laughed and kicked water at him. "Yeah, it was, Mr Tough guy – you crapped it! Admit it!"

He frowned and shook his head. "Na; didn't care one way or the other." His scowl faded and melted into a grin. "Okay; maybe a little bit."

She smiled and swam close to him, again throwing her arms round him, he pulled her close and their lips met.

Later, as they lay on the grass, her head on his chest while he used their clothes as a pillow he sighed contentedly. "This is The Life, eh?"

"Yeah," she said dreamily.

"Just think, this time last week we were sitting in group talking shit about taking shit."

"Oh don't go there, babe," she protested. "Don't bring that crap here."

"Sorry," he muttered.

They lay in silence, Guy stared at the cloudless sky, his mind wandering. Eva stared at him and tried to bring up the question, something that had been bothering her and now she felt she had to ask. "Babe," she said softly.

"Hmm?"

"Do you still get the itch?" She asked, referring to their mutual habit.

Silence.

"Well do you?"

"I thought we weren't bringing that shit up?"

She lay back down and stared at the sky, wishing she felt the calm that he seemed to feel.

He turned his head a few inches and squinted at her through one open eye. "I take it you do?"

She nodded. "I don't think it'll ever go away."

He reached out and took her hand in his. "It's gonna be ok. I promise." He turned fully round, smiled at her and kissed her passionately. She responded…

Later as she cuddled into him she felt a lot better. I guess that's the way to keep the damn itch away!

"So how long are we staying with your mum?"

"Haven't really thought about it to be honest," he replied. "Why, you in a hurry to leave?"

"Nooooo," she replied. "I love it here."

"Me too," he whispered and closed his eyes, letting the sun beat down on him.

Eva remained silent as she listened to the rhythm of his breathing. Eventually she said: "That farm looks like a lot of work for your mum."

"It is," he replied, "especially at harvest time. She usually gets some help then."

"She ever thought of, you know… selling?"

"Never. She loves it here, anyway, I thought we could stay and help this year, harvest time is only five weeks away."

"Me? Farm?" she said laughing.

"Why not? I'll teach you."

"Yeah, sure," she said.

"Anyway, it'll be good practice."

"For what?"

"For when we own it."

"We?"

"Yeah, my mum won't be here forever."

She smiled silently. "And you think I will?"

He grabbed her close, she responded and while her smile lit up her face, his eyes fell and a sad moue touched the corner of his mouth. When she pulled away to kiss him his expression had changed to one of happiness.

"I love you so much," she said.

"I love you, too, Eva; I really do," he closed his eyes but not before a rogue tear escaped and slipped, unnoticed, down his cheek.

History

From the front porch of the farmhouse, Eva paused to take in the fresh smell of the early summer morning. She felt amazing, so much better than she had in, well, in forever!

For the hundredth time she lifted her hand and stared at her wedding ring and smiled again. She loved the ring, it was obviously worth a fortune and very valuable from a sentimental point of view. She leaned on the railing and surveyed the fields in front of her. It was mid-summer, a bright July morning and they were fully and beautifully tilled, she marvelled at their perfect angles, neat rows, and colours. One small point caught her attention, it was to the far left and downhill from the house, an overgrown, unsightly patch that looked as though it shouldn't belong there, it looked like some artist had just handed his brush to an infant who then splattered the area.

She jumped down from the porch and walked over to investigate further. The area had been allowed to grow freely with no human hand to guide or inhibit it. On the outside edge, weeds had formed an irregular circle around a deep depression in the ground from which various swamp-like reeds grew in a sickly haphazard fashion. The water looked deep and menacing. On the far side a large stone which at one point long ago must have stood straight and erect, was now leaning to one side and falling forward, an oily, tarry liquid seemed to lie just below the weeds and there was a pungent smell bordering on a miasma. A feeling of revulsion overcame her as she shuddered and stepped backward.

"Whoa! Steady there, babe!" he cried.

"Jesus! You scared the shit out of me!" She grabbed him tightly, his warm body felt good against hers in the sudden chill. She turned her head back to look at the swamp. "What is all that? Can't you fix it or something?"

He laughed. "Fix that? That is the family mystery, my love; a tale older than you and I combined."

"Oh?"

"Yeah! Wanna hear it?"

"Yeah, go on then."

He took her hand and led her over to a small bench she hadn't noticed before that lay to the far left of the area.

He cleared his throat. "Do you know what a Sapper is?" he asked softly.

Her brow furrowed slightly, "No," she replied.

"Well, I'm not up on current military ranks or that, but back in World War One, a Sapper had probably one of the worst jobs in the army." He shifted on his seat as he lit a cigarette, taking a deep puff before continuing.

"When The Great War began in 1914, the general consensus was it would all be over by Christmas; a quick kick up the Kaiser's ass, and home again. Well, depending on how much you know, that 'over by Christmas' idea turned out a load of bollocks and it turned into a long, drawn-out bloody mess that carried on until 1919; the fighting itself finished in '18, but the whole mess ended in '19 with the Treaty of Versailles.

"Anyway, by 1916 the Western Front was a mess; long, deep trenches were dug and fortified by both sides and the fighting was done pretty much there. One side would launch a huge bombardment and follow it up by sending soldiers up and over to attack the enemy, then they would reciprocate. The whole area between them was known as 'No Man's Land', and from all accounts, was a total horror story in itself: men lying dead and dying from the many attempts to go over the trenches, caught up in barbed wire and gunned down; animals stuck in the mud, making noises; poison gas, sink-holes, explosions." He shuddered. "Horrible."

"The Sommer!" she cried.

He smiled. "Nearly right: The Somme – it was one of the most notorious battles and yeah, that one was in '16. It was about that time that the politicians and the public were getting fed up with it dragging on and on, so someone came up the brilliant idea of a Sapper. Their job was basically to dig tunnels underneath the trenches, try to locate a German trench, plant explosives and get out before it blew the whole lot to hell."

"Jesus," she muttered. "Fuck doing that!"

"Yeah," he said sadly, "my great-great-grandfather did just that." He took an old yellowed black and white photograph from inside his jacket. It showed a fresh-faced young man standing proudly in his army uniform.

"Cute," she said.

"That was him one week before shipping out. My mum still has all his letters he wrote to his parents, his wife, and siblings.

"At first the letters were all full of hope and full of the usual wonders a twenty-year-old man feels in a situation like that. He talked of the pals, the battalions where they all knew each other and of how much fun they were having at training; they talked of how sad he would be when the war was quickly over. Pretty soon, though, the letters became shorter and shorter, with less hope, you know, and full of... of fear." He frowned deeply. "They thought he was going mad."

She leaned in closer to hear him as his voice dropped to barely a whisper. "Why? What happened?"

He shot her a glance. "He said the men and him... they... they started to think there was something there with them; something in the trenches - just outside in 'No Man's Land'."

She blinked and swallowed hard. "What was it?"

"Nothing they could see. They said it was something they could feel, especially after a day of heavy fighting and when the scent of death was at its highest. They said that on the days when the most suffering and deaths occurred was the feeling was worse. Then, suddenly, when they were charging the enemy trenches, the mud would be thicker; would suck at their boots, almost like it wanted to pull the men down.

"He described a black liquid that would form in shell-holes, bomb craters, and into which 'no sane man would 'ere risk a leg'; he said that even when a shell-burst filled the night, the black pools would show no reflection, as though light itself could not penetrate that oily darkness. He said that the wounded that fell in 'No Man's Land' seemed to die more slowly than others before. Often, they could be heard whimpering in the night for hours on end, out of reach of help until either they died of their wounds, or the cold. Now, he said, it was as if the dying were being taken. Next day they'd look for survivors and lots of times see only a few fingers or a boot protruding out from the ground, or worse still, a face – all this on ground that wasn't saturated enough to sink a body.

"That's creepy as hell!"

He nodded. "They wrote stories and even poems about it. My Granda wrote that," he said, handing her an old open diary, from it she read:

Come the morning, we knew it'd be there
That fear, that loathing, that horror, that despair.
Terrible and sickly - the fog covered ground
Taking away those men who make nae a sound.
And we who know but did not see the beast from the black
Know still, at any time that fearful fog will come, to take us all back!

She shuddered again. "That's freaking me out."

"There were loads like that."

"So what happened; did he get out?"

"Well, one day he gets summoned to the General who has a plan. He wants my great-great-grandfather to take a small squad and tunnel toward the largest and most heavily fortified of the trenches. He's to plant the biggest load of explosives that literally the world had ever known.

"So at night they start the tunnel, some digging, others taking the dirt out while others were to bring the explosives up. Eventually, they get there. They're so close that they can hear the German soldiers muffled voices through the walls.

They work slowly and as deathly silent as they possibly could and eventually, they bring all the explosives into the end of the tunnel and set them all up. All this while just a few metres away from an entire enemy army.

"When it's almost time, my Granda orders all the others to clear the tunnel while he sets the fuse. It's at that point one of the guys notices black liquid droplets on the roof of the tunnel, he nearly gives the whole game away; he steps back and puts his hand into a puddle of the stuff, and that's when he starts freaking out; he's whimpering and starts saying 'it's here! It's here!'; they grab him and hiss at him to shut up, but he's fighting and wriggling trying to run away, eventually one of the guys has to give him a smack on the head to knock him out, but it doesn't, and he yells out, one of the guys covers his mouth, they hear the Germans go quiet and then start yelling, my Granda yells at his men to get out, as they start running, some German rifles and bayonets start literally pushing through the dirt walls, suddenly there's bullets flying in the dark, men are screaming and some are going down, while others try to scramble over the bodies."

Her eyes widened in shock, "Go on," she urged.

"He knew there was no time to waste! He gets all his men behind him and they start crawling out as fast as they can, while he starts to back out of the tunnel, keeping an eye on where they've came from, and when he sees the first German helmet appear, he just slam-punches that trigger – blows the whole damn lot to hell!"

She fell back slightly. "My God!" she gasped. "What happened?"

"As the Allied commanders had hoped, it was the biggest man-made explosion the Earth had ever seen. Countless Germans dead, even more wounded; their biggest trench disappeared. Men, equipment, everything was first blown hundreds of feet in the air with most of it falling back to vanish into the gaping maw of the huge crater it left. It's still visible to this day."

"What of your Granda, did he die?"

He turned slightly and took her hand in his. "They found him, or rather what was left of him. The explosion had somehow propelled him out of the tunnel. He lost both eyes, both legs, an arm, most of the fingers on his remaining hand, and pretty much most of his face. He was in hospital for… God – forever! They fitted him with this horrible prosthetic on his face to cover where his eyes and nose used to be. From what I hear, it gave my grandmother nightmares.

"Eventually he came home to this farm. He could barely talk and when he did, he would just whisper, 'I see it!', 'it's here!' or 'Leave me, leave me alone!' "

He turned to look at her. "You want to know what freaked me out the most?"

She nodded slowly.

"He said right when his man flipped and yelled 'it's here!' back in that tunnel, he said he felt something was there too. All he would ever say was "'all that death and suffering and horror and blood must've attracted something right out of hell'"; he said they all lost parts of their own humanity in those trenches."

He shook his head to clear it. "Anyway, he came home and pretty much all he did was just come out in the sunshine and sit in his wheelchair, in that exact spot," he said, indicating the overgrowth. "Over the years his wheelchair made a depression in the ground. He would just sit there, alone, for hours. Sometimes he looked like he was talking to someone: crying, sobbing and occasionally a maniacal laugh would just burst out from him, quickly followed by yells and cries and he'd pound his chair with his one hand before yelling to be taken inside. My Grandmother said he was just talking to his men, you know; letting them know he thought about them.

"From what my mother's mother told her, it was a horrible existence. She said he just kept on getting skinnier and appeared frailer every year, just withering away. He lived like that for years, and years. He came back from the war hospital in 1917, and just died a little every day until he eventually passed in 1939, ironically, on the day World War Two broke out."

"That's weird!"

He nodded. "My grandmother used to say it was because his heart just broke when he heard his 'War to end All Wars' wasn't that after all."

"What do you think?"

He shrugged. "He was just a sick old man who clung to a bit of life for as long as he could." He motioned to the overgrowth. "They buried him here, in his favourite spot. See that big rock? That's his gravestone, although I wouldn't recommend stepping in there to read it."

"Why not?"

"Because," he said as he grabbed her and pretended to throw her in, "Look at that black water! It might be that creature!" He burst out laughing as she fought him off and ran back to the porch, suddenly cold and shivering. He playfully walked back up and sat beside her on the porch. "It's all just really old family histories, that's all. Don't freak out about it."

She scowled. "Yeah, well, when we ship that old dear of yours off to her Care Home, that horrible place is getting filled in."

Jumping to his feet he frowned: "Don't start that shit again!" He made to storm off but she grabbed his arm.

"This place could be ours; should be ours! Look at it, she's too old to handle this place."

"It's her home!"

"Yeah? Well, it should be our fucking home if you just grew a pair of balls!"

He stormed away but after a few steps he paused then turned. "Look, this is an argument for another time. I came to say I need to go away for a few days."

She looked at him incredulously."

"Why - where are you going?"

"I've a friend who's having some trouble with his bar, I need to go help him. I'll be back in three or four days."

She looked at him in disbelief. "You? In a bar? Are you crazy?"

He gently gripped her shoulders. "Babe, we're clean remember, I'm not interested in getting pissed or high. I just need to help my mate."

"Some mate! If he really was your mate, he'd leave you the fuck alone and not tempt you! And what am I supposed to do here?"

"Help my mum, you know - get used to the place."

"So now I'm the fucking hired help?"

"Don't start, Eva." He reached out and took her by the shoulders. "I'll be back before you know it and I'll be good for you - some bonding time."

"There's nothing to do here, Guy!"

"It's a different life," he admitted, "but trust me, you'll enjoy it. Just use the time to relax, get plenty of sleep and not worry about anything."

She sighed her acceptance. "You better make it up to me when you get back."

He broke into a grin. "I will; I promise."

Day One

Eva lay in bed feigning a headache and needing sleep. He had been gone only two hours and already she wondered how she would ever get through this. His mother had already chapped the door offering tea.

Fuck off! She thought!

"I'll leave it outside your door, dear," she said before shuffling away.

Dear? She laughed out loud. Who calls anyone 'dear' nowadays? Old bat, god, this place could be amazing for us if could get rid of her!

After lying there for another few hours she reluctantly got up, as she left the room, she kicked over the cold cup of tea that had been left for her. She sighed as she bent down to pick up the broken cup.

As she walked into the kitchen, Joan was sitting at the farmhouse style table, a

newspaper open before her. She lowered her glasses and stared at the broken cup.

"I, uh…" began Eva.

The older woman jumped up and took the cup form her. "Don't worry about it, dear, it's an old cup. I should've collected it when I didn't hear you get up for it."

Is it my imagination or is that almost a sneer?

"I'm sorry. I meant to get it, but I feel back asleep. It was kind of you to bring it."

Joan dismissed her with a wave of her hand. "I'll make you a fresh cup."

Eva smiled. "I'll make it. I…"

"No!" Snapped the old woman. "It's my kitchen!"

Eve recoiled and the old woman caught herself, she tried to smile softly, but it was lost on Eva. "Sorry, dear, it's just that this kitchen has been my domain for many, many years. I'm not used to sharing it, and anyway, you're our guest." She emphasised the word a little too much for Eva's liking.

She stared hard at Eva, who felt obliged to shrug and smile back. "I understand." She stood there a few moments longer, uneasy and unsure what to do. The old woman stared at her in such a peculiar way. After what seemed like an eternity, she patted the back of a wooden chair. "Sit here, honey. I'll make you tea and fix you up a wee breakfast."

As she sat in the kitchen, she felt restless and her sense of nervousness increased. The old woman cut and chopped while humming some incessant tune, casting occasional and uncomfortable stares at Eva. She couldn't take any more. "I'm just going out to stretch my legs before breakfast if that's ok?"

"You go right ahead, my darling," she said, cracking an egg into a bowl. "Don't go too far; I'll shout for you when it's ready." Joan cast a glance out the window, "besides, I don't like the look of that sky; I think we're in for some terrible weather."

Eva bolted from the house. Once outside she took a deep breath. It was a beautiful morning and she savoured the warmth and brightness of the late morning sun and took in the peppery smell of the farm. What is it with that old woman? Thought he said she was lovely? She's weird and creepy! Eva raised her face to let the sunlight cover her. Bad weather! Yeah, right!

As she walked, she found herself drawn to the sunken marsh that held the remains of the old grandfather - all that pain and suffering - it was almost too much to imagine. She shivered as she neared it and wrinkled her nose as the sweet smell was replaced with a smell like rotten vegetation. She shivered despite the heat of the morning. As she felt the hairs on the back of her neck rise suddenly, she quickly turned round, to see the old woman peering at her intently from way up on the porch. Freak! She thought as she walked over to the bench and sat down, taking her phone from her pocket, she unlocked it and read the single text message:

Got here safe, babe. Miss u already! See u soon x

She heard the old woman call to her and wave from the porch. With a sigh of resignation, Eva headed up to the house. She had already decided to feign another headache and go to her room and avoid the old bag. As she walked up the hill, she swatted at the midges that had seemed to come out of nowhere from the marshy ground. As she scratched at her neck, she chalked up another reason to hate the place.

Day Two

Her phone bleeped loudly and she awoke with a start. A dull, grey and mournful morning lit the room in feeble light, and light rain dripped down the windows. Eva she yawned and rubbed at her temples.

It was hard to recall such an unpleasant night. The wind had howled and screamed all night and every time she almost fell asleep, the noises had seemed louder and woke her.

The dreams were the worst. Horrible dreams of being chased, and of imminent danger. Several times the wind and her nightmares seemed to come together to turn them into a physical presence.

With an effort she pulled herself up, swung her legs and sat on the edge of the bed.

She felt tired and unrested and her head pounded. Absently she scratched and clawed at the various insect bites that had plagued her all night. Yesterday had been the longest day of her life and she had relished the relative privacy of the bedroom. The thought of another day with that woman! She checked her phone for a message from Guy - there wasn't, and he hadn't returned her missed calls from last night.

As she made her way reluctantly down the stairs, for the first time in a long time Eva felt the all too familiar pang deep in the pit of her stomach. It was the cry of the addict in her. She knew it wasn't dead; would never die and was only sleeping. All she wanted right now was a quiet place and a crack pipe!

No I don't! It's not me! It won't ever be me again! She tried to focus on coffee. A hot cup of coffee was all she needed

Walking into the kitchen she was forced to put down a feeling of annoyance when she realised the old woman was already there, humming her unrecognisable tunes as she walked around with her ever-present cloth wiping furiously back and forth. She smiled a sickly-sweet smile. "Good morning, dear. Did you sleep ok?"

"Not bad," she said as she moved to the kettle.

"Oh, are you looking for coffee? We're all out, I'm afraid."

Great! "I'll go get some," said Eva.

"In that rain? The shop's miles away; you'll be soaked!"

"Perhaps I could borrow your car?"

The wiping stopped and she turned. "My car? It's not working, dear. Something about the timing belt or something. I'll phone Guy later and tell him to pick you up some, maybe even that McStarbuck or Coster coffee or whatever it is you young people like. All that money for a cup of coffee! You're mad!"

Eva fought down a wail. No car! "It's fine; I'll get a bus or a taxi."

The old woman laughed. "A bus? No buses up here, dear, and no taxis either." Her cloth paused mid-wipe as she thought. "There's Tricia who sometimes taxis part time. Ah, no but she's away caring for her mother in Callander." She leaned forward and lowered her voice, as though spilling secrets she shouldn't. "Got dementia, you know. Said to be in a terrible way."

Eva felt trapped, captive; a prisoner here and as if to add insult to injury, the old woman said: "just you and me together. All on our own," and she actually chuckled.

I got to get out of here! "I'm going to take a walk."

"You going to visit grandfather again?"

Eva paused mid-step. "Sorry?"

"My grandfather - Are you going to his grave again? I noticed you seem to like it there." That smile again!

"I uh, I'm not sure."

"You go right ahead, dear. He likes you, you know." And with that the cloth began again as the humming started in earnest.

Eva fled the house and into the dreary and dank morning.

Later, after her walk she made her excuses and went up to bed and tried to call Guy. All she got was his voice mail followed shortly by a text.

Up to my eyes here, babe. Call you later x

She crawled under the covers and tried to read. Then the headache came, followed shortly by a cold sweat, and by late afternoon, she had the duvet pulled up close, was drenched in sweat and shivering uncontrollably. She remembered seeing the cable and plug of an electric blanket and she struggled with the controls, which frustratingly refused to work until she dropped it in disgust. She pushed herself further down into the covers and tried to control her shivering.

As she began to drift off to sleep her mind wandered and she couldn't tell if she was awake or asleep the rain had come on suddenly and drummed mercilessly against the window further adding to her misery. The room seemed cold and unforgiving and no matter what she tried she could never get warm. Guy's story about his great-grandfather played in her mind and she semi-dreamed of soldiers and mud before the cold, or her headache or the damn itching from the bites forced her awake.

"Insect bites? My, I've never been bothered with them here, dear; must be something in your blood!" So much for a soothing ointment or analgesic, old Joan had actually laughed at the request.

Eva moaned gently as she shifted in the bed, she had been asleep for an hour or so, and as she rolled to her side, she half opened her eyes and screamed. There beside her, bloodied, eyeless and horrific, lay the figure of Guy's great-grandfather. He reached over with his mangled arm and screamed! She awoke with a start.

"Think you've got a bit of a fever there, dear."

The old woman was seated on Eva's bed, her cold, clammy hand on Eva's forehead.

Eva recoiled from the touch. "What are you doing?" She gasped for breath after that horrible nightmare. She scratched at the ugly red weal on her left arm. Those damned bugs!

"I came to ask about dinner. My, my, you're burning up! That's what happens when you go walking in this weather practically naked! You young people, honesty! Not even an overcoat!" She shook her head and handed Eva a cup of steaming liquid. "Here you are, dear, some camomile tea."

Eva wrinkled her nose as she took the cup. Camomile tea? Tea for old fucking women! She thought.

Joan moved and fussed around the bed, and then began pumping up Eva's pillows. "I don't know what you were thinking going out in that weather!"

"Have you heard from Guy?" Eva asked.

Joan froze and blinked at her several times. "Uh. No, actually but he's always the same when he goes off with those friends of his. Sometimes I don't see him for a week!"

"He said he'll only be four days and anyway, I thought it was business?"

Joan smiled. "Yes. Drink your tea, dear; there's a good girl."

Eva fought off the nausea wishing the old woman would just go and let her sleep. She sighed and took a drink of the tea. She retched and looked down into the cup. Instead of tea, it was filled with oozing black liquid. With a yell, Eva hurled the cup across the room. It smashed off the wall, and the tea went everywhere.

"Eva!" Cried Joan in disbelief.

Eva stared at the light stain as it dripped down the wall. "I… it was… it wasn't tea… it"

"Wasn't tea? Of course it was tea!"

Eva stared at her as the nausea began. She groaned and fell back against the pillow.

"No dinner for you," said Joan, shaking her head. "Sleep, I think, I'll bring you some hot water and lemon later on. You just shout if you need me." With that she collected the broken teacup. "At this rate I'll be needing a new tea set!" she stood and walked to the door, that infernal whistling again! With her head swimming and the nausea overwhelming her, Eva closed her eyes...

The trench was long, muddy; dirty. Some of the soldiers slept where they sat, on overturned munitions crates or their own packs, while others stood ready, guns pointed towards the German trenches. The dead lay where they'd fallen, rats scurried back and forward, the living paid them no more attention than did the dead, and the rain was torrential.

Eva, wearing a white wedding dress and carrying a bouquet, walked calmly through the trench, ignored by all the soldiers. Flares lit up the sky for a few seconds, making eerie sculptures of the barbed wire from which some entangled bodies seemed to dance and sway to unheard music from the constant thump-thump of artillery and small arms fire.

Eva hummed a tune as she strolled, coming face to face with Guy. He was dressed in a captain's uniform. He smiled when he saw her. "Eva!" he said.

She awoke with a start as a thunderclap rang through the house.

She gasped and wiped her forehead. She was soaked with sweat and shivering. Outside, the rain pounded furiously upon the window, while the wind screamed in angry gusts.

Day Three

Morning, when it eventually came, brought with it little respite. The skies were grey to an almost black, and the light strained just to break through. Although it was late July, it seemed cold and autumnal. Eva lay in bed, exhausted. She still shivered uncontrollably, her head and neck ached and her mouth was parched; the insect bites itched and oozed. She hadn't eaten or drunk in over twenty-four hours and the promised hot water and lemon had failed to materialise. As she tried to prop herself up in bed, her strength failed her and she collapsed back down, out of breath. Her back hurt when she moved.

Desperate for a drink of water, she managed to swing her legs round to plant her feet on the floor, but as she tried to stand, her legs gave way and she fell painfully to the floor. As she grabbed at the sheets to pull herself up, her mother-in-law appeared. "Oh, Eva, my dear! Look at you!" She rushed over and tried to lift the helpless girl.

With the older woman helping, Eva managed to get to her feet, although she had to lean heavily. Somehow, she made it to the toilet.

"You just sit there a moment, dear," called the old woman, "I'm just changing these sheets. My, you were sweating last night. Good for you; get all that nasty fever out!" She whistled away as she worked.

The weather front remained, like some stubborn child refusing to get up and so again the wind howled down on the farm and the rain beat furiously upon the windows as though desperate to get in. If she was concerned for any crops that grew or for any animals she had, the old woman didn't show it and she remained frustratingly close, whistling and humming as she strolled, apparently carefree through the house.

Guy's phone remained off with only the annoyingly friendly voice of the answering service. Eva's texts went unanswered. She remained in bed all afternoon, unable to get up, between the illness and the mother-in-law she couldn't tell which was worse.

She did know what was worse, and that was the oily, snaking way her want of a crack pipe was pulling at her, making her numb. Even at the lowest of her many falls she hadn't felt as sick or as low as she did right now. Cold, lost, alone, and sick on a farm in the middle of nowhere. She began to wish she had never laid eyes on Guy. The feeling of isolation and of utter abandonment hung at the edge of her senses. She felt so utterly alone and helpless and was struggling mentally.

> *Hey babe, mum says you're sick. I'll wrap things up here and head back soon. If u need anything let mum know. Love ya x*

She threw the phone onto the empty side of the bed. Wrap things up? Yeah, well seeing where your priorities lie! Eva closed her eyes and tried to sleep, she resisted the urge to scratch, determined to sleep. Only one thought remained in her mind: For Guy to turn up, grab her and get her out of this place, never to come back! She tried to recall how pleasant and welcoming the farm had looked when they'd first arrived, but she couldn't. Is this how a mouse feels when it sees the cheese in the trap?

With a start she sat bolt upright and breathed heavily. What was that? At first the noise fitted into the nightmare she was having, of being chased through an empty building with someone or something chasing her. Some part of her brain had registered the sound as being external. They say the fight or flight response lies deep within the limbic system - the most primitive part of the brain, and in the midst of her fears, it was acutely tuned.

She lay in the dark listening, then she heard it again a noise like something wet, something horrible slithering across the ground and it was coming closer!

Downstairs, in the kitchen, the old woman sat at her table, a warm cup of coffee in her hand. She sat as though dazed with a strange look on her face. She too heard the noises from outside and in contrast to the terrified girl upstairs, she seemed pleased. "Good girl," she said with a smile and sipped at her coffee.

She turned slightly as the figure of a man appeared in the doorway. Her smile widened and she nodded. "It won't be long now," she said pleasantly.

The bomb the soldiers called a "whizz-bang" exploded, sending pieces of dirt and meat from dead men and animals over the trench. The bomb was followed seconds later by another, then another, and another.

Eva walked barefoot through the mud, her white dress pristine and clean in direct contrast to the mud-splattered and bloodied soldiers who were as oblivious to her as she was to them.

Another whizz-bang shrieked through the air before exploding, men were thrown like rag dolls and their screams rang out. As though unaware of where she was, Eva slowly walked down into the deep depression of a bomb crater, a soft smile fixed on her face, she stared straight ahead when suddenly her left foot seemed to sink into the mud. As she tried to walk on, her right foot sunk lower into the mud. As if only suddenly aware, she blinked and tried to pull her left leg free, the mud made a horrible slurping noise as her foot sunk further in. As she tried to move, she lost her balance and fell forward into the wall of the bomb crater, her hands disappeared into the mud and she tried to pull them out but they remained firmly stuck. With a sense of panic she tried vigorously to free herself, when suddenly, from out of the dripping mud in front of her, a face appeared, worm-eaten and half decayed, the eyeless skull leering at her. Slime and mud oozed from the open mouth as she fought to pull away. More hands and faces appeared from within the mud, and skeletal fingers grasped her tightly, mouths opened on corpses as they shrieked and screamed at her. She was being pulled further and further in, unable to scream or even breathe. The mud wall got closer and closer and then, she suddenly disappeared into the mud…

Eva screamed as she fell from the bed onto the hard floor of her bedroom. She was shivering and soaked with sweat. Her heart pounded as she gasped for breath. Lacking the strength to even move she collapsed onto her back and lay on the floor sobbing.

She paused and held her breath as the hacking, mewling noises from her dream continued. They seemed to be coming from outside her window, coming closer and closer. The rain lashed furiously against the window and the wind, like some malignant force with terrible fists, pounded and rattled against the windows. Eva lay there, terrified and trying to catch her breath. Her legs made futile scrambling gestures as she tried to flee. A sense of terror and of fear and loneliness welled up inside her. Something on the duvet, which had fallen with her from the bed, caught her eye.

There, all across the bottom of it was a black, wet and tarry stain. With a start she looked at her outstretched arms, and from the red and swollen insect bites, there oozed a deep and dark black liquid!

The Last Day

Eva screamed and somehow staggered to her feet. With her head pounding, her vision swimming, and her legs threatening to give way, she fled the room, desperate to escape. She had to get away from this place!

She half ran, half fell down the stairs while the noises continued from upstairs. As she reached the kitchen, she was only vaguely aware of her mother-in-law sitting silently in the dark.

Eva raced past her and tugged at the door handle.

"Are you going out, dear?" she asked in a lilting voice.

Eva spun to face her. "Let me out of here, you old bag! Let me out!"

Joan smiled pleasantly. "Language! My, my. You should be in bed."

"I'm not spending another minute in this house with you! This place is fucked up! You're fucked up! I don't care if I have to run ten miles! You open this door. NOW!"

"You'll catch your death out there! Are you sure you want to go out?" She asked, holding the key in her hand.

Eva lunged at her and grabbed her forcibly. "Give me that key! Give me it!"

She pulled and shoved the old woman until she let go of the key and fell to the floor. "You evil old bitch!" Eva turned and opened the door, then ran out into the stormy night.

The freezing shock of the wind and rain paralysed her for a moment, and she gasped. Looking around she tried to spot some familiar landmark, but it was pitch black in the dark, and the rain impeded her vision.

"Eva!" yelled the old woman from the porch. Eva spun to see her standing there, a black silhouette framed against the light from within. She held a shotgun in her hand!

"Eva! Come here, girl, this instant! You can't leave. You have to stay here!"

"Why? You don't even like me, why do you want me to stay?"

With her gun aimed at Eva, the old woman shook her head with a look of complete sadness etched on her face. "You have to stay, it's… well, it is what it is." She motioned back toward the house. "Come on, I'll make us some coffee. I found some, and you can call Guy."

Eva nodded slowly as though giving her acceptance. As the old woman turned toward the house, Eva's temper flared, with a scream she raced forward and putting both hands on the old woman's back she shoved her forcibly against the door frame. The older woman fell to the decking, stunned, blood dripping from a gash on the bridge of her nose. Eva turned and took off into the night. As she turned and ran, she failed to notice the outline of a man watching her from one of the upstairs windows.

Eva stopped running and looked around her, trying to find a way to go but her eyes failed to penetrate through the dark. There were no lights from far away houses, no cars signalling roads; nothing. The only light came from that hellish house and there was no way she would head back there!

Guy! Where are you? What the fuck?

A loud explosion shocked Eva. The mad, old cow had fired the gun! From out in the blackness she heard: "I'll find you, Eva! Think you can take my son from me; think you're worthy? You're nothing but a junkie tramp!" Another report from the gun echoed through the dark. "Where do you think you can run to?"

Eva headed in the opposite direction. She wished she had her phone. Why didn't I lift my damn phone? What an idiot!

She ran on, down, and away from the house. The rain had stopped suddenly while she has been running, she couldn't recall the moment it had stopped, but now, in the relative silence she heard so much more. She could make out the slurping noises of the crazy old woman as she stomped through the muddy field. From in the dark came another sound: the same, horrible mewling nightmare noises. And it seemed to be getting closer.

Eva felt terror and fear rise up from the pit of her stomach, but the fear drove her and she ran on.

The door was thrust angrily aside as Joan entered the house. Her face was ruddy and set in anger. Sweat dripped from her face, and she wiped the blood from her nose on the back of a sleeve. She stomped into the hallway and paused on the second step. "I need you to come out to help me," she yelled up the stairs. "She's out there somewhere- - stupid girl! Why is this one so much worse than the others?"

Eva paused and looked uphill. The moon had appeared from behind the clouds and illuminated the farmhouse. What once had seemed so quaint and welcoming now loomed eerily in the dark, the building squatting like some nightmare creature. Eva gasped as she saw the silhouette of the old woman appear from the door and stand there looking around her, the shotgun in her hand.

Realising she was beside the dead grandfather's grave, Eva crouched down behind the bench. "Go away, you old bag!" She hissed. She watched as the old woman scanned the field looking for her.

"Eva? Eva, sweetie. Come on, this is silly. We'll both get pneumonia! I found some coffee; I had it all along. What say you I make us both a nice hot cup?" Eva couldn't ignore the underlying menace in the voice. "I know where you are, Eva!" She swung the barrel of the gun towards where Eva hid.

She very slowly backed away, she didn't hear the old woman - her attention was focussed on the muddy pit from which there came a series of strange noises. The surface bubbled and oozed and the surface seemed black and foreboding. From deep in its centre something appeared. It was round and white, and covered with slim. As she stared at it, a worm crawled over its surface and marine snails stuck to it like glue. Unable to even move, Eva stood in petrified horror it seemed to move closer and closer. It rose slightly higher in the murky water, and two symmetrical holes emerged. Eva almost screamed as the nose and top row teeth of a human skull appeared. She turned to flee and as she did two familiar strong arms grabbed hold of her…

Eva screamed and began to pound the chest of her captor.

"Hey, babe! Steady, it's me!"

Opening her eyes, she saw the smiling face of Guy looking down at her. She almost collapsed. "Guy?"

"It's me, sweetheart. Calm down; are you ok?"

She cried as she embraced him. "Guy! Get me out of here, oh please, please, get me out of here!"

"You're ok," he said, whispering soft reassurances in her ear.

She held on close and sobbed. Is this real? Oh god, please be real!" His arms felt so good!

"Hello, mother," he said softly.

Eva pulled away and turned to see Joan's smiling face. "There you are!"

"Get her away from me! Guy, get her away!"

"Shh, calm down."

"Calm down? She's a fucking head case!"

Joan smiled and tried to place a hand on Eva's back. Eva pulled away. "Don't you fucking touch me!"

"What's this all about?" demanded Guy.

"She's trying to kill me!"

"Kill you?" Guy laughed. "I don't think so, Eva."

"Yeah? Why's she carrying that gun?" Said Eva jabbing a finger toward the shotgun in Joan's hand.

"This old thing? Why, it's to protect you and me, dear, there are dogs and foxes out here. If you hadn't gone running away in the middle of night I wouldn't have had to come and try to protect you."

"Protect me?" Yelled Eva in disbelief, "you nearly killed me!"

"I'm sorry you're so ungrateful," said Joan as she sniffed, "I only wanted to help, Guy - you know that!"

Before Guy could speak a terrible wail came from the tarry grave. Remembering what she had seen, Eva grabbed Guy's jacket. "We need to get out of here; we need to run!"

"Run?" Said Guy in disbelief. He took Eva by the hand and walked toward the grave. Eva resisted, but Guy pulled her.

"Guy, stop! There's something in there!"

She watched in horror as Joan smiled and walked over to the edge, she crouched down. "There's nothing in there, dear..." she turned and smiled a sweet and happy smile toward Eva and said: "except for my dear, sweet Granddaddy." She dipped a hand in.

Eva shook her head. What's wrong with these people? "Guy, we need to go! We need to go now!"

Guy hadn't heard her, his attention was focused on his mother.

Eva grabbed his hand and tugged hard. "Come on."

He blinked and looked down at her. "I love you, Eva. You've been the best of them all."

Joan smiled. "See? Guy's home now, Eva. There's nothing to be afraid of."

Eva stood shivering and desperately holding onto Guy.

"You've been so unwell, I called Guy and told him."

"And I came straight back," he said soothingly.

Eva sobbed. "I guess I have been ill, I feel terrible, Guy, I really need to get out of here,"

He brushed a strand of her hair. "It's ok, babe, I'll look after you."

"Can we please just leave?"

"Oh, Babe." Guy kissed her forehead. "I'm sorry, but this is your home now."

"That's right, dear," said Joan with a smile. "He really likes you, you know."

Guy embraced her tightly, and then taking her hands in his, he deftly slipped the wedding ring off her hand and whispered: "You'll never leave here!"

"What?" She looked into his eyes and was still wondering at it as he pulled back, a strange and sad look on his face, took her by the throat, and with a sudden effort pushed her back forcibly, casting her into the black water.

Down into the muddy depth she went, black water rushed into her mouth, she felt herself being pulled down into the terrible dark. With the last of her strength she pushed hard towards the surface, her head and shoulders broke through the as she gasped for air. Guy and Joan stood at the edge, him with his arm around his mother, her lying her head on his chest as they watched her struggle in the freezing, oily black water. They looked so happy!

"Guy! Guy help!"

Guy took his mother's hand, her head turned to gaze lovingly at her son, while Guy's eyes stared hard at Eva as she struggled in the water. His eyes wet with tears, and a deep sob escaped him. Still, he did not move.

As she tried to swim, an arm appeared from the murk and grabbed her around the neck. She screamed as a muddied face, missing two eyes and most of the lower jaw appeared. A terrible laboured noise was forced from the creature, with a scream Eva and the creature both disappeared into the depths. The black water slowly dissipated, leaving only clear water reflected by moonlight.

Joan smiled, and taking her son's face in her hands, gently pulled him down and kissed his forehead. "Well done, Son. Granddaddy is happy now."

Guy nodded. He fiddled with her wedding ring in his two hands and blinked back a tear. "I really liked her, mum."

"Aw, I know you did, my darling. But grandfather comes first; you know that, and we made sure Eva had no family to worry over her, and now we have her things to sell, and, as her husband, her life insurance will come to you." Joan rubbed his back, and gently plucked the wedding ring from his hand and held out her other hand into which he dropped his own wedding ring.

Joan smiled warmly. "If I told you how expensive this farm is! My, you would never sleep, perhaps if your father had been as strong as you… well, we mustn't dwell on it.

"Come on, let's go, I'll make you a nice supper."

Guy nodded. He walked to the edge of the grave. "Goodnight, Granda. I hope you like Eva, she was… she was my favourite."

A large bubble formed and then popped in the silent and deep water, the only response he was to get.

As they walked back to the farmhouse the old woman cuddled into her son "I think you should stay a bit longer this time before you go back again. I'm sure granddaddy will understand."

Guy nodded. "I'd like that mum."

As they reached the house, Joan walked over to the mantelpiece below which a fire was roaring and burning hot. She smiled at an old photograph of a young woman standing next to a smartly dressed soldier. She blew a kiss at the couple, and dropped the two wedding rings into a small, ornamental box and before walking into the kitchen whistling and humming. Guy stood in the doorway and stared out into the night. From out in the dark something howled.

He gently closed the door.

Epilogue.

She sat arrogantly on a red plastic chair, her foot nervously tapping. She chewed gum loudly and popped a large bubble, hoping the actions would hide the shaking of her hands.

Her eyes were sunken and she looked terrible. She looked around at the other addicts and shook her head. She was supposed to get help here? She had almost decided to leave when a new guy walked in. She could tell he was a looker, normally. But right now it was obvious he was as fucked up on crack as she was.

He grabbed a chair from the stack and arrogantly slammed it down onto the floor as he looked around. She could almost tell what he was thinking.

He sat down and began to sigh and paused as they made eye contact. He smiled nervously and nodded at her.

"You're new," she said.

"So are you," he replied.

"You look fucked!" she said laughing.

"So do you!"

"First time in rehab?" she asked.

"Second. You?"

"Yup, second."

"And last, right? Cause we're gonna do it this time?"

She laughed, picked up her chair and placed it beside him, extending her hand she said: "Sadie."

Taking her hand he replied: "Guy."

"I'm gonna enjoy you, Guy."

He smiled. "Oh, I know you will!"

Flipside II

Prologue

The small, family run pub, The Turtle Inn, located in The Trossachs area of Scotland was well known to the locals and a favourite of the seasonal tourist trade. It was much the same that afternoon. The people were the same, the music was the same; the small town was the same.

Such was the routine here on an off-season Friday that, when the door unexpectedly creaked and opened at three twenty, most of the patrons recoiled in surprise.

All eyes were focused on the new arrival as he walked in and sat down at the bar, apparently oblivious to the incredulous stares cast his way from the few local people who looked up from their glasses, or dominos, to take in the intruder.

The tall, balding bar man with a huge moustache approached the unwelcome guest.

"Yes?" he said aggressively.

The stranger eyed the bar up and down, finally resting on the real ales. He half raised his eyes to take in the bar man. "I need a drink," he muttered.

Seeing where his gaze fell, the barman picked up a pint glass, almost as an afterthought he demanded: "How you paying for this?"

The stranger fumbled in his pocket and eventually dropped some coins in front of the amused bar man.

The bar man looked at him, a mixture of humour and annoyance on his face. His left eye ticked. "You being funny?"

The man raised his eyes to look the bar man in the face. His mouth set in a grim line, worry lines had etched their path into his cheeks and the corner of his eyes betrayed his anxiety. He may only be in his mid-forties or so, but his face suggested he was much, much older. Only the penetrating stare of his eyes, full of pain, said otherwise. He lowered his head. "I really need a drink," he said, almost whispering.

The bar man made to snap, but the silent dignity, or lack of, screamed to him. Just as he was deciding what to do, the stranger spoke.

"Gilmour said you'd help." Again the voice held its strange mixture of near dignity and humility.

At this point the bar man would have accepted anything. Not knowing what else to do, he broke into an uneasy smile. "Danny Gilmour, eh, heard that sorry bastard died."

The outsider flinched, he shuddered as though dancing to music or images only he could see. "Yeah, I was there," he said flatly.

The patrons, who, until now, had seemed to be watching the drama around them with slight amusement, sensed an immediate change. The air became charged with unasked questions. Even the semi-regulars at the far end took notice of the unwelcome change to the atmosphere and looked up from their drinks or partners. All around there seemed to be a shared knowledge that things had altered here.

It was a few seconds before the bar man spoke, when he did his low voice seemed to reverberate through the bar. "So, how'd it happen? I heard a ton of shit from the papers. Let's hear the real story then."

"How about that drink?"

The bar man nodded solemnly, quickly poured a pint of his strongest and handed it over.

The stranger accepted the glass and took a long drink. He replaced it, half empty, on the bar.

Looking up at the barman, it was easy to see he looked a lot better, more life in his eyes. He studied the tall bar man silently eventually he said: "You're Malcolm, aren't you?"

Malcolm nodded.

"Yeah, Danny told me all about this place." He took the bar in with one glance, "said if I ever needed anything to come here." He took another drink. "Thought that a bit presumptuous myself, you know, vouching for another. But that was always the problem with Danny, wasn't it? Vouching for things he knew nothing about."

Malcolm forced a half smile. "Who are you?"

Downing his glass he extended his hand. "Brooks."

Malcolm's eyes widened in surprise as he said: "Steven Brooks, Reice Ellis's mate?"

Silence.

The bar man drew a grimace. Without warning he poured another drink and placed it before Brooks. This time he selected something different for him.

Brooks looked at the drink.

The bar man tried to smile, though his nervousness betrayed him. Indicating the change, he said: "Your tastes are well known, Mr. Brooks."

Brooks accepted the drink. He could see in Malcolm's eyes that he was desperate to find out what had happened to his friend. There was also a hint of fear, personal or otherwise, though well hidden. He admired his restraint.

Brooks took a deep breath.

"Take your time, Mr. Brooks," said Malcolm softly. "We've all the time in the world."

Brooks took a long drink and smiled. "If only that were true, Malcolm. You see, I've always been a stubborn bastard.

"My problem now is that I'm already dead, but like I said, I'm just stubborn." He turned and pointed to the clock behind him. "See that, Malcolm? I'm willing to bet that you're here to see that clock show five thirty. Would I be right?"

Malcolm remained silent, not knowing where this was leading.

"I, on the other hand, if fate follows prediction, will be thirty minutes dead by then!" He smiled. "But anyway, your hospitality begs a story." He downed the remainder of his glass and sighed…

Part One

It was a quiet morning in the popular tourist trap of Puerto Del Carmen, Lanzarote. Not quite eight am, the air was still cooled from the lazy summer evening of the night before and the sun was not yet high enough to deliver its promise of the day's heat. Of the many bars and restaurants along the strip, some were showing sign of life, their owners busily preparing for the restless morning tourists in search of an early breakfast or hangover cure.

The Ocean Blue was one such unassuming establishment. Loud, full of life in the evenings and long into the night; quiet and family oriented during the day, offering a variety of meals and coffees.

As was his custom, the manager and owner entered the premises carrying his copy of The Sun newspaper. He headed straight for the bar to carry out his morning ritual of checking the previous night's takings. He was seldom present during the loud nights, preferring the quiet times during the day: less hassle, friendlier people. He had left the loud nights and long evenings far behind him. Too many memories lurking in the thump-thump beats of club music, the paper-thin attention of the ladies, and more importantly, in the bottom of the beer bottles.

He had chosen a pair of light denims, white trainers and a short white cotton shirt, open to expose his ample tan, suggesting he was already aware of the imminent heat. As with all ex-pats, he had never quite lost his native look, differing from the local population, though not as obviously as some. His hair was dyed a light, dusty blond.

He smiled with unrivalled pleasure as his gaze locked on the ample figure of a young woman who was busily preparing a pot of fresh coffee. He sniffed deeply, inhaling the delicious aroma. On seeing him, she turned and walked seductively toward him. He reached out and embraced her, gazing, as he always did, into the deep blue eyes that seemed to look straight into his soul, the full lips parted to show her brilliant white teeth, she flicked her tongue over her already moist lips and he found himself staring playfully at the laughter lines that took over her features as her smile grew warmer. He playfully patted her rear as she pulled away. Melissa. His gorgeous, unbelievable wife! She kissed his neck as she brought out his coffee. He accepted it and took a sip while nodding with pleasure at the till receipts. It was promising to be another good week.

He cupped his chin in his hands and looked out the window to the not-so-distant Atlantic Ocean with its sunlit waves. He subconsciously followed a distant cruise ship as it made its slow, meandering voyage across the horizon, laden as it obviously was with hungry, thirsty, and fresh holiday makers eager to shake off the yearlong stench of long working hours and life back home. Yes, it was going to be a good week.

A plane taxied along the runway, before coming to a halt at Gate 5 of Arrecife airport in Lanzarote. On-board were the usual clichéd tourist types that swarmed to the Island from, among others, Prestwick airport in Scotland. Families arguing, children crying after the four-hour flight, couples looking at each other in anticipation of a good holiday, young and hungry twenty somethings desperate for sun, sex and alcohol. They were the loudest already. Just the usual bunch, really.

Seat 27A on the other hand stood aloof and seemed in sharp contrast to his fellow passengers. Its occupant looked neither excited nor annoyed. He wore a light grey business suit, white shirt open at the collar, no tie. His tray, also in contrast to the chaotic mess of his fellow passengers was neat and sparse. One empty cup of coffee sat to his left, the sugar and milk carton carefully placed inside. He folded the newspaper neatly in half and placed it in the fold of the seat in front of him. He stretched his arms over his head and sighed.

The passengers disembarked with surprising speed, all anxious to get off and start the sun tanning, or drinking, or both. Once through the somewhat lax passport control, most people had surged ahead and now stood anxiously waiting for their seemingly lost luggage while the onslaught of husband and wife bickering, and the cacophony of ignored and disoriented children, continued unabated. Seat 27A, however, walked straight past the collection area and made his way outside; bypassing the assembled holiday reps and politely refusing all offers from the army of touts. He smiled pleasantly at the large security guard as he left the airport. Pausing only to take his sunglasses from his suit jacket, he made his way purposefully to the assembled taxis. He entered the first available one and lowered the window.

"Puerto Del Carmen," he said softly. The driver nodded and took off. 27A took an envelope from his pocket, opened it and again studied the large photograph and short note. He turned to look out of the window and, ever so slightly, smiled.

While 27A was making his way through the airport, in one of the small bars, positioned at just the right location to catch all the exit gates, and at the best table to observe the exodus, Juan Armand Asante sat in his usual seat, drinking his usual drink and trying his usual chat up lines on the incoming tourists. Normally his attempts were met with giggles, laughs, the occasional argument and generally resulted Juan being able to focus on his easy, well-paid job as lookout. His one instruction: watch for any single passenger who looks completely out of place.

For this simple task, Juan would earn more money in a day than most of his friends made in a week.

Normally Juan excelled at his task, mainly due to the fact that there had never been a single passenger who looked completely out of place exit the airport during his lengthy watch.

Today, however, he met Julie Smith. She was twenty years old, cute, tanned with large breasts that poked through her too small top, and more importantly, just out of a serious relationship and looking for any local who would take her mind off Chris Geoffrey Stone - the Pig!

At first, she smiled at Juan. Then she laughed at his terrible joke, and then she nodded as he motioned to the seat next to her. After drinking her third Cosmo, paid for by Juan and his generous employer, she relented to his kiss.

As their lips locked and his hand wandered, Seat 27A strolled past, just as oblivious to Juan and Julie as they were to him, and Juan would never again boast to his friends about his "easy money." His nice little earner would vanish as quickly as his interest in Julie Smith.

As the taxi pulled a U-turn and drove off, 27A checked into the small, unassuming hotel. "No kids allowed" proclaimed the sign in the tiled foyer. It had a large swimming pool, minimum facilities, but came highly recommended. He stood at the check in desk and handed his details to the receptionist.

"Morning, sir. Name please?"

"Sullivan."

"How many in your party?" she asked.

"Just me," he replied softly.

She eyed him with suspicion, said stiffly: "You here for one or two weeks?"

"Two for the moment, I may wish to stay longer. Will that be a problem?"

She shook her head. "You have family here?" she asked.

He favoured her with a smile. "May I request a room on the upper level, preferably with a view to the street, top floor if possible?"

She shrugged off his refusal of small talk. "No problem," she said. "Room seventeen, on the top floor, there are only two rooms up there. Bit of a climb, you sure you wouldn't like one near the bar or the pool?"

He shook his head. "That will be fine." He accepted the key from her, lifted his small hand luggage and walked to the door. He paused and turned. "Pardon me. Are there any local bars here run by a British gentleman?"

She looked up and frowning, said: "There are lots of good bars here."

He smiled, though it didn't look quite natural. "I had a friend move here, bought a small place, I forget the name."

"Your friend; what was his name?"

Sullivan smiled. "Thank you for your time." With that he walked from the room as the receptionist reached for the phone.

Right after slamming the phone down and moments after ordering a "serious kicking for that fucking halfwit Asante!", Steven Brooks, owner of the Ocean Blue and Ex-Pat, made his way immediately to the small storage room he had at the rear of the kitchen. Inside, he yelled at the chef for no apparent reason, ordered him down to the supermarket for some bleach and a "fucking cloth" then once he was gone, he pulled a small box from its concealed hiding place behind the door. He quickly opened the combination lock and with the smallest of sighs emptied the contents of the box onto the floor.

With practised ease he slammed the magazine cartridge into the Desert Eagle .50 handgun and hid it in his jacket pocket. He picked up the unused credit card, the excellently forged driver's licence, and the small flick knife. He gathered up the rest of the contents and threw them back in the box which was then returned to its hiding place.

When he returned to the bar, Melissa was looking understandably worried. "You sure?" she said simply.

Brooks nodded. "Yeah, I'm sure. It's for real this time!"

She blinked several times, fighting down the fear that, until now, had existed only in the back of her mind and in her occasional nightmares.

"You know what to do, Mel," Brooks said sternly. "We knew this could happen."

"We talked about it, yeah. But I guess I always thought it wouldn't happen. You were so careful…"

"It doesn't matter. I always knew there would be a reckoning for what I did. I expected it sooner, to be honest. The Ellis brothers, Danny Gilmour…" He shook his head sadly. "What the fuck was I thinking making a deal with that prick Brent Thomas?"

"Anyone would have done what you did," Melissa said. She knew what she was doing, dragging it out, but she didn't want him to leave.

As though he knew that Brooks smiled sadly. "Would they? No. Looking back now, I could've gone two other ways, both better than this. I could've gone over to Reice, hell! I spent so long with him and did so much illegal shit anyway, or I could've called the police, given them the complete, fully wrapped up package and become the hero of the moment…" he sighed deeply. "But no. All I saw was the bigger payoff and a way to get back at everyone who had written me off and laughed at me; a way out of the shit I had fallen into. I grabbed that memory stick, ran off and finalised the deal Karl had organised then screwed Thomas over. I took the idiot option; the short end money and the easy pay off. But that's a pile of shit; an empty dream. I've spent the last four years watching every fucking tourist, shitting myself every time my phone goes or God forbid, the door gets knocked. I got all this money, and time and all I can do is spend it worrying, regretting and fretting!"

Melissa turned to the bar, poured a large Jack Daniels and offered it to Brooks. He smiled as he took the glass and instead of drinking it, he placed it on the polished black surface of the bar. He winked at her. "I don't think so, Babe. I need my head clear this time. One hundred per cent clear." He shuddered as he recalled his last flight from the sordid underworld. The drugs, the drink the… No, he would never fall again. He looked at Melissa and saw her staring at his left hand. He followed her stare and saw to his surprise that it was trembling uncontrollably. He cleared his throat and shrugged. Melissa smiled in understanding. "More coffee then?" she asked softly.

"Please, and get me my phone, will you?" Brooks headed to the door and bolted it shut just as a hugely obese tourist family arrived at the door. The father rattled the door, gesturing angrily at Brooks who smiled and closed the blinds. "Arseholes," he muttered.

Melissa had poured the fresh coffee and had brought a sandwich for her husband. Brooks ignored it and sipped the coffee, again finding it perfect to his tastes. He picked up his mobile phone and with a heavy sigh, turned it on. It began beeping incessantly as a stream of missed calls and text messages arrived. He pressed clear and ignored them, choosing instead to sift through his address book.

Ray - Straight to answer phone.

Brooks sighed.

Mick – Unobtainable.

Donnie - Same story.

Pete – it rang and rang. No answer.

With a deep frown etched on his face, Brooks tried the remainder of his co-called Friends - It was the same story from every one of them. He dropped the phone on the desk and rubbed his eyes.

No one, not one fucking answer from any of them! Some were hardly a surprise, the unreliable-last-port-of-call types, but Ray, ever-ready, always available Ray? It was then that Brooks began to get the horrible, deep feeling in the pit of his stomach.

He grabbed his phone and punched the call button. His fear was replaced with anger as again it went to answer phone. "Asante! Where are you, you little shit? I told you, never to ignore me! Get your arse over here right now or so help me God!" He threw the phone on the bar. "Fuck!" he yelled.

"Calm down," said Melissa quietly.

Brooks stared at her. "Calm down? No answer from anyone? Even that numb-nut Asante's not answering. I don't like this, Mel. Not one bit!"

Just then there came a soft, distinguished knock on the door.

"We're closed!" yelled Brooks.

Again the knock sounded, more insistent this time. "Get rid of them, Mel. Will you?"

Melissa nodded as she went to the door. Brooks turned his back on the door and picked up his phone and called the airport. "Yeah, it's me. Listen, have you seen Asante this morning? He's…"

"Steven," said Mel.

Brooks waved her to silence over his shoulder.

"Put the phone down, Mr. Brooks," said an authoritative voice.

Brooks spun on his seat and reached for his gun. His hand stopped as he focused on the pistol pointed right at him.

"Hang up the phone, please," said the man sternly.

Brooks cut the call and dropped the phone. The man was tall, easily six feet, dressed in a white shirt and smart trousers. He wore designer sunglasses and evidently carried the heat well. His hair was cropped and dark, his chiselled features showed a hint of designer stubble. The gun was held casually but firmly in his left hand, while his other hand gripped Melissa's arm. She tried to move but he pulled her sharply back, causing her to cry out.

"Stay where you are, Mr. Brooks," said the man when Brooks made to stand.

"Who are you and what the fuck do you want?" demanded Brooks.

"My name is Sullivan, Mr. Brooks. My employer has need of both you and Mrs. Brooks"

"For what?" spat Brooks.

"I truly have no idea. That is not my concern. Mrs. Brooks will accompany me for a short and pleasant stay while you will remain here. Any attempt to call for help, or if you leave here, things will not go well for Mrs. Brooks."

Brooks stared vehemently at Sullivan. "If you hurt her…"

"Threats are irrelevant, Mr Brooks. I am stating facts and I advise you to listen carefully. Mrs. Brooks will not be harmed, provided you carry out my instructions."

"I'm not entirely helpless, Sullivan!" spat Brooks. "I only need to make a phone call…"

"Were you able to contact any of your friends, Mr. Brooks? I daresay the answer remains an intangible no. Ray Gordon, for example, died most cowardly."

Brooks snarled an insult.

"So, Mr. Brooks, you will remain here while your wife accompanies me on a little trip," said Sullivan softly, his voice leaving no room for argument. "An old friend of yours will be along shortly then you will have the answers to all your questions. So long as you do exactly as I have said and if your wife does her part then I see no reason why this cannot go smoothly for all concerned."

"Who is your employer?" demanded Brooks through gritted teeth.

In reply, Sullivan smiled softly. "Do not try to be a hero, Mr. Brooks. Just do what is expected." He turned toward the door, pulling a struggling Melissa with him.

"Mel. Don't fight him. Do what he says, everything will be fine. I promise." The words were torn from him and he stared angrily and helplessly at Sullivan.

Sullivan nodded at him. "A very good start, Mr. Brooks, I commend you on your admirable restraint." With that he turned and left.

Brooks paused a moment, anger and rage overcoming him. He ran to the door, gun in hand and pulled it open. He hesitantly lifted the gun and aimed it at the unsuspecting Sullivan who was still forcibly pulling Melissa across the deserted street. She turned and looked at her husband with a mixture of fear and rage.

Sullivan either ignored him or was unaware of the threat. He pushed Melissa into the rear of a black rental car and closed the door. He glanced once at Brooks and flicked his gaze over the aimed gun. He shook his head minimally and calmly walked to the driver's door before getting in.

Brooks, with tears of rage blinding his eyes, turned and walked back into the bar, slamming the door violently behind him. With a scream he hurled the gun against the optics behind the bar. An explosion of glass and liquid followed. He fell to the ground, back against the door. Great sobs wracked him as he lay.

"What the fuck have I done?" he yelled. The bar became nightmarish, claustrophobic. He struggled to breathe. The air was too hot; too heavy, miasmic, not enough. The walls closed in and the ceiling lowered. As he lay there, he was vaguely aware of a large people carrier pull up just outside, across from the bar. He jumped to his feet and ran behind the bar. He stepped over the broken glass and pooled alcohol, stooped to retrieve his wet pistol. He rubbed it across his chest to dry it off.

Running to the door, he stopped and stared in sheer disbelief at the adapted rear of the vehicle which was now slowly opening.

From within, a wheelchair was being lowered to the ground, an all too familiar arrogant face on the ruined body sitting on it.

His jaw fell open as the gun slipped from his fingers and fell to the ground. He staggered back. "No, no, no!" he whispered. "It can't be!"

Outside, two large, burly security-type men were helping the man in the wheelchair descend from the ramp onto the sun-baked street. One walked over with an arrogant swagger and threw the bar door open. He stood there, holding it, his sun-glass shaded eyes staring at Brooks who stood in shocked, stupefied silence.

Meanwhile the other man, though projecting a similarly arrogant pose, helped to turn the wheelchair around. The man in the chair said something to him and his arrogance vanished to be replaced with subdued chagrin. He meekly nodded and manoeuvred the wheelchair up the small curb and into the bar, where upon its occupant gained control of it, controlling the motion via a small joystick, The other man stepped back and with his swagger restored, closed the door behind him and pressed against it.

The man in the wheelchair might well be crippled, his body unmoving, but the eyes betrayed the violence of his past and he had lost none of his inherent, vehement rage. He stared unwaveringly at Brooks, bringing the chair to a stop mere feet away.

When he spoke it was with a voice well-used to being obeyed and one that never had to repeat itself. "Sit down, Steven," he said. The voice had deteriorated somewhat, and its owner had to clear his throat several times as though it were full of some gritty contaminant.

Brooks found himself obeying without question as one of the burly men slammed a chair into the ground just behind him; Brooks fell dejectedly into it. His eyes asking the questions he could not. Eventually he found his voice which came out in a whimper of disbelief and fear.

"How?" was all he could muster.

The man laughed, wheezing, he said: "After all these years that's all you have for me?"

"You're... You're dead! I watched you die!" Brooks stared at the apparition from his past; still doubting what his senses were telling him. There was no way this man was alive! Yet here he was! A face from his nightmares; a face from his past and one that he could never exorcise no matter how much he tried.

"You honestly think Karl would kill me, his own flesh and blood?" Reice Ellis shook his head in a jarring motion.

Hearing the voice made the nightmare all the more real. "How did you survive? I saw him shoot you; I saw you fall."

As if suddenly aware of the two henchmen behind him, Reice moved his head marginally to the side. "Outside, you two," he barked.

"Sir…" ventured one.

"Outside, I said. Steven here's an old friend," Reice said sarcastically. "I'll be fine."

With a glance at each other the two men went outside and returned to the vehicle.

Reice turned back. "The bullet missed my heart but did sever some vital blood vessels. I lay on that floor slowly bleeding to death, unable to move. I lost consciousness. Hours I lay there, drifting in and out. Your old mob came with their forensics and their investigators and their inane bullshit! No one looked twice at me lying amid all those bodies. Eventually, I must've twitched or something, a young police woman saw me and yelled for help. She looked so much like young Gemma. You remember her, I'm sure."

Brooks winced at the name of the dead police officer.

"Anyway, that's when they eventually got me an ambulance but by then it was almost too late. I'd lost so much blood and I had had a series of minor strokes. Then the funny thing was, and you're gonna love this! Just as I was on the road to recovery I got hit with this massive fucking stroke, hence the reason for this piece of shit," he said, motioning at the chair, "paralyzed on the entire right side of my body, no movement of any kind, and reduced motor control on my left." As he spoke he stared hard into Brooks' eyes, almost daring him to smirk or show any emotion. Brooks held onto his composure.

Slowly, almost disappointedly, Reice continued: "Eventually I recovered enough to be sent to prison, though your old boys kept me off the record, seems they wanted no knowledge of my survival to come out, they were well into picking off Karl's team by then and they were worried the news of my survival would cost them their momentum.

"It was a decision that cost them dearly, I'm telling you. My brother had one amazing legal team! They got me my freedom, denial of my civil and human rights and all that horse shit! Cost me most of my fortune fighting them though, fat prick, Jacob!" He coughed violently and again tried to clear his throat. With obvious pain and effort, he raised a handkerchief to his mouth and wiped some spittle. His arrogant, authoritative demeanour slipped for a second, but was quickly restored, "Which brings us nicely to the reason for my visiting you and the current Mrs. Brooks."

Brooks, who'd been caught up in the narrative and return to his past had almost forgotten the kidnapping of his wife. Again, the deep knot in his stomach twisted painfully. "What are you going to do to my wife?"

"That depends entirely on you," said Reice. He leaned forward in his chair. "You're going to get something for me; something you and your sister are about the only two people in the world who can!"

"My sister? Reice, what the fuck does my wife - and now my sister - have to do with you?" yelled Brooks.

"Listen you turncoat, thieving, twisted prick! Don't forget who you're talking to, even from this fucking chair, I could kick your ass without breaking a sweat!"

Brooks paled as a hundred memories of this violent, sadistic thug poured through his subconscious: stabbings, beatings, shootings, and just plain sick brutality that Reice had seemed to revel in. He shuddered as he recalled one guy losing his eye to a hot cigar as Reice just laughed before throwing him from a moving car.

Submissively, Brooks lowered his eyes as the brutal stare burned into him. "What do you want from me?" he asked pitifully.

Reice looked scornfully at Brooks. "Your sister, I believe, works as a P.A to Brent Thomas of First National Bank in sunny Glasgow, does she not?"

Brooks' eyes widened. "I, uh, I'm not sure she…"

"Sure she does! She's been there for over ten years, working her way up from work experience temp, through Customer Services to her current esteemed position. Drives a Mini Cooper, two years old, under finance to Black Horse, she owes, I believe, six thousand four hundred. It's red if I remember. Her house has only recently been re-mortgaged through, surprise, surprise, First National - but we'll come back to that.

"She's married to Philip R Harris, albeit estranged, a Quantity Surveyor originally from Leeds. They have two children: Alex, who's five and little Tom is going on two. A lovely wedding that, in The Dominican Republic, you enjoyed it from what I hear. The first Mrs. Brooks never did find out about that slut from reception, did she? Tut tut, Steven. That was terrible what you did, I wonder if Melissa would approve?

"Anyway, back to your sister. Well, ever since she considered leaving the unbelievably boring Philip R Harris, she's been a bit of a bad girl, ran up some debt so she did. That re-mortgage. Poor Philip doesn't know anything about that, or the savings account that's been a bit depleted. Luckily for her that lovely Brent Thomas arranged her re-mortgage on the quiet, even though technically she's now on a finance blacklist, even though technically Philip never signed it, but what the hell, perks of the job eh? She keeps her four-bedroom detached suburban dream that no doubt will land her way once the divorce is finalized and Brent Thomas gets his end away on that huge mahogany table in his office whenever he gets a bit horny. You wouldn't blame him really if you saw Mrs. Thomas; big, fat, ugly fucker that one, probably hasn't been down in those knickers for years!"

Brooks felt rage burning, threatening to overwhelm him. He wanted to punch that sanctimonious face, knock that smile right off! Push the chair over and stamp on that twisted skull. Kick his jaw again and again and again and…

"Why are you looking at me like that, Steven? I'm just telling you what's been happening back home. You're looking like one of those old Emperors who kept a pike handy to skewer messengers bringing bad news. You should really be thanking me, Steven. Your poor mother would be turning in her grave to see what's been happening to her family. Old Valerie would have you and Simone over hot coals for what you've been up to."

It was too much. "You leave my mother out of this you twisted fuck!" he yelled.

A sudden death-head grin enveloped Reice. "That's it, Steven! That's what I need! I need your rage, your way of thinking from the old days! The sun-drenched, gay boy barman look doesn't suit you! I need the aggression!"

"Aggression?" said Brooks in disbelief. "You make me sound like you, I was nothing like you!"

"Oh you do yourself an injustice! You were the consummate professional! That undercover cop layer quickly vanished when you got into The Life with me! Even after the Old Bill kicked you out, pressed charges, sent you for psychiatric evaluation you still stayed with me!"

"To bring you down!" yelled Brooks.

"How many chances did you have? You could've taken me a hundred times over, but you were addicted to it, but enough of this blame-game. Ancient history can wait 'til another time!"

"Fine with me, what do you want?"

Reice coughed, and again weakly wiped his mouth, "Jack Daniels, straight, plenty of ice."

Brooks looked at him in disbelief, and then with a shake of his head, poured the glass from one of the remaining optics his gun didn't break. He slammed the glass down beside Reice.

"Get a straw and hold it to my mouth," ordered Reice.

Brooks did as he was told and stared out Reice as he drained the glass.

"Ah, fucking lovely!"

"You going to tell me what the hell you want from me?"

"Your darling sister's employer ain't as squeaky clean as his fucking office portrait in Who's Who of the banking industry. He has something that belongs to me; well, of a sort. It was Karl's and, by proxy, is mine and seeing as you gave it fucking back to Thomas, you're going to get that sister with the gorgeous arse to get it for me."

Brooks stared at him incredulously, "That all? I have the original of Karl's program, the one I gave to Thomas was a virused copy! You can have the original right now!"

"Not good enough, Steven! The same job we planned all those years ago in Danny's club is still on, only this time Thomas' bank is the target and he's not in charge, I am! And it's up to you to carry it out!"

"You what? Yelled Brooks incredulously.

"You heard me! You're going to help me take that double-crossing arsehole down. I want the money I'm owed, and I want him exposed, run out and fucking completely ruined! Thinks he can rob from me and walk away without a fucking scratch? I want him hurt! I want him bleeding! I want him screaming for his fucking mother! That two faced, goddamned piece of..." Reice coughed violently and began to thrash violently in his chair, his eyes rolled in his head and unintelligible noises were torn from him. It was only then that Brooks noticed the restraining belt on the chair holding him in, the only thing that kept him from falling to the floor.

Brooks ran to the door, yanked it open, startling the aides in the car. "Get in here!" he yelled. "He's dying or something!"

The two men in black raced in. One held Reice while he snapped the restraining belt open and leaned him forward in his chair, the other pulled his trousers down, and administered some kind of treatment while Brooks looked on in disbelief.

When they had finished, they leaned him back in his chair. His eyes were rolling, and he was drooling badly. One of them wiped his mouth before stepping back.

Reice lay with his head resting on the headrest. With obvious effort he opened his eyes and, with difficulty, focused on Brooks. When he spoke, it was barely audible: "You'll do it, you fuck. You'll do it or I'll make a phone call and our mutual friend will slit your whore of a wife's throat and post her body back to you in pieces!" With that his eyes closed, and he fell into post epileptic sleep.

Brooks picked up the bottle of Jack Daniels, pulled the optic nozzle off and took a generous swig from the half empty bottle. Looking at the silent form of Reice and his two dumb aides he shook his head, sighed deeply, and said simply: "Fuck!"

Part Two

He sat in total darkness, staring out the small window at the world passing him by. The rain was relentless and had been coming down in torrents most of the day; he sat listening to the sound as it pattered off the window and dripped down in waves. At this hour, traffic was light, the cars few and far between, their wipers going full speed just to keep up with the storm. People passed with such a lax approach, and no one was in a hurry at this time of night. 3am yet again.

A distant roll of thunder followed a flash that lit up the night sky for a brief second. He nursed the glass of vodka and coke with lots of ice in his left hand and, for the umpteenth time, he sighed deeply as he pondered his position. How did things get to this?

The house he was renting here in the Greenfaulds area of Cumbernauld, Glasgow annoyed him, he was paying way over the odds and knew it, though desperate times and all. He tried not to think of the home he had left behind. The dream house he had spent years searching for, then discarded in the blink of an eye, and for what? He desperately tried not to think of everything he had lost, of all the memories that he had ruined through his inability to control his all-consuming need for revenge. Now his mind was once again full of dark thoughts and things he no longer wanted to think of, that he was tired of thinking of, things that had cost him yet another relationship. It's a son's duty to avenge his father!

The acid in his stomach attacked him with its usual ferocity as he took a long drink from his glass, futilely hoping it would help. He winced, a mixture of the strong alcohol and the stomach pain. A sudden flash of forked lightning and the following rolling grumble of thunder distracted him for a brief second.

The call should come soon. His mobile phone lay beside him on the small sofa. The six missed calls and the mounting unread text messages from everyone but she held no interest. He thought once more about throwing the phone off the nearest wall, but something stopped him. He cursed as he moved his foot and knocked over one of the many beer bottles that littered his feet.

He stood quickly, drained the glass, lifted his mobile phone and walked into the small kitchen for a refill. His stomach growled again, this time to remind him he still had not eaten, though he pushed that thought aside also.

Another heavy sigh and another long drink.

How long had he spent planning this? The blackmails, the favours, the money! But none of that would matter soon. Soon the past would be set right, and all the nightmares would end.

As his phone bleeped and the text came in, he smiled and slowly made his way to the kitchen. Opening the large cupboard, he pulled out the green canister of petrol. He quickly unscrewed the cap and proceeded to pour it over the furnishings, the floor and then into the hall where it soaked into the carpet. Next the living room and its sofa, and throwing the empty container, he mounted the stairs to the front door. With a satisfied smile he lit the lighter and threw it down the stairs. The flames spread quickly, simultaneously engulfing the kitchen and the living room. He watched for a few moments until the flames began their upward climb. With a deep sigh of satisfaction he headed out into the night, slamming the door on the horror that was his rented....

He jumped as his phone really did bleep, bringing him out of his day dream. He smiled as he saw the number. It was not the smile of a contented man.

The message said simply: Done.

He walked over to the kitchen sink and looked out of the window. With another long drink to settle the nerves, he smiled again and muttered: "Finally."

D'Loca is a well-known and much-loved Italian restaurant in the Bishopbriggs area of Glasgow. Always much in demand so the chances of getting a table on the weekend nights without booking were remote and slim. Only well-known returning customers had a chance, through a wink and a nod, of even getting the chance of an unusual, late cancellation. Simone was well known and was one such customer. She sat in her favourite seat by the window and stared out at the passing traffic, oblivious to the chatter going on around her. Normally relishing her favourite meal with epicurean delight, she had barely touched her Mussels in White Sauce and now her Jimmy Style Spaghetti Carbonara and Pizza Romana was cooling slowly. She clutched her glass of House Merlot and sighed. Marks on her chin revealed the passage of time as she stared out the window. She failed to notice him walk past outside and rush back into the restaurant. Only the slamming down of his chair as he forcibly fell into it jolted her from her reverie.

He threw his mobile phone onto the table. "I still can't get a fucking answer!" he spat loudly.

An elderly couple at the next table looked up from their antipasti in annoyance. He ignored them and lifted his glass of Nastro Assura and half drained it before slamming it down on the table. Finesse and softly were not in his vocabulary. "Why the fuck can no one confirm this bullshit?" he yelled.

Simone grew aware of several stares and shakes of head. "Sean, calm down, people are looking."

"Like I give a fuck!" He stared hard at the old man at the next table who looked away, muttering his complaint. "Anyway, how can I calm down? Your brother, back from exile and demanding your help!"

Simone winced at his idiotic dramatics. She frowned and glanced around her to see who was listening. "Will you keep quiet, for God's sake?"

"Months we've been planning things and then your fucking brother turns up out of the blue demanding we drop everything and help him! What's he doing back here anyway? If the Old Bill find out their most wanted arsehole is back in town..."

"He knows that! He had no choice."

"Yeah? Well, one phone call to them and he isn't a problem anymore!"

It was Simone's turn to slam her glass down. "Sean! Don't you even joke about that, I'm warning you!"

He shook his head. "You know I won't," he said, softening slightly. "I know what you owe him; I just can't believe the timing!"

Simone sighed deeply just as the waiter turned up with another glass of Assura which its recipient was ready for, he topped up Simone's wine glass and left with a smile.

"I know. This is unreal!"

"So, what now?" he asked.

"That all you care about?"

He scowled. "We have different motives but the same goal, Si, don't forget that. We need to think about this and find a way. It's going to take time. So, can I stay at your place tonight?"

"Why? You finally burned that house down did you?"

He shrugged and raised his hand, his finger and thumb were millimetres apart. "This close."

She choked on her wine and stared at him incredulously.

Part Three

Brooks paced back and forth in the small hotel room. It hadn't been easy, the furtive flight back to the United Kingdom, as good as his forged passport was and how different he looked from his old mugshot, there was still the risk that some overzealous immigration officer would feel the need to check further or even that the police sketch artist would somehow have imagined his new look. The memories of Prestwick Airport were not pleasant, nor was the long drive to Cumbernauld and now the hotel felt cramped, dirty and cheap. And it was cold, freezing even. He had forgotten how cold it was in Scotland. Every time he blinked, he saw the sun-drenched streets of Lanzarote with its remembered illusion of security. No, every time he blinked he saw Melissa dragged into that car by Sullivan, and Reice's twisted face haunted every waking moment.

He grabbed the bottle of wine from the small dressing table and poured another glass into the tumbler from the bathroom and gulped furiously. Cursing, he checked the time on the small television screen mounted on the wall. He cursed again, and poured another glass, almost dropping it as a knock sounded on the door.

He grabbed his small knife and held it behind his back before gingerly opening the door. He sighed and threw the door open, grabbing Simone by the arm. He gasped as he saw the man behind her.

"Who the fuck are you?" he demanded threateningly, holding up the knife.

"Calm down, Steven. He's with me," said Simone. "Jeezo, it's good to see you too!"

Brooks stared hard. "Get in, both of you," he hissed as he closed the door, locking it behind him. "You better start talking, Simone. I mean it!"

"You better put that knife down, man!" said Sean.

Simone elbowed him. "Sean, be quiet for once, will you!" She turned to Brooks. "Steven, I need you to trust me, he's with me and needs to be here."

Brooks gestured to the bed for them both to sit down with a sarcastic flourish and a shake of his head. With a quick look through the peephole to make sure they weren't being watched, he locked the door and leaned with his back to it amid the uncomfortable silence.

"So, who wants to start?" ventured Simone.

"Start?" spat Brooks. "Never mind start, Simone this was meant to be between you and me, one simple thing to do and we were in the clear!"

"You were in the clear maybe," ventured Sean.

Brooks glowered at him. "You don't even figure in this, pal, you…"

"Listen, Brooks! This isn't all about you! We…"

"They have my wife!" yelled Brooks. "And unless I get them what they want they're going to kill her, that serious enough for you?"

Simone gasped. "Why didn't you tell me?"

Brooks fell into a chair. "Didn't think I had to; you were nervous enough without me adding to it."

Sean frowned. "As much as we understand your situation, Brooks, we are in this together and uh, maybe I can help, you know? I got my own ideas for getting back at Thomas."

Simone and Brooks looked at him.

Brooks laughed. "Really, you have a plan?" He laughed again. "My sister couldn't break into a piggy bank, so what are you, some kind of super thief? Ok, big man, tell me your plan? How are you going to get into Thomas' system, how are you going to get the money out, how are you going to do all that without getting caught? You some kind of computer genius who can bypass the best systems money can buy? Do you know how to avoid the marked accounts, the traceable ones?"

Sean blinked as his cheeks reddened. "What I mean, is that… well, maybe we can work this out to suit all of us here. I mean, if you've got a plan already, let's hear it."

"Just what is your agenda anyway?" said Brooks.

"Well, you want to rescue your old lady, Simone wants money and a way out of her crap life. Me, well, all I want is plain old-fashioned revenge. I want Brent Thomas taken down! That bastard owes me!"

Brooks shook his head. "Sorry, I don't do revenge, mate!"

"Well, looks to me like you got no choice! You need Simone to do this and she's with me," he said, grabbing her hand. "So lucky for you, you get two for one!"

Brooks stared at him, deep in thought. "Why do you want Thomas taken down?"

"Let's just say…"

"No. Let's not just say. If you're to be in on this I need to know what you're into."

Sean sighed deeply, let go of Simone and stood up, crossing to the window. He leaned against it. "When I was six, my dad died, which screwed me and my mum big time. She lost the house and everything else all because dear old dad thought more of cocaine than he did of life insurance. So, we get bounced back and forth between shit council dumps and even shittier rented houses, my mum did all she could to try and make ends meet. Then one day, while in one of the three jobs she had at the time, she ends up working as a cleaner at First National for, you guessed it, Brent Thomas.

"Suddenly she's the flavour of the month; he ends up buying her everything, a car, jewellery, a nice house. She's his dirty little secret. He turns up whenever he likes and I get play stations, smart phones, money, anything to keep me quiet and out of the way. It's a great life until my mother makes one huge fuck up: She ends up pregnant."

Simone stared at him, caught up in what was obviously news to her. Brooks looked on impassively.

"Thomas goes off the fucking deep end! There's no way he wants an illegitimate kid fucking everything up. He goes mental, accusing my mother of trapping him, starts smashing up the place, I get a broken jaw for getting between him and my mother and she gets three broken ribs, a punctured lung and a broken nose for trying to get him off me.

"Then it's all over. The car gets taken back; some big bald pricks come for our stuff; we get thrown out the house while the locks get changed. Thomas stops returning our calls. And there you have it. My mother lost the baby in the assault, decided to follow my dear old dad and dies of cocaethylene poisoning a while later, leaving me to get passed around foster parents like a scud book with fuck all to my name except revenge."

He placed both hands on the dressing table and stared hard into the mirror. "So, if you think for one second you can cut me out of this, you got another thing coming!" He punched the wall hard. "I'm taking that bastard down; you can have whatever you want. I want Thomas!" He swallowed hard. "You got any drink here?"

Brooks motioned to the half empty bottle of Rioja, said: "Only wine."

"I need a real fucking drink!"

"There's a pub next door," said Brooks, "go knock yourself out."

"Or there are some supermarkets just across the road, Babe," said Simone. "I'll come with you."

He motioned her back with a wave of his hand. "You stay here and talk happy families; I need to clear my head!" With that he stormed out the room, slamming the door behind him.

Brooks stared at Simone and sighed deeply; he walked to the bathroom and came back with another glass which he filled with the wine before handing to Simone.

She accepted it with a smile and took a small sip. "Bet this is terrible compared to the stuff you get in your bar."

He smiled weakly. "Yeah," he said before taking a large gulp from his own glass. "What a fucking mess!"

"I know," said Simone quietly. "I knew he had some reason to hate Brent, but I had no idea."

"Simone, he's an accident waiting to happen! How the hell can we trust him?"

"I can handle him, Steven, don't worry. I'm the only one actually going in; he won't be anywhere near Brent or the office. Steven, we can get out of this, I promise. Brent totally trusts me, I have the run of the place and no one's going to question me or stop me. I can do what none of you can, I can literally walk right into his office! You couldn't do that with a small army!

"So let me do this, Steven! We can bring Thomas down, get you what you need to free Melissa and it'll get me free and clear too."

Brooks frowned. "I'm coming with you."

She shook her head sharply. "You're too much of a risk. Think about it, not only are you on every wanted list from London to Glasgow, but Thomas knows what you look like."

"That was a long time ago, he dealt with Danny and Karl, not me, besides I look so different now, he won't recognise me."

"No, Steven. We can't take that risk."

Brooks stood and crossed to the window. After a long, clear struggle with his emotions, he sighed and turned, picking up a bag, he rummaged in it for a while before taking out a memory stick. With a mixture of emotions, he stared at it before turning to Simone: "Use this when you get into Thomas' computer. A lot of people died for this damn thing, it's been a few years admittedly, but it will work."

Simone's eyes widened.

He shook his head. "It's not cash; it's my bargaining chip for Reice Ellis."

"What is it?"

"Nothing I can talk about. It's the whole reason Karl got involved with Reice again, why Danny Gilmour died, why," he winced, "why Gemma died. I gave a version of it to Thomas so he would leave me alone, but I corrupted it with a destructive worm and it locked down so completely that it's untraceable. He had access just long enough for me to get away; I kept the original."

"What makes you think it'll work now? Whatever it was, it's unlikely Thomas will still have it."

"He does have it, he just doesn't know it. Plus I modified his copy with a tracker program; once you install it, it will launch the tracker and download the data directly to the memory stick and scramble the data, only we'll have access."

Simone looked down. "What about us?"

"There's a subroutine on it I copied from Karl's original, it's basically a grab program, it'll get us access to anything from say one to twenty million depending on what Thomas has going on at the moment. It's an old program but a good one. It was Karl's insurance for himself; he didn't think I knew about it. You and lover boy will be ok. I just need the memory stick back."

Simone smiled. "My kind of deal, brother"

He smiled back. "Ok, let's go through the plan."

The car slowed and eventually pulled up on the corner of St Vincent Street in the centre of Glasgow, a short distance from First National. It was late – well past midnight, and apart from a few late revellers and omnipresent taxis, the street was quiet. A light wind had settled in, and it made dust devils from discarded litter. After a quick check in the rear-view mirror, Sean turned to Simone. "You ready?"

She nodded and stared at him with more confidence than she actually felt. "I'm ready."

"In and out, a quick hour or so and we are home free! I'll wait here for you, and don't worry; we've been over this a hundred times, nothing can go wrong."

"What if Brent is in there, though?"

"He's not."

"How do you know?"

He grabbed her hand. "I know, trust me, Si."

She kissed him quickly on the cheek. "See you soon," she said, opening the door. The wind seemed to howl through the open door, and she shivered, as much from the cold as from the adrenaline.

He watched her leave, staring hard as she half walked, half ran though the street. He took a deep breath to calm his nerves and leaned back, preparing himself for a long vigil. All the planning, the waiting, the bribes, the gambles, they all came down to this.

Almost there!

It wouldn't be long now and he could dump the whole fake identity and go back to being his real self. He wouldn't miss 'Sean' at all, based as he was, upon the people he despised.

Simone Harris ran though the light rain and tried to look confident as she scanned her I.D card and the doors opened, allowing her entry into First National Bank. She successfully fielded the security guard's joking comments about the time and why she was here as she placed her handbag in her locker as per security's rules. "You know Mr. Thomas," she said, "work never sleeps!" It was enough to kill off any possible suspicion on the guard's part. Thomas' insane work ethic and constant pushing of employees was legendary, and the sight of a stressed-out P.A running into the office through the night was not that unusual.

Simone rushed into her small office which was adjacent to Tyrant Thomas' own. She relaxed slightly as she saw his office bathed in darkness, the only light coming from a computer standby light. She glanced at her watch and smiled weakly. 3am! Sean's "Favourite time of the night!" what was so special about that time? He'd told her once, but she hadn't really paid attention; something to do with dogs or wolves. She didn't care.

It's really happening! She thought. Suddenly her stomach knotted. Lying talking about it in the warm safety of her bed, thinking about it during work, fantasizing about Brent Thomas' face when he realised what they had done… it all seemed so easy, but now it was actually happening, it took on a new life!

She felt her heart thunder in her chest and thought she felt it in the back of her throat. She was perspiring and she knew it. A few deep breaths to calm her and she began a losing battle to keep her composure. But now was not the time to be worrying over such things! Finally, Brent Thomas would get his; would get what was coming to him and Simone Harris would finally no longer have to pay for "all the extra help" he had given her. The thought of revenge and the belief that he deserved what was coming did little to dispel her unease. Then there would be the added pleasure of finally being away from the reaches of her dead-beat husband, every day the same with no excitement and no possible way out. Right now, she imagined him at his temporary home, dreaming of the neat little savings accounts and its monthly interest accumulation. Everything with him revolved around saving money, never spending it. She could barely remember any real passion; it had been so long ago. And fun? A long-lost memory that had been replaced with emails. Emails!! All about "our next step," he couldn't even fight properly, had to do it all through neat little emails, indexed and cross-linked with little coloured pie-charts and diagrams showing how the split could and should run. It was beyond boring!

Simone came out of her reverie and winced as she imagined the security cameras turn and focus on her, their lens zooming in closer and closer to see what exactly she was doing, an overzealous security guard reaching for the phone to call Brent Thomas for clarification and then the silent alarm as the police were called.

It was all in her mind of course, no one had the slightest clue that anything was about to happen. To the mindless zombies in the control room, it was just another dull and boring night at First National Bank, the most excitement they could expect tonight would be when the pizza arrived.

With an almost amateurish glance around the room she began what until now had been a fool-proof and easy plan. One simple job, then a lifetime of stress-free living! With another furtive glance to make sure she wasn't being watched, Simone rushed over to the door that opened into Thomas' office. Once inside she turned his computer on. With heart pounding and palms sweating she reached into her pocket wishing she knew why computers took three times longer to boot up when you were in a hurry! She inhaled sharply and her heartbeat tore at her chest as panic threatened to engulf her.

It's not here! Oh my God! Sudden realisation took her as she remembered her handbag and the memory stick it held.

Turning off his computer she ran back into her office and after switching off the light, fell into her chair desperately trying to swallow her panic. She imagined the security guards racing towards her, the police already summoned. She opened a file and pretended to look through it and tried to calm her breathing. It was, after all, just a short walk back to the security office to pick up her memory stick. She could handle the guard at the door easily, make up some stupid excuse about forgetting her keys; flutter her eyelashes; show a bit of leg. He was too easy anyway.

Her footsteps echoed loudly in the near empty building, she heard the lashing of the rain on the windows; the clap of thunder and for a brief moment considered not going back in, just run back to the car and beg Sean to take them somewhere where she could lose herself in sex and wine for a few hours, forget all this!

Shivering in the late-night chill, she stopped at her locker and fumbled with the lock; she had unlocked the door and reached inside when suddenly, she felt a hand grip her arm tightly.

At the exact same time, Brooks leaned back against his pillow and sighed heavily. What the hell am I doing? Reice you bastard, why couldn't you just have died like the rest? Why did you survive? Why not Gemma? He winced as a picture of her flashed through his head; he could never exorcise the image of her face, surprised as the bullets hit her. Again, Brooks shook his head and wondered why he had shot her. Did I really fall so far? Was I so deeply immersed in my part that shooting a police officer came naturally - My first instinct was to shoot?

He jumped from the bed and poured more coffee. Not for the first time today he felt a horribly familiar feeling in the pit of his stomach, no, not his stomach, it seemed to come from everywhere, a radiating tingle that crawled down to his fingertips, an insidious and alluring call.

Maybe just a couple of lines…

Angrily, he threw himself on the bed. No fucking chance! I'm not a junkie! I was never a junkie! I played a part, nothing else! But still the craving held him, twisted itself in his stomach until even his groin tingled in anticipation.

Throwing his hands up to his face he sobbed deeply as his mind tortured him once more with a vision of Melissa being led to the car; that helpless, agonised look.

He grabbed his phone to check the time. Surely, she was out and on her way by now? Fifteen to twenty minutes to get to St. Vincent Street, another five; ten at the most to get past security and into the office, less than an twenty to download the memory stick and get the data, another ten to get out and then fifteen, twenty back here.

"Simone, where in the hell are you?" he growled. His thoughts turned to Sean, what did he know about him really, what did Simone know? She wasn't long away from that arsehole husband and vulnerable; add to that her historically bad taste in men! Brooks' stomach tightened another notch.

He walked to the bathroom and threw cold water on his face and after an unsuccessful attempt to look himself in the eye, he returned to the bed.

I need a drink! But he knew he couldn't, the last thing he needed was to be off his guard, he still felt the lingering of the wine from earlier.

He picked the TV remote up from the bed and began flicking through the channels, his impatience apparent in the speed he went through them. Nothing held his attention although he managed to give five minutes to the Sky News channel and a report on the latest plans for a manned Mars mission before angrily turning the TV off again, he walked over to stare out the window, yet the darkness and solitude did nothing to appease him and he once more he flopped onto the bed as the cravings returned in earnest.

He jumped up and drained the remainder of the coffee, his thoughts returning to Sean.

Who are you? Who are you really? He couldn't explain why, but every time he looked at him his mind screamed: Don't trust him! Why? What was it, the smile, the eyes? Or was it his body language? Suddenly he realised what had been bothering him about the man. He swung his legs round and sat up on the bed. He felt suddenly sick.

That was it! His words don't match his movements! There seemed to be a depth to the man that stood in stark contrast to the angry, impatient, and brutish nature he gave off. At this realisation a deep panic began to set in. It grew and grew until it threatened to overwhelm him, in a moment of desperation, he grabbed his jacket from the chair and threw it on, the sudden action made him feel better, as he made for the door; suddenly it was knocked twice, loudly.

Brooks instinctively staggered back. He took a deep breath, grabbed his knife and opened the door a crack, the adrenaline left him to be replaced with elation as he saw Sean standing there. With a deep breath he opened the door and managed a smile which vanished quickly as Sean closed the door gently behind him. There was a strange look of creamy satisfaction in his dark, grey eyes.

Panic once more engulfed Brooks. "Where's Simone; what happened?"

In a very soft and controlled voice, very unlike his usual tone, it was more clipped and formal with less of an accent, he said: "Sit down, Steven and kindly hand me that knife. Slowly, please."

Automatically, Brooks handed the knife over and fell into the chair.

Sean crossed over and sat stiffly on the edge of the bed. "The first thing you need to know is that Simone is safe and well as we speak. How long she remains that way is entirely up to you. Do you understand?"

Brooks nodded numbly.

"Good. First things first," he said as he pulled a memory stick from his pocket. "Simone carried out the plan to the letter. On this stick is the information required by Reice Ellis."

Brooks jumped with a start. "How…"

"How do I know about Reice Ellis? Believe me, Steven; I know a lot about Reice Ellis. I know all about him, Karl, his brother; Danny Gilmour, and I know all about you, Officer Wilton."

Brooks' hands began to tremble, seeing this Sean leaned into his bag and brought out a bottle of Jim Beam bourbon which he proceeded to pour into a glass then hand to Brooks. "Take it; you'll feel a lot better."

Brooks downed it in one gulp and held the glass while Sean refilled it. "Better?"

Brooks nodded, unable to speak past a tightening in his throat.

"Good." He said, pouring a glass for himself. He took a small sip. "I am afraid that I have not been entirely honest with either you or Simone. My name is not Sean, nor did I know Brent Thomas growing up, in fact aside from seeing his face in the media I've never seen him."

"Then who…"

"Several years ago, close to twenty actually, Karl and Reice Ellis came to meet a man called Duncan Blake who, at the time, owned a large and very popular bar and night club called The Rooftops in the west end of Glasgow, you do actually know the club in question and know it very well, but we'll come to that. Now, and I admit I cannot supply you with exact details, but somehow Karl Ellis came to frequent The Rooftops and became very friendly with Duncan Blake. It was not long before an insidious partnership was born and The Rooftops became the main base of operations for The Ellis brothers, and Duncan Blake quickly rose to prominence in their empire.

"However, soon the pressures began to take their toll on Duncan Blake, more and more was asked of him, and he went from small time crook and club owner to hit-man and the go-to man the Ellis' used when they needed something done…or someone gone.

"Eventually what with the hours and the pressures and the realisation that he was in too deep with people he couldn't escape, Duncan Blake turned more and more to cocaine and alcohol, he became paranoid, obsessive and ultimately convinced that Karl Ellis was determined to oust him from his business and no doubt kill him. He therefore went after Karl and very nearly succeeded." Sean paused to pour himself some of the Jim Beam which he quickly drained. He turned to stare directly at Brooks. "But ultimately, Duncan Blake - my father, was killed by Karl Ellis. So, the part I told you earlier about losing my father to cocaethylene was essentially true as cocaine and alcohol proved to be the catalysts that propelled him toward his death. The club and all my family's assets were turned over to Brent Thomas; he himself then sold The Rooftops to… Danny Gilmour, so as I said; you know the club well, and that club you frequented with Reice was once my father's, and thanks to the death of Gilmour, it has now returned to Thomas."

Brooks stared hard at Sean as all the old memories came back to torment him once more. He wanted to vomit, he wanted to hurl himself at Sean and tear him apart, but most of all he wanted to hide in his bar on Lanzarote and not feel this hurt ever again.

"So now, Steven, we come to my true motivations: Karl Ellis received his just rewards and paid the ultimate price, Reice Ellis however, has not. When I first heard the rumours that he was not really dead, I set out to try and find him. He is, you can imagine, very closely guarded and not very easy to get to, and when I heard of his desires to revisit you, well, it was just too good an opportunity to miss. My close associate, Mr. Sullivan, was able to arrange the meeting between you and Reice."

Again, Brooks gasped and lurched to his feet. "You bastard, you kidnapped my wife! It was all you!"

"Sit down, Steven!" Sean barked. "Your wife is perfectly safe, as promised! You try anything against me, and Sullivan will carry out his threat! Plus, you will never see Simone again either. It is a trying time I know, but there is no reason why we can't all come out of this for the better."

Brooks collapsed into his chair and threw his hands to his face. "What do you want from me?"

Sean nodded. "You will contact Reice and tell him you have been successful. You will arrange to meet him to give him this."

He held up the memory stick. "I will accompany you and have my final discussion with him. That is all you have to do."

"And my family?"

Sean nodded and took his phone from his pocket, he quickly dialled a number. "Sullivan, it's me," he said, "everything's fine here. Put her on," He handed the phone to Brooks.

"Hello?" he said.

"Steven? Steven is that you?"

"Melissa? My God, are you ok?

She sobbed down the phone: "I'm ok, he hasn't hurt me. He…" the phone was snatched from his hands.

Brooks stared at Sean.

"Good. Now, if you agree to my terms, then I will arrange for the immediate release of your wife, she will be returned to your bar or wherever she likes, unharmed as promised."

"And Simone?"

"Upon the completion of our task then of course, she will be released. You will also be free to go. I'll release your wife as a sign of good faith."

A sad moue touched Brooks' mouth: "Once again, it seems I have no choice."

Sean smiled and nodded his approval; he again lifted the phone, said: "Release Mrs. Brooks; take her home. She is free to go." He hung up and faced Brooks. "Get your things, Steven. I'll be back shortly once I have made final preparations. I urge you to try and remain calm; this thing will go much more smoothly if you can lose the anger. Once I'm back, you can call Reice from the car and then this will be almost over." He paused on the way out. "I remind you that Simone is still in danger; do not do anything stupid like trying to call someone. Sit tight, calm down and this will all be over soon."

Part Four

In less than two hours they were in Sean's car and headed north along the M80 motorway. The rain had passed, and the morning sun shone brightly. The roads were quiet with the exception of large freight vehicles and the occasional car.

A quick call to Reice Ellis had established that they were to meet in the picturesque town of Callander, in the Trossachs. Brooks was to make his way to the Queen Mary Hotel, room seventeen and there, business was to be concluded. Sean apparently knew exactly where Reice would be and was unsurprised at the remote location, the fact they were headed that way seemed to support this.

Neither of them spoke for several miles, the radio remained off and the silence added to the gloomy atmosphere that was in sharp contrast to the warmth outside. Brooks felt a mixture of elation at Melissa's release; she had phoned him from their apartment in Lanzarote to say Sullivan had dropped her there and had apparently left. In stark contrast, Simone's whereabouts and condition remained unknown and played on his mind. A quick look at Sean showed a plethora of emotions under his usually calm surface, it was clear he was high on adrenaline, no doubt he had planned the murder of Reice many times in his head, and the opportunity to avenge his dead father finally and fully must be intoxicating. His breathing was calm but with a suggestion of what? Fear, maybe doubt?

What do I do? Do I try and talk this madman out of his plan? Can he be reasoned with, even made to see sense?

Even as he thought it, Brooks knew it was hopeless; clearly revenge was driving this man and had done so for a long, long time.

As they drove under the Castlecary Arches, Brooks ventured a conversation: "So, what age were you when your father was killed?"

Sean took a deep breath. "We're not going there, Brooks. He was killed by Karl Ellis and Reice is now accountable, that's all you need to know. Now shut the fuck up and let me think!"

Brooks raised an eyebrow but said nothing, outside he could make out landmarks from the side of the motorway, after an unbroken silence of several miles he caught sight of a sign for a Safari Park and then a sign for Callander itself. He felt his stomach knot return then.

What would happen in that hotel? In spite of Reice's apparent incapacity, he still felt fear and loathing toward the man. The thought of his murder really didn't affect him much, after all, until recently he had believed the man long dead, it was more the thought of being back in a situation like that again, like being back in the nightmare at Danny's club when all that madness went down, the choking, burning smell of gunfire and of blood, the sounds, the flashes, the bodies falling…

Brooks sighed heavily and shook his head to clear it and to remove the flash memory image of Gemma falling to the floor, the crimson red blossom forming underneath her porcelain white tunic, the look of shock as her life slipped away.

Fuck it! One last dance and it all goes away forever! Reice, Brent Thomas, the ghost of Gemma and this prick beside me! One more act of violence and I'm gone, I'll take what money we took from Thomas and disappear, properly this time. Not that it matters, there'll be no one chasing me anymore!

Brooks summoned his strength and sat up straight. "So, what exactly are we going to do in Callander? I doubt that Reice is just going to let us both walk in and kill him."

Sean shot him a side glance. "All you need to do is knock on the door, let Reice's boys pat you down and let you in, smile sweetly and enjoy the fun."

"That all?"

"That's all," said Sean and he smiled, said: "We're here."

They drove into Callander, passing a large petrol station and a sign for The Turtle Inn that promised home cooked food, Danny Gilmour used to rave about the "best food in my hometown!" Brooks became conscious of an empty pang in the pit of his stomach. How long had it been since he had eaten?

Sean turned the car into a small side street car park, offset by charity and tea shops. He motioned with a nod of his head. "That's it. That's the Queen Mary Hotel. Leave your stuff."

Brooks made to open his door, but Sean's hand gripped his arm tightly. "I don't need to remind you not to fuck up here, do I? Just remember, I showed good faith and released your wife, I still have your sister and it would be a shame if she had to die because you couldn't follow simple instructions. Do I make myself clear?"

Brooks pulled himself free. "Perfectly, but you need to know that I will kill you twice if you screw me over!"

Sean nodded. "It seems we do have a perfect understanding of the facts. Like I promised, both you and Simone will be free to go once Reice Ellis dies." With that, he opened his door and stepped out into the pleasant mid-morning air.

Brooks followed him and together they walked toward the large green doors of the Queen Mary Hotel. Once inside, they were greeted by the middle-aged barman who, as his picture on the wall proclaimed, was the hotel manager. They both refused his invitation of a drink and walked through the bar and the lounge and began climbing the stairs to the hotel rooms.

It wasn't long before they located room seventeen. Sean motioned for silence and pulled something small and black from his pocket which he proceeded to manoeuvre into place at the door lock, once satisfied he stepped back and pulled Brooks to the door. With his lips almost touching his ear, he whispered: "Knock and go in, gently close the door behind you and make sure you step at least two paces into the room, let them search you and then talk to Reice. I want him calm and relaxed. Play him, Brooks, you did it before and you can do it again." He handed him the memory stick.

"One thing, Sean," whispered Brooks with more confidence than he felt. "When this is over, I'm keeping that memory stick! It's haunted my god damn life for years and more than that, I earned it."

Sean nodded. "It's yours; I don't want it. Now go!"

Brooks took a deep breath and knocked on the door while Sean crouched down and hid out of sight. The door was opened by the same dumb idiot who had walked into the bar in Lanzarote, the same glazed look. Brooks nodded, "Hello again."

The man motioned for Brooks to enter and closed the door, only Brooks seemed to notice the lack of the usual snick as the door failed to lock properly.

Brooks looked straight ahead at his nemesis in the wheelchair, positioned in front of the window and giving off the same air of violence and danger which seemed to cloak him like some putrid cloud that not even a stroke nor wheelchair could completely erase. To his left stood another hired muscle, arms crossed in front of him as he stared impassively at Brooks.

"Steven," said Reice humourlessly. "Arms up and try not to get a hard on." He motioned to the man behind Brooks who started the search. "Can't be too careful of course, you might be a shit ex-copper and a junkie, but I've seen you shoot."

The muscle brained idiot finished his search and crossed over to stand on the right-hand side of Reice. Brooks tried not to smile; the whole image of the two clowns proudly standing beside the ruined figure of Reice in matching black suits was almost comical. Do you hire these guys from a shop? He wanted to ask. Fuck Wits Are Us?

"Well? You gonna stand there like a dumb prick all day or you gonna tell me some good news?" said Reice with a scowl.

As Brooks reached into his pocket the action brought Dumb and Dumber to the balls of their feet and poised for violence. "Steady, girls," he said, pulling the memory stick from his pocket. "I have it."

Reice motioned, and the man on his left reached out and took the memory stick which he handed to Reice who then stared at it hard, as though a million memories had been jogged. He stared at Brooks, "Thomas?"

"Keep your eye on the news channel; you should be hearing something real soon. Brent Thomas won't be a problem anymore."

Reice laughed. "Good boy, only wish I'd strangled that bastard myself when I had the chance!"

Brooks saw his moment. "So, this is over now? There is nothing left between us."

"Over?" yelled Reice. "I say when this is over you fucking cock-sucker! You think for one second…"

In a flash the door suddenly flew open, Brooks dropped to his knees and was only vaguely aware of a "pfft pfft" sound and a sharp gust of air that blew past his left ear. The men at either side of Reice went down like toy soldiers and in an instant Sean was in the room, beside Brooks with his silenced pistol aimed at Reice's chest.

Reice's eyes betrayed total shock and for a moment he lost all the toughness, all the bravura that made him so intimidating, his frightened eyes went from Brooks to Sean and back again as he pathetically tried to move himself further into his wheelchair.

"Pull that clip off the door, Steven, and let it lock this time," said Sean through gritted teeth.

Brooks obeyed and leaned his back against the door. Immediately the smell of the gun assailed his nostrils, the sound of the bodies falling hit him and he began breathing hard, his head swam and for a moment he was back in that bar; Gilmour's bar – the bar that used to be Duncan Blake's! He could almost hear Danny Gilmour: "Get me a fucking doctor here! I'm dying!"

Reice stared hard at Sean and suddenly regained himself, although with subtle differences. "You want to explain this, dickhead? Who the fuck are you?"

"We've never met, Mr. Ellis," said Sean calmly. It was clear he had played this moment over and over in his head, his words almost read like a script. His eyes glazed over. He was on autopilot. "We have, however, spoken."

Reice squinted in one eye. "Ah, you're the guy who told me where Steven was hiding; you told me you could arrange the meeting!" Then, seeing a possible ally he turned to Brooks. "This prick kidnapped your wife!"

Brooks felt nauseous. "I know," was all he could manage.

"You know? Then fucking hit him! If it were my wife, I'd rip his balls off!" spat Reice.

Sean raised a finger to his lips, "Shhh! That's all ancient history, Mr. Ellis. Mrs. Brooks is safely at home, I'd be far more concerned with my own skin if I were you."

"Yeah? So you gonna tell me what the fuck this is all about?" Reice coughed violently then and Brooks feared a repeat of the seizure he had suffered in Lanzarote, he glanced at the dead aides on the floor. No one would be pulling Reice out of it this time.

Luckily the seizure never came. "Water!" barked Reice.

Brooks jumped at the remembered authority and immediately crossed to the worktop, lifted a glass and gave Reice a sip.

Sean looked on in amusement.

Reice leaned back and stared at Sean. "What? We gonna play charades now? Have I to guess?"

Sean smiled again. "My name, Mr Ellis," he then looked at Brooks, "is not Sean. My real first name is not important; my surname however is, as it will remove all need for further explanation." Again, the script-like recital came back. "My surname, Reice Ellis… is Blake!"

Reice recoiled as though struck. "Blake!"

Blake nodded in appreciation as the name had its desired effect.

"Jesus fucking Christ!" said Reice coughing.

"I want to know the exact truth surrounding Duncan Blake… surrounding my father's death, Mr. Ellis! You and your brother used him, emptied him and finally, after ruining him completely, your brother killed him - I hold you accountable!"

"It wasn't like that, I swear!" yelled Reice. "Yeah, we used him; used his club. He was only too keen to get involved, he wanted it! But then he went fucking crazy! Every time I'd see him, he'd be coked out his head, drinking like fuck! Then he started accusing Karl of ripping him off, of wanting his club, wanting him dead."

Blake shook his head. "You did do all that, my father wasn't imagining it!"

"No, you've got it all wrong, I swear! We needed him, we wanted him in the club; he knew how to play the game, kept the law from the place, kept it clean. Then he got all fucking weird and shit! He started turning on us, demanded a meeting with Karl, and then went completely fucking mental, yelling that he was gonna kill Karl and stormed off; that's when Karl came to me."

Blake's hand tightened on the gun until his knuckles turned white. The effort to remain calm was etched on his face. "Go on," he said hoarsely.

"What's to tell? I was watching Karl's back and got word Duncan was coming for him, I told Karl and we waited, sure enough Duncan comes blazing in, before Karl could even speak he launches at him and smacks him right in the mouth, before I knew what was happening they were rolling about, punching and kicking all over the place, as I tried to decide what to do I sees your father back on his feet, Karl on the ground and Blake pulls a gun from his pocket, what was I to do?"

Blake's eyes widened in shock, clearly this was new to him. "You fired?"

"Yeah, I fired! Just to wound him was all, next minute Karl pulls his gun and fires four shots and Blake goes down. He..." Reice caught himself as the import of his words hit him. "Now wait a minute, I only fired to wound him, to stop him killing Karl, and it was a flesh wound; I didn't kill him!"

A tear coursed down Blake's face as he lost control of his composure; Reice saw his eyes harden. "I told you, you were accountable, and don't even try to claim you don't deserve this!"

Reice made to speak, though stopped and lowered his head. He made no sound as Blake fired four times into his chest. He sobbed once, ever so softly, and then fired once more at the prone figure of Reice, this time the bullet struck him on the top of his skull, blood splattered the wall behind as Reice's body jerked once.

Blake lowered his gun and closed his eyes in silent conversation. When he opened his eyes they were reddened, he wiped them on the sleeve of his jacket. Silently, he crossed and retrieved the memory stick which he handed to Brooks. "It's over."

"My sister?"

Blake nodded as he pulled his phone from the pocket and punched in the number. Into the phone he said: "Its' finished; start the clean-up." As he dropped the phone into his pocket he turned to Brooks. "I need a drink, and then we'll talk." He turned and walked out the door, and without looking at the carnage behind him, Brooks followed, closing the door on the nightmares of his past.

Part Five

A short walk and a short time later, Brooks was sitting outside the beer garden of The Lakeside Inn, looking across at the meandering river, the pathway was crowded with families both young and old who were enjoying the afternoon sun which was slowly approaching its zenith. The air had a fresh feeling, warm with the pleasant smell of early summer. He watched as a small child dipped a fishing net into the river as her father kept a tight but loving grip upon her yellow jacket. The father turned and smiled as the mother came over with the ice creams. Brooks savoured the sight; a sharp contrast to the blood shed he had witnessed only minutes before.

His reverie was shattered as Blake sat down in front, blocking his view. He took two pints of beer and two double whiskies from the tray he carried and placed them in front of them.

Blake took a generous swig from his whiskey and followed it with a gulp from his pint, he motioned to Brooks.

"First I want to know about Simone. You have what you wanted; you got your revenge."

Blake nodded, although he had calmed somewhat, Brooks couldn't help but notice the lack of elation in the man. "You are here, Steven, for the final chapter." He pushed the whiskey glass closer to Brooks. "A Toast," he said, "a Toast to vindication and to redemption, for both of us."

Brooks glared at him as he lifted his glass and hit Blake's glass in a mock salute before downing his own in one gulp."

Blake gave a creamy, self-satisfied smile and looked down.

"There," said Brooks impatiently, "now about Simone."

"In a moment, Steven, there is one last thing we need to discuss."

Brooks recoiled. "Now what, you promised me once Reice was dealt with that would be it!"

"And I intend to keep my word, Simone's part in this is finished," Blake said as he reached into his pocket and then dropped a key which was attached to a large piece of plastic with the word "Edradour" etched into it, onto the table. "You sister is across there in the Neptune Hotel, that is the key to the bridal suite."

Brooks grabbed it and made to stand when Blake stopped him. "Like I said, Steven, your sister's part in this is over. However, there is still one person accountable."

Brooks frowned. "I had nothing to do with your father's death! I never even knew him!"

"I know that. But there is something else you need to know. You see, my father, while embracing his life with the Ellis brothers, was only too aware of what they were like and how they were likely to coerce him. He was fiercely protective of his personal life… and his family. So much so that Karl and Reice were unaware that he was married or that he had a child. He kept up the pretence of a single life by using his club's own women."

Brooks blinked. The thought of a mother hadn't even occurred to him.

"My mother was devoted to my father, even with the cocaine and the drink and the increasing instability; even though, at the end, she had no choice but to leave him she never stopped loving him and firmly believed that her leaving would be the trigger he needed to finally break away from his life and habits and would come back to her.

"As you can imagine she took his death very hard. As I've already told you, Brent Thomas assumed ownership of The Rooftops thanks to that slimy, fat lawyer who claimed to have "found" a stupid hand-written will my father had supposedly written one night, and we pretty much lost everything. Add to that my father's paranoia, which had kept him writing an actual will. The money that came from a few trusted people dried up as they themselves were killed, arrested, or left to join Karl Ellis fully, until in the end, we ended up destitute and relying on the charity of others.

"My mother never gave up her thoughts of revenge. She left me with my paternal grandparents while she fought hard to place herself in a position to strike back at the people who had taken everything from her."

His mother! Brooks felt the beginnings of realisation.

"I think you can guess what happens next, Steven," said Blake. His eyes burned as he stared hard at Brooks. "You could say, I suppose, that she achieved her revenge. She did manage to kill Karl, although it was short lived… thanks to you!" And he spat the last word with vehement hatred.

Brooks gasped. Gemma! Again, he saw her fall, saw the blood; saw the look of shock in her eyes. He came out of his reverie to find Blake's stare burning through him.

"Sean… I…"

"I told you, my name is not Sean! You killed my mother, Brooks! My Grandfather was a Detective Chief Inspector; he was able to get the CCTV footage from Gilmour's club. I saw everything! Everything! I saw Karl shoot Reice; I saw Gilmour fall; I saw my mother shoot Karl, and of course, I saw you murder her! Over and over, I watched that part; in my dreams, my nightmares; all the time!" He took a deep breath to calm himself.

Brooks swallowed hard. "I am so sorry. There hasn't been a day that I don't regret what I did! Gemma haunts me too, every time I fall asleep, I see her…"

"Stop talking, Steven. There is nothing you can say to me that can possibly justify your actions. You decided in that split second who you really are!"

Brooks swallowed hard as he accepted his fate. "Are you going to shoot me? Here, in front of all these people?"

"I'm not going to shoot you, Brooks," said Blake as he stood up and pulled his sunglasses from his shirt pocket. He looked around him and then turned back. "What I did do however… was poison you." He motioned to the empty whiskey glass and then looked at his wristwatch. "Half past one now, by five pm, you'll be reunited with Karl, Reice and Danny in Hell where you all belong! Go get your sister, Steven, and enjoy that memory stick that you worked so hard for. I only have one thing left to say." He leaned down to within an inch of Brooks' face. "Fuck you!" With that he turned and walked away.

Brooks barely saw him leave, didn't see him climb onto a motorbike that was parked in the car park and then disappear down the street. Instead, he stared at the empty glass in front of him. With a sudden, deep breath, he turned and staggered through the bar, ignoring the startled looks from the customers, once on the street he focussed on the imposing Jacobean white-washed building of the Neptune hotel that loomed front of him. Cars blasted horns and drivers yelled as he staggered across the road and flung open the hotel doors, he ignored the duty manager as he raced up the first flight of stairs and up the second as he followed the signs for "Edradour", before finally pulling open the first door and climbing the stairs. At the room door, he paused as he shakily tried the key a number of times before successfully opening the door. As he stumbled into the room, his eyes fell upon the prostrate figure of Simone lying outstretched on the large queen-sized bed. The curtains were drawn and the room was gloomy in spite of the warm sun outside. With tears blinding him he gingerly sat beside her. How peaceful she looked.

As he moved to check her pulse she moaned slightly and turned her head to the side as Brooks sobbed with elation.

He caressed her hair softly and within a few minutes she opened her eyes, through drug fogged consciousness she looked first at him, then around the room, then back to him. She smiled.

"You ok, Sis?" asked Brooks softly.

"Yeah," she rubbed her forehead. "Where am I?"

"The Trossachs," he said softly.

"The Trossachs?" she said with a giggle, "that's for old people!"

"I know."

"Where's Sean?" She asked. "I got back in the car after getting out of Brent's office for the second time, after that idiot security guard tried to ask me out. Sean had a coffee waiting for me, then…" she frowned as she tried to remember. "Then I woke up here."

Brooks took her hand. "Don't worry; you were a bit out of it after all the excitement." He reached into his pocket and placed the memory stick in her hand. "Here, you deserve this, Sis. I reckon there's at least a couple of million on it. Just load it into a computer and launch the program, it'll create multiple accounts, follow the on-screen prompts."

She yawned and stretched. "There's four million on it, I checked."

Brooks feigned a laugh. "You're free and clear then!"

"What about you?" she asked.

He shrugged. "I don't need it, remember, I got my other thing."

"Oh, the mysterious 'thing' you can't talk about," she said laughing.

He nodded. "That's right, top secret." He climbed to his feet. "Anyway, I got to go, got to get this thing moving quickly."

"Can't you stay? Sean should be back soon."

"I… I can't, Sis. I'll call you." He backed toward the door, smiling at her.

"You ok, Steven? You look weird?"

"Fine, I'm fine! Just... you know, I just got to… to get this thing sorted, tight window of opportunity." He fumbled in his pocket and then dropped the car keys on the bed. "Go on, get out of here and go get your money and get the kids from Philip! Mel would love to see you."

"You mean you'd both love to see me, right?"

Brooks nodded. "Yeah, you and the kids could all spend a few weeks at our place, get used to being rich."

She stretched and smiled. "A millionaire, it sounds good! Go, get out of here!"

He smiled once more and ran from the room, the sound of his own heart thundering in his ears.

The flight from the hotel was a blur as he walked and walked, past shops, houses, hotels and streets. His thoughts were turbulent. Was he really going to die? Should he try and sort it? Was there anyone he could call? Should he go to a hospital; where was the hospital? He laughed maniacally as he remembered a joke: "quick, someone get me the phone number for 999!" He half walked, half ran with no idea of where he was headed.

Suddenly, he caught sight of a sign he had seen a few hours before: "Turtle Inn, Home cooked food" he walked to the door and took a deep breath before opening it…

Epilogue

The barman, Malcolm stood wide eyed, unsure of what to believe, was this some kind of joke?

Brooks downed his glass, which was quickly replaced. He was about to speak when he caught sight of the television. "Turn that up, will you?"

"… Just a few minutes ago, Police Scotland entered the home of famed politician and city banker Brent Thomas with an arrest warrant relating to alleged charges of Money Laundering and embezzlement. Sources close to Brent Thomas have strenuously denied these charges and say they will find out who is behind this latest smear against one of Holyrood's more colourful politicians. The market has reacted strongly to these developments and…

Brooks waved at Malcolm. "Turn it off."

He smiled and then laughed heartily. Well done, Simone! Well done! One more arsehole taken care of! Brooks climbed to his feet.

"You off?" asked Malcolm.

Brooks blinked. "Where's the toilet?"

"Up back," said Malcolm pointing.

As Brooks staggered towards the door, Malcolm cleared his throat. "Uh… Mr. Brooks. It's just gone five o clock!"

Brooks paused and turned. He blinked a few times as he looked around the bar as though savouring the view. "Thanks, Malcolm."

And with that the door slammed closed behind him.

The XIIIth Parable

Prologue

The secure unit was in the small village of Kisiljavo in Serbia, and it was exactly that - secure. There was no way in or out unless one possessed a verified access card. The building itself was built by fear, fear of people getting in and, worse, of people getting out. The windows were all made too small to allow a person of adult size to either enter or exit, the doors were limited and fitted to the very limit of acceptable agreement by the fire department, and of the health and safety laws. Those doors which the staff used, were few and they were well guarded. It was safe to say that no one was getting in without the proper clearance.

That was all too abundantly clear to one who needed in, but who also had no legitimate means to enter. So, it waited, and it watched. Imitating and copying humans was easy if all it entailed was a passing copy, but when faced with the same people over a period of time, it took more of an effort.

So, for now, it waited, finding at last a socially awkward and somewhat simplistic member of staff. Subduing him would be easy, copying his mannerisms and voice, equally easy. The memories? Well, it all depended on how easily they imprinted upon the blood. It is a little-known fact that erythrocytes - red blood cells, contain no DNA, whereas the leukocytes - the white cells, do. So, it was a waiting game, gently picking and picking at his victim from within dark shadows and at night when he was most vulnerable, until eventually he succumbed to a nasty blood infection which triggered, quite naturally, an immediate immunological response from the white cells. It was then a very simple process of silently attacking him as he slept, draining the blood, and absorbing the memories from the cells.

After a day or two of "sick leave" Doctor Arnold Frombald returned to work feeling "much, much better, thank you." He was not only a lot only more attentive of his patients, but often stayed on late to help one of the more famous and long-time patients, poor Dr Alexander Jeffries who had mysteriously taken a turn for the worse.

The Client

It was one o'clock exactly when I returned to the small and pathetic place that I called an office. Rachel, my secretary, promptly reminded me that I was late and that my twelve-thirty client impatiently awaited me.

Full of a hangover and in a seriously bad mood, the last thing I wanted was her moaning and complaining. I nodded. "Uh, uh," and walked to the small bathroom to throw up and to wet my face.

Within five minutes I was seated behind my old stained solid mahogany desk. The only real thing I ever kept from my father. I tried to ignore the various cigarette marks on it, the only other thing I inherited from him since I never smoked.

Now, in my particular line of work, I tend to find myself with the most idiotic clientele that you could ever hope to meet. Something about a sign that says Private Detective, such as the one outside my door, is usually enough to bring them in. "Help, my sister is not really my sister!" or "My cat is trying to kill me!" are just some of the assignments I have refused, and on those occasions, I tend to explain how I am not as good as my close associate, and former fellow soldier, Calvin Thomas and refer them to him, he does the same – pathetic, I know, but in this job, you take all the laughs you can get.

So, when Rachel informed me that my client today, Mr Roderick Jacobson, was most insistent that he talk to me and that my life was in mortal danger, I was expecting this to be one of Cal's stupid practical jokes.

Imagine my surprise when, instead of the tinfoil hat anorak type I expected, before me sat the most well-dressed of gentlemen. He stood perhaps six feet tall with short dark hair with white patches near the temple, cropped at the sides with short neatly trimmed sideburns. A similar black moustache covered his top lip. Piercing blue eyes lay slightly into the jutting forehead and when he spoke, it was short, clipped and to the point. I immediately thought: military.

"Mr Anderson," he said. "I come before you today as a man at his wits' end. I have tried all other avenues open to me and had long wished to avoid what I now must do. I cannot find a satisfactory alternative and am forced then to draw you into what I am sure you will come to view as 'the stuff of nightmares.'

Were there a way to spare you from this, I would do it, but time itself has become our enemy."

I sat and waited for him to continue. He, however, remained silent, forcing me to speak. "I'll do what I can," I said, it was the only thing I could think of. "What exactly can I do?"

"Mr Anderson. This is not easy for me, to come here I mean... I am a proud man with many years of military service under my belt."

Strike one for the assessment then!

"But you do need help. There is no question of that. My family is well respected in this town, and indeed in Serbia where I have many interests. Although it is abhorrent to me to speak of this and should word of this ever get out…"

"Mr Jacobson," I said, very formally, if not a little pretentiously, "I pride myself on the utmost discretion. Have no fear. What is said here goes no further, I assure you."

He seemed to relax. "That is very good to hear, Mr Anderson. Too many people know of this already." He leaned back, having apparently come to a decision. "Here is my story…"

Calvin

I sat alone in that small, dingy office. Rachel had left some time ago, turning off the lights in the reception and hallway on her way out. I failed to notice the encroaching darkness, light from some small lamp in the corner cast a feeble glow upon the frayed carpet of my office. The sun was almost gone and the evening seemed to give a promise of rain.

Half a bottle of vodka inside me and I was still no better off, my gaze returning often to the chair vacated by Mr Jacobson. Was it really only a few hours since he had left? I found it hard to believe.

His story! I have never heard such a tale, and I thought, after so many years in this mad job, I had heard them all. Had it not been for his quiet dignity and the sincerity in his voice, I would have laughed. There was also the strange feeling I had of it being true – that - and the fact I had heard some of it before, a long, long time ago. I stood, suddenly aware of a growing hunger. It was then I noticed the small packet of chicken salad sandwiches on my desk. I smiled. Rachel - She always knew my needs.

I quickly ate them and washed them down with a pot of aged coffee. Grabbing my jacket, I hurried in the direction of the Drowning Duck. Once inside, I peered at the bar. As I made my way over to speak to the barman, a hand holding a glass of scotch shot out to block my way. Looking along the arm, I saw my intended target. Taking the glass, I sat down. "Well, Don, how goes it, mate? You look like shit, by the way." He said laughing.

I winced. "I know." Due to our long association and friendship, he heard an entire conversation in those two little words.

Calvin Thomas nodded. "Ok, I'm listening."

I took a long drink from my glass and coughed before wiping my mouth. Cal's years of army intelligence skills came through and he said. "Ok. Now I'm really listening, and I promise no piss-taking."

I smiled weakly. This was the Cal I needed.

By the time I had told my tale, the normally fastidious Cal looked as shit as I did. He had listened with the promised intensity and had on several occasions clawed at his tie and collar as though they were choking him, and now his tie hung low around his neck and the top two buttons on his shirt were open to reveal dewlap. His normally well combed sandy hair lay in disarray across his forehead. He leaned back and shook his head. "Jesus H Christ!"

I waited expectantly on the laughter I was sure would follow; instead, he remained silent for a few moments. It was then that I noticed he seemed to be somewhat pale. "Hell of a thing, that."

"No pun intended, I take it?" I asked.

"What the hell, Don?"

I drank long and deep from the glass given to me. We both found the same spot on the floor to stare at for a while with neither of us wanting to talk of it, but both desperate to.

"So," said Cal after what felt like another eternity. "Was he from the Navy?"

"A Colonel from the Army," I replied, somewhat distantly.

He took a long drink from his glass and motioned to the barman for another round. "Did you believe the part about the demonic-like creatures, what did he call them; blood-eaters?"

I nodded. "Or him being – what was it – close to two thousand years old? Fuck off!" He laughed, but I heard the effort in it. "Thirteenth Parable indeed! Some immortal dude needing the blood of twelve families! What did he call it again?"

"The twelve become the Thirteenth," I said, unconsciously mimicking Jacobson's tone.

"Freaked the shit out of me!" said Cal, taking a large drink from his glass.

I could tell Cal was desperate for me to laugh out loud. Instead, I favoured him with a stare. I drained my glass and swapped it for the fresh one. "He seemed to believe it. I swear he actually broke into a sweat telling me, and his hands... the way they shook!"

I fought down the urge to blurt out the rest of what Jacobson had told me, but the truth was, I didn't know what to make of it myself - and there was Cal's mental state to consider. He was ex-army with considerable PTSD, and I didn't think he could handle it. So, I tried to steer the conversation away from blood-eaters and demons, but he was fixated now and wouldn't deviate.

"What else did he say about the Thirteenth Parable?"

"You know, the worst thing is," I swallowed hard, "I've heard that mentioned before - the Thirteenth Parable. My mother mentioned it sometimes when she had those, you know, moments, there was the odd talk of it between the older family members during gatherings and things. It always stopped when I appeared, almost as though they felt guilty talking about it." I shook my head. "It all started around the time my uncle disappeared after an incident in Serbia.

"So your uncle was involved in it?" asked Cal.

I nodded. "He became obsessed with finding a forgotten and ruined castle that seemingly no one had heard of. He worked at the museum in Glasgow and somehow talked his bosses into funding it. He eventually found it, some people got killed and he stated talking about 'The Creature', and about demons and shit. He refused to come home and in the end they locked him up and the whole thing got covered up."

"And you never found out the truth about it all?"

"My mother refused to let me be drawn into it and banned anyone from talking about it - sober, at least. To tell you the truth, I'd forgotten all about it until Jacobson walked in."

"First thing in the morning, I'm going online to look this shit up." Cal took a drink. "So maybe your uncle Alex wasn't that mad after all."

I smiled. "He is mad!" I said, "He gets accused of robbing an ancient castle, of stirring up all kinds of international incidents; of murdering his friends and of inventing a vampire story to cover his tracks! His lawyer even got the murder charges down to reduced capacity, claimed he was half dead from hypoxia from breathing old stale air and from coming into contact with whatever toxic mould or whatever was down there in the ruins and all my uncle had to do was admit it and he could be returned to the U.K and given an appropriate sentence here, but instead he keeps on getting into trouble with the local police, attacking people he thinks are his 'creature', until one time in court he pushes it too far. Starts yelling and screaming so much the judge found him certifiable and locked him up there and then for psychological assessments. Even then he refused to back down and tried to escape. He stabbed an orderly and beat up a security guard with his own baton. They ended up locking him up for life."

Cal shook his head. "And now we got Jacobson's mad talk."

I nodded. "Yeah, I haven't told you the worst part yet."

Cal motioned to the waitress and ordered another couple of doubles for us. His lips were tightly closed as he waited for me to speak. A heavy reluctance had come over me and I had to fight myself to speak. “Uncle Alex kept begging me to go see him and when my mother refused, he wrote to me. He kept warning me and telling me things to look out for and that he could help keep the demon away.”

“Away from what; from you?”

“Yeah.” I swallowed convulsively, the desire to shut up was overpowering. “He said that the Thirteenth Parable affected me.”

As I looked at him, I grew aware of a sudden hush that had come over the place. It seemed as though the entire pub was listening into us, and the air was becoming filled with an almost supernatural stillness. Somewhere toward the rear, a glass was dropped and smashed off the floor, no one seemed to notice.

Cal frowned. “I think the first thing we do, is try and find out a bit more about our Mr R Jacobson. I'll try and find out a bit more about his military background. I’ve still got some mates in army Intel who owe me a favour or two, we should..." Cal trailed off as one of the oldest looking men I have ever seen came and sat opposite us. He clutched a pint glass, half full, in his skeletal-like hand. The other, he placed on the table between us. Veins stood out on his grey, milk-like skin. The nails were broken and brittle looking, with dirt clinging to the underside. His long white hair hung like wispy straw down to his curved shoulders, and for some reason I couldn’t explain, his breath came out like a cold vapour, as though we were in sub zero temperatures, except it was quite warm in the pub.

Cal looked at him with amusement. "Can I help you?"

The old man stared at him, and then turned to me.

"Hello?" said Cal loudly. "Can we help you?"

"Your voice carries, friend," he said in a husky, quivering voice, as though speaking through vocal chords that hadn’t been used in a long time.

"And?" said Cal, getting a little annoyed. Subtlety was never a strong point.

"That name. It is not one you should speak of loudly, nor indeed lightly," he set his mouth in a grim line. "My advice is quick, and it is simple - it is also free. Leave Mr Jacobson to his delusions. Forget what you heard of the Thirteenth Parable. Do not get involved; others will see that he gets what he requires. This is your first and final warning. Next time... will not be as pleasant." He smiled then, a cold and sickly smile showing broken, near green teeth. With that, he jumped to his feet with more power and speed than I could ever have imagined possible. He turned and was gone.

"Cheeky son of a bitch!" yelled Cal, as he jumped up and ran after the old man. I followed and soon we were standing outside in the evening's pouring rain with Cal staring down the one-way street. There was no sign of the old man. Cal scratched his forehead, looked at me and shivered. As we both turned to re-enter the bar we heard a loud wailing screech, almost bird-like, that seemed to come from far above and it reverberated through us both. It was a sound that chilled me to my very bones. We both ran back into the pub to see others looking up, wondering about the horrible scream.

"Jesus H!" cursed Cal. He motioned to the barman. "Two more, Tony."

"Doubles, Tony," I added. "And Cal's paying!"

We returned to our seats and conversation naturally turned to our client and the old man. The rest of the evening passed without incident and at roughly one a.m., after several more doubles, courtesy of an unusually generous Cal, I staggered back home full of whisky and with an uneasy feeling of being watched and followed. My dreams that night were vivid and troubling, with Mr R Jacobson haunting me in a few of them, and the old man in others. Six a.m. woke me with a start as my mind once again replayed the hideous scream. The old man seemed to be standing in the shadowy corner of my room. I blinked a few times and took a deep breath to convince myself he wasn't actually there. I lay for a few minutes wondering if the scream was in fact a memory or did actually occur. Despite my best efforts I was unable to return to sleep.

Seven o'clock in the morning

By seven a.m. I was in my office, having showered and shaved. Rachel did a double take as she turned up for work at seven thirty, her usual time. Though I did not actually start paying her until nine, she still turned up at this time. As for why, I never bothered to ask. I tipped my head and motioned to the coffee pot.

"Fresh," I muttered as I continued typing on my antiquated laptop.

She favoured me with a stare as she poured her coffee. She replaced my half empty, cold coffee with a fresh one. Without asking, she fell into the chair opposite mine and she stared that damn stare!

I tried my level best to ignore her in spite of the constant irritating clearing of her throat as she tried to get my attention. It worked. I slammed the lid down on the laptop and stared back.

"What?" I demanded.

She licked her lips and smiled. Let me tell you, working with your ex-girlfriend, ex-best friend, ex-fiancée or whatever, should most definitely be avoided - most especially when that person is all three.

"How was the pub last night?" she asked.

"For God's sake!" I cried. "Sometimes I think you should be the god-damned detective and I'll make the coffee and do the filing!"

She grimaced at her cup. "Not a good idea."

I favoured her with a look I knew she hated.

"So, are we taking that crazy old man's case?" she asked.

"If you are referring to my esteemed client…"

"I'm referring to that old nut who I saw talking to himself and chasing away imaginary insects."

I looked at her again.

"I mean it, he was whispering angrily and swatting at something before you came in. Walking to and fro and looking out the window. He's a nut."

"And he's paying us a fortune!" I looked up as the door opened, "ah, Cal – right on time."

My friend and rival looked the worse for wear, it didn't take a detective to see that he had continued drinking when he went home and had barely slept. I imagine he saw that on my face and appearance too.

"Rachel," I said firmly, "coffee for my friend, please."

She stared him up and down before tutting loudly. "I think he's suffered enough!"

"That bad, is it?" said Cal with a smile.

She shot him a look that's better left unsaid.

"What the fuck are we into, Don?" he asked me. I frowned at him in concern as I noticed he was shaking. My first thought was not a pleasant one: is he back on heroin again? I was almost afraid to ask.

He looked up at me and winced. "No, before you ask, I am not back on the smack."

"What's wrong?" I asked.

"Something's stalking me," he said, his voice barely a whisper. "Last night it was watching me, I heard it and saw it hiding in the bins waiting for me. I ran toward it yelling, I thought 'I'm not getting stabbed in the back' so I took it on my terms."

"What happened?" I asked.

"It was the damnedest thing! It jumped backwards and then ran off… up the god-damned wall! The fucking wall!" The last few words he shrieked at me.

It brought Rachel running back in. "What's happened?" she asked.

"Nothing; it's fine," I said, waving her off.

"The hell it is!" she snorted, she sat down beside Cal and put her arms round him and shot me a look that had a full conversation in it.

Ex-army!

PTSD!

You ought to know better!

He's not strong enough for your bullshit!

You're meant to look after him!

I stood there in dumb silence. My look back to her, full of remorse, said: I know.

The Detective

Detective Jerome Jonas staggered out onto the front porch, leaning heavily on the door frame. His head fell forward and he wretched several times before he was able to sink down onto the top step of the quaint, but modest, suburban home. His hands shook as he reached into his pocket and he fumbled with the cigarettes. It took four attempts before the Zippo's flame caught and he was able to light the cigarette. Inhaling deeply, he held his breath as the nausea again swept over him. Eighteen years he had been doing this job and he had long since entered into that stage of life when most thoughts are given to the years passed and the retirement looming as opposed to eyes fixed on the career ladder and impressing superiors.

Eighteen years and he thought he had seen it all – the murders, the rapes, the weird and the stupid, but this!

How can one old man hold so much blood? He wondered, yet again. As the images played through his mind, he leaned forward and coughed up the bile that filled his mouth - The dead eyes, the horror-stricken mouth, the unnatural layout of the corpse, the innards. The images played almost stroboscopic-like in his mind and threatened to overwhelm him. He took another deep drag of his cigarette and flicked the end onto the street. Fumbling in his pocket, he pulled out the evidence bag that contained the bent and blood-soaked business card that had been in the pocket of the dead man. He turned it over and sighed. "Ok, Mr Don Anderson – Private Detective. Let's see how you figure in this messed up shit!" Taking another cigarette from his pocket he shook his head to clear it.

How can one old man hold so much blood?

An older man, with a large pot belly was leaning lazily against a police car and smoking a cigarette. As Jonas stepped out of the house, he wandered over.

"Fucking mess eh?" he said laughing.

Jonas put down the feeling of resentment. "Bit of respect, Bill, eh? A man is dead."

Bill shrugged. "Maybe," he said as he reached into his jacket pocket, "this all sounds like a load of shit to me. Read the latest from that bitch captain – said it before – she's lost it big time!" He thrust a sheet of paper in Jonas' hands and walked off chuckling. "Pub time – see you later, Big Shot!"

Jonas watched him waddle off and he shook his head before turning his attention to the faxed sheet of paper. His eyes widened and his mouth fell open. "What the…" he said as he read:

MEMO

Police Scotland District 12

From: Captain F Herbert

Internal – Officers level 4 and above.

DO NOT CIRCULATE

The following are comments (redacted for Data Protection) from various social media formats. The dates and times have been removed, however all range from three thirty am on the sixth of June until eight am on the seventh.

Anyone else hear that noise from ---- street last night? Sounded like Satan!

Just seen a freaky bald guy run across the motorway tonight! Scared the shit out of me!

Lol, must be pissed! Thought I saw some mad old dude climb a drainpipe up six floors. I'm buzzing, man, lol

Anyone seen ----? Was talking to him on the phone and got cut off after hearing some mad noises. Seriously worried!

WTF! Just saw some bald guy taken out at 60mph by a van. He got up and ran off! I want what he's on!

Early reports suggest some common features among the person sighted. These are:

Person, or person who is aged and hairless or of little hair

Possessing great agility and strength

Multiple sightings

47% increase in violence and missing person calls 6th June to 7th June.

All sightings to be reported immediately and extra care to be taken. Use code word Porcelain to report additional information.

Use of deadly force if contact initiated is authorised.

Captain F Herbert

Family Secrets

Every family has its fair share of secrets, and more than a few have that one relative who is never spoken of, nor referenced and remains an embarrassing blot on the genealogy tree. For me it was my late mother's brother, Dr Alexander Jeffries, once such an esteemed doctor in his particular field of anthropology. The rumours were that he went mad, killed some of his fellow scientists and has been in and out of various mental hospitals ever since. Since my mother died and my elder brother was killed in Iraq, the crazy uncle became my responsibility. My embarrassment was made all the worse when the hospital in Kisiljavo called me insisting that my uncle desperately had to speak to me right in the middle of Cal's visit. No amount of my promising to call back satisfied the doctor, who said it was extremely important I take the call in order to calm my uncle down else they would have to heavily sedate him and his weakened heart might not take it.

With a feeling of being guilt-tripped into it, I accepted the call. "Uncle Alex," I said with as much fake enthusiasm as I could muster. "How are you; it's been…"

"Listen to me, Donald!" his voice was shaking and full of nervous energy, "you must listen to me! He's coming, Donald! He's coming for you! The demon – I found the demon in the castle! We dug down and released him! He killed my friends – killed them all. He's been watching me… One of his minions is here now, it killed my doctor and has taken his place, but no one will believe me!"

I sighed – I didn't have time for this nonsense. It was always the same: The demon; The Vampire; the man from the castle; the creatures. "Yes, uncle, don't you worry about it. Are you taking your medication?"

"Listen to me, Donald!" he hissed, "To hell with the medication! I know what you think – the mad old fool! I've been protecting you your whole life and you don't even know it! I've hidden away, making sure he couldn't find you, but now he will! … His allies have found me, monsters, Donald! Demons!"

I rolled my eyes as Cal stared at me expectantly.

"He knows about you now. You may have the noble blood! He thought I did, but I don't. Oh I tried to stay away, but your mother wrote to me about you, and I tried to not read the letters; tried not to learn anything they could use, but the temptation and the boredom and the desire to know you – they got the better of me, but I didn't tell him! I destroyed all the letters; I told no one, but his blood-eater minion attacked me in my room, held me down and learned of you from my blood, and now they know of your existence – they're looking for you! Read my notes, son! Read about the blood-eaters, they're more common than you think! They're looking for you now! They can take memories from blood, he knows all about you now after his minion read my blood memories, thankfully I've made sure I don't know where you live and have deliberately kept you away and safe. I wish I could've done more to stop him, I was too weakened to fight back! It sat there, perched on the end of my bed, just as I remembered all those years ago; all emaciated… the smell of death!

"He's coming for you, it's the Thirteenth Parable, Donald! The Thirteenth Parable!! I'm too old and too weak to fight him now, but I understand now why he left me alive all those years ago, you must run! Wait… I'm not finished… get off me!" He had been getting more and more animated and louder on the phone and I guess the orderly had decided to get him off the phone. There was a sound of a scuffle and I heard him yell: "Don't let him find you, Donald! Don't let him find you! Watch out for the smell! Listen for the screams! They're… Nooooo!"

A few moments later a calm voice came over the telephone. "Mr Anderson?"

"I'm still here," I replied.

"Nurse Blagojević - your uncle's mental health nurse. We're going to have to sedate him after all, I apologise; I had thought the phone call would've been enough to calm him, but it appears to have aggravated him instead."

I admit to being somewhat disconcerted by it all. "Will he be ok?" I asked.

"He is a very sick old man," she replied solemnly, "he is also doing some serious self-harming. It is a worrying new symptom. Please try not to worry; I am in discussion with Dr Frombald and we will make it ok."

"In what way is he self-harming?" I asked in surprise.

"He has been banging his head on something and has a large, red mark - like a handprint, and when the nurse was changing him, she called me. He has an ugly wound on his chest, like teeth marks. Strange, such a wound should bleed a lot, but there was no sign of any blood."

I felt a cold chill and shuddered unconsciously just as Rachel rapped on my door and opened it, a tall, dark-skinned man pushed past her while flashing a police badge in my face.

I muttered something to the nurse about looking after him and to call me with updates, then hung up the phone. "Can I help you, officer?" I stammered.

He smiled. "It's Detective," he said, showing his badge.

I motioned him to a seat and called Rachel to bring some coffee for the detective. I knew she'd not miss an opportunity to ear-wig, so she might as well be useful. After handing him the coffee, she made no motion to leave. I chose to ignore her.

"So, what's this all about?" I asked.

He motioned to Cal. "Who is this gentleman?"

"A co-worker of sorts," I replied. "He can be trusted."

The detective shrugged. "I'm here about Colonel Jacobson, I believe you know him."

As it wasn't a question, I remained silent.

Jonas pulled a blood-spattered card, which was sealed in one of those clear plastic police bags, from his pocket. "Yours, I believe. We found it in the Colonel's house last night. We were called there after reports of an assault."

Cal and I exchanged looks. "Is he alright?" I ventured.

"No, he was very brutally, and very violently murdered last night."

Sinister Happenings

I have no idea how long the three of us sat there. Somehow, and I have no idea how, but we must've answered all of the detective's questions and he left. The sun had begun to set while we all went through periods of manic chatter alternating with sombre silences. For Rachel it was more excitement, she often talked of how boring her job was and goaded me several times on the banality of the assignments I accepted. This one however, seemed exciting enough for her.

Cal was shocked, I had cursed the detective under my breath when he showed us some of the photographs of Jacobson's murder and was concerned for my friend. We had both done two tours of Iraq and Afghanistan before being honourably discharged. I went first in a much less dramatic fashion than Cal. He got out following a terrible incident which killed several of his friends and left him traumatised. He had returned for two years as private security in an attempt to fix the damage it had done to his skull (his words), until he was himself badly wounded. I was one of the few who knew the extent of his mental health issues, and now those photographs and the case itself could be affecting him in ways I could not imagine. He caught me looking at him and interpreted my look, he smiled in understanding and nodded firmly as though saying, I'm fine; don't worry about me! Well, I couldn't help it. Now, with the detective away and Rachel out the room preparing to leave, I said so.

"Honestly," he said, "I'm ok. I want to get to the bottom of this, we owe it to our client after all."

For me, the pictures had been almost hypnotic, and the blood spatters seemed like a hidden language that seemed to speak to me on some atavistic level, as though I could unconsciously hear the thump-thump of ancient drums, and the rhythm of music that weaved and threaded through the blood trail. It had taken all my effort to tear my glance from the pictures. I felt like my heart was racing and all my senses were elevated.

As I made to speak, from the direction of the reception office, I heard a loud, piercing scream. Cal froze while I jumped to my feet and ran through,

Rachel was standing facing the small side window and shaking uncontrollably. I gripped her by the shoulders. "What's wrong; Rachel what happened?"

She pointed to the window, her arm shaking and with teeth chattering said: "It was… it was there…in the window!"

I turned to look at the small window. "What was there?"

"A face… a man's face! It was hideous!"

"Rachel, there's nothing there - nothing can be there; we're two floors up."

She shot me a look as she pushed past me. "I know that! But it was there! A horrible old man with yellow teeth and mad bits of white hair!" She pulled the window up and leaned out. "Try that again you old bastard! I'm ready for you now!"

Aghast and more worried about the neighbours than I was about ghostly old men, I pulled her back in. "Jesus!" She folded her arms defiantly. "I know what I saw!" she said again, and as I made to close the window, I heard another horrible scream from out in the dark, the same one from the pub. I shivered and slammed the window closed, although not before I imagined an old man squatting on the roof of a building several streets away. I blinked and rubbed my eyes to clear the spectral vision. When it didn't disappear, I closed the curtains instead.

I stayed long into the evening after the others had left. Cal insisted on walking Rachel home, which I knew I should've done, but I wasn't ready to leave, mostly because I had neglected my other clients. I spent the evening lying via phone calls and emails, falsely claiming I was "working diligently on your behalf!" Truth was I had lost all interest in them and was obsessing over this one. I couldn't explain it, but every cell of my being vibrated with a kind of nervous energy something I had never experienced before. I felt like something was coming, like a kind of unconscious drumbeat was playing far, far back in the depths of my mind. It was all I could think about.

I decided enough was enough and that the claustrophobia of my office had done me in. With a burst of energy. I threw on my coat, punched out the lights and headed off.

I walked briskly, owing to the cold and the inclemency of the weather. I strode past Owens, the bakers, down by Mulberry Lane and past the plethora of corner coffee shops and late-night takeaway places, feeling self-conscious against the stares of the people out to fuel their carnal and ostentatious desires. I began to feel watched and a sensation akin to what a rodent must feel as a serpent slithers toward it, or how a gazelle must feel as it searches in vain for a glimpse of the lion. The feeling gnawed at my insides and caused me to increase my step until I was literally barging past people, muttering "sorry" as I did so. And then I saw it! Or at least a glimpse of it. A skeletal figure just outside my peripheral vision. I caught a flashing glimpse from the street ahead, then it was behind me, above me, coming closer to me. I was literally running down the street, my lungs burning from the pain; my legs on fire and my chest pounding hard, sweat blinded me, my breaths coming out in short gasps that hurt my ribs as I inhaled. I imagined more of those terrible screams above me, sometimes from left or right, or in front, or behind. They varied in length, pitch and sound – could it be a language? Some part of my brain was still working and went into overdrive.

I had no sooner reached the imagined sanctuary of my front door and had begun fumbling with my keys – my hands shook so much the damned lock seemed to move when someone appeared and grabbed me from behind. As I made to scream, a powerful hand clamped itself to my face.

"Do not scream, Mr Anderson," said a soft and familiar voice. The hand fell from my face, and I turned to stare into the face of Mr Jacobson.

"They said you were dead!" I blurted.

With a furtive glance down the gloomy street, he said: "perhaps we could go inside?" I was aware his eyes kept glancing upward.

With my hands shaking, I managed to unlock the door. It took me nearly three attempts to turn off the alarm but thankfully I managed it. A phone call or a police car investigating was something I could do without right now.

Once inside, I made straight for my sideboard and the decanters. I poured two rather large whiskies and, after thrusting one into the hand of my client, I took a severely generous swig before refilling my glass and collapsing into my chair. The deep and burning stare of Mr Jacobson followed my every move.

Before I could speak, he stood up in one fluid movement, which was a surprise given his age, and strolled to my window, peered through the blinds for a few moments and when he seemed satisfied, he sat back down in the seat opposite me.

I sat there, too shocked and too afraid to speak. Who was this guy?

He held the glass in a vice-like grip, his knuckles almost blue under the tight skin. It was then I was aware of some blood under his long fingernails. As I looked, I realised the nail on his middle finger was missing, as though pulled, or perhaps torn off violently. It appeared to be a fresh wound.

"I was visited this evening, Mr Anderson, by what we call a blood-eater. They are detestable parasites who plague me and others like me and have done so for a long, long time. They dwell in the dark places; the hidden places, feeding upon those whose blood is noble, pure, and from a long unbroken line of ascendancy. You appear ill at ease, and it is for that reason I am loath to use certain words such as 'supernatural' or 'demonic', however I am at a loss as to any possible euphemism which may suffice. Perhaps you can claim some comfort from the fact I am not talking of heaven and hell; God and Satan so to speak, although those terms did originate from an attempt to adequately describe me and others like me."

I sat in silence, a heavy reluctance to speak had overcome me.

"I was aware from our initial meeting that you appeared undecided about believing me or were uncertain of the things of which I spoke."

I think I nodded in some dumb and idiotic manner. In any case, he continued. "The blood-eater came to my home; it attacked me and tried to copy me. I managed to kill it, although not before it did me considerable damage. It was rather far along in its attempted facsimile of me, which resulted in sufficient tissue for a detective to identify the remains as me. We noble-born heal somewhat faster as do you mort… you."

I'm asleep! I thought. This is some crazy, stupid dream!

"I assure you this is no dream," he said softly.

I laughed bitterly. "You're right," I said, "It's more of a damn nightmare!"

He nodded solemnly and a sad moue touched the corners of his mouth. "I know. Some of us are tired and want nothing to do with what's coming. That's why I sought you out. It is time."

"Time for what?"

"You already know the answer to that, don't you?"

I looked at him fearfully. My heart beat faster, sweat formed on my brow and from within the deep, dark recess of my mind, something was screaming at me. Like a fragment of memory - such as when you try to recall a song lyric or place someone's face.

"You've seen the civil unrest, the climate change; the gradual collapse of our society. The cycle is coming again.

"The ancients knew it. We tried to warn you all with the pyramid, Easter Island, Machu Pichu, you nearly understood the message."

Still grasping to fully understand, I blurted out: "Doomsday Clock!"

He nodded. "Every twenty-six thousand years this chaos comes around and within each Great Year there are only a few cycles in which this Parable can be done. He failed last cycle. Now the time is nearly upon us again, he needs the blood of the twelve families - the twelve make the Thirteen. Three hundred and thirty-three years ago we stopped him and imprisoned him. We thought we could finally let it all die." He paused and took a long drink.

"And then my uncle released him!"

"Precisely. Although weakened, he knew your family bloodline was attached to the thirteen and so he manipulated your uncle into finding and releasing him. When he tasted the blood of your uncle, he knew his blood strain was not strong enough for a rebirth. He had to look further." He stopped and stared at me.

Realisation hit hard.

"Me!"

Braničevo, Serbia

Dr Alex Jeffries lay against the medicine cabinet, breathing hard. He was still weakened by a mixture of the drugs the hospital had poured into him, from the nightly attacks of the creature and the resulting infection, and from the violent attack he had inflicted upon Sonders, the night security guard. Beside him lay the unfortunate Sonders. He hadn't meant to kill him, but the man had been so strong and unrelenting, yet Alex knew how vital it was that he get the message out.

Another death I failed to prevent! He felt the burden of so many deaths and tried to take solace from the fact his pain would end. Not far to go now and I shall be rid of you forever! You who have taken my life - who has taken so many lives and haunted my dreams! I shall soon be rid of you!

Suddenly he heard loud banging noises coming from the locked security doors. He had locked them and then broken the keys inside the lock to keep them out, but he knew it was only a matter of time. He gently touched the gaping cut on his head that had he suffered as he fell fighting the guard. He heard the police yelling from through the gate and heard the call to summon a locksmith. I don't have a lot of time.

With a strong effort he tried to climb to his feet while keeping the guard's gun in his hand. "Keep back or I'll shoot!" He yelled.

"No one wants that, Doctor," yelled the police negotiator. "Let us help you. We need to see the guard. Is he ok?"

"He's dead. I have his gun and if you come in, I'll use it!" It was an empty threat. He staggered over to the small medicine cupboard and unlocked it, aiming the gun at the frightened nurse he had imprisoned.

"Out!"

He crawled out, obviously terrified. Alex waved the gun at him. "Get up and unlock that computer. Right now!"

The nurse threw up his hands. "Ok, ok."

Alex ignored the banging and attempted plea bargaining. There was nothing they could offer.

The nurse typed and the computer screen unlocked. "Access my file."

He nodded and did as he was told. "What is it you think you will find, Doctor?"

Alex shook his head. "You lot have nothing on me that I want to know." He motioned to the screen. "Get me my nephew's phone number."

"The phones won't work at this time of night,"

Alex laughed. "I know you, Miroslav. I've seen you make calls from that hidden mobile phone you carry. Get me the number and give me your phone."

"I don't have it, I swear!"

Alex aimed the gun. "I don't have time; my nephew doesn't have time and you sure as hell won't if you lie to me again. You might just survive this, Miroslav, you've always been one of the good ones, but lie to me again and you won't."

He swallowed hard. "I have your nephew's number"

"Good. Now hand me the phone."

He handed it over, thought for a moment about reaching for the gun, but thought better of it.

"How do I dial the U.K?" asked Alex

"Plus, then four, four."

"Very good," he said as he aimed the gun at the nurse. "Get back in the cupboard."

"Come on, Alex! I..."

Alex fired the gun to the right of Miroslav. "Get in the cupboard, or I'll shoot! I haven't the time for this!"

Miroslav stumbled backward, and Alex pushed him into the medicine cupboard and locked the door.

As he turned to the screen to type the number into the phone, there was a loud explosion as the security gate burst open. Smoke filled the corridor.

Bloodlines

"You're telling me that I'm part of this bloodline?" I asked

Jacobson nodded.

"And I am…"

"The last of the twelve. He has secured their blood and just needs you. You will complete the…"

He paused as the phone loudly rang, shattering the silence of the room. Instinctively I grabbed it. "Hello?"

"Donald. I need you to be quiet and listen to me right now!"

"Uncle Alex?" I said. "How did you…"

"We don't have time! Listen to me." There were a lot of loud noises and then what sounded like a gunshot." Get back! I'm warning you - next one in here I kill!"

"Uncle Alex, you need…"

"No! You need to listen! I'm dead already, you need to be ready! He's coming for you, Donald! He knows where you live! This is why I stayed in Serbia, in Kisiljavo; why I never tried to come home. I needed to stay far away from you! To protect you! I tried to fight him, I refused to tell him where you were, but he just kept coming and coming! Every night he would haunt me, sometimes in my dreams and sometimes he'd be here! I told him I would never betray you, and yet I did - he got it from my blood! Don't trust anyone! Don't trust anyone!"

I heard a loud commotion, lots of yelling and then a gunshot. Everything went quiet. Then after what felt like an eternity. I heard fingers grasp the phone and drag it. Then I heard my uncle's breathing. It was laboured and came out in gasps. "He's coming, Donald," he whispered. There was further commotion, yelling and shouting, then I heard my uncle again, he gasped for breath and whispered: "Run!" Before I could speak there came another three or four gunshots then silence.

"Hello? Uncle Alex? Hello?"

"This is Sergeant Floki, to whom am I speaking?

"Is my uncle ok?

"Dr Jeffries is dead."

I let my hand drop and the phone fell to the floor. "My uncle…"

Jacobson frowned. Somehow, he already knew. "Then he is already on his way. You must listen to me, Donald, if you want to live."

"How can he be here if he was in Kisiljavo, it will take him a long time to get here!"

Jacobson shook his head. "You cannot think like that, he can be wherever he wants to be – more quickly than you can imagine."

I looked at him incredulously. "Yeah? Well, why didn't he beam himself out of that castle my uncle found him in, eh? He sounds pretty thick to me!"

Jacobson shook his head as though I were the stupid one. "He was under tons of earth and weakened from attempting the ceremony. That was why we attacked him then."

"So he can be here? Right now?" I yelled.

"Precisely. He now knows where you are and who you are. Come." He grabbed me by the arm and pulled me to my feet.

My head swam, the room began to move, and I lurched forward and would've fallen had it not been for the swift action and speed of my client. He grabbed me mid-fall and lowered me down to the chair, his grip painful in its intensity. I shook my head, "What the fuck is really going on, Jacobson – Really?"

He frowned deeply and his lips drew to a thin line. He fell heavily into the chair opposite mine, and when he spoke it was precise and slow.

"The things you have heard – from you mother; from your uncle, and from me well, they are all true. I am of a race called Noble Born, which requires a long and complex explanation, for which we do not have time. Suffice it to say we are, what you and your kind would probably call, 'immortal'. We are not that as such. We can live extraordinarily long lives, I myself shall be a thousand years old in a decade or two, there are others much, much older and some who do not live that long."

"There are also among us some who possess even greater skills, things that you would see as fantastical: mind reading, telekinesis, mimicry, that kind of thing,

"There was a world-order centuries back in which some of us ruled the continents, and the humans of the time called us gods, and we do in fact form the basis of many of the archaic religions. Some of us even adopted the mantles that the humans called us. I met many of the ones whom history has called gods, and none of them were any more of a god than I am, and yet they are, and were, worshipped for centuries."

I sat in disbelief. If I had ever dreamed of adventure and excitement, I regretted it now. All I wanted was a nice easy cheating spouse case, or a missing cat, but Jacobson had more to tell me.

Ambush

It sat there, concealed behind some bins and discarded rubbish and was completely invisible in the late-night gloom. The only light came from far off to the right – the large, illuminated Police Scotland sign and the occasional flickering light from the tall and inadequate car park lamp posts. For a supposedly secure building, there was not much light, and that suited the creature perfectly.

More like a hunting animal than a man, it was thin, painfully thin, with long fingernails, a short stub of a nose and close-set eyes that were almost black. It crouched in a position that any normal person would find painful: squatted down on haunches, hands splayed on the ground in front. Its head weaved from side to side, mouth slightly open, making strange short and rapid breaths as though tasting the air. It sat in perfect stillness, apart from the head motions. And it waited.

The wait was not long, from above and to the left a strange, short, shrill scream was heard, and was repeated a few seconds later, although this time it was closer.

The creature paused and turned its stare toward the entrance of the police building, a man could be seen exiting the large glass doors. The creature paused, becoming completely still, even it's breathing stopped. And it waited.

A car door slammed, and footsteps approached, the creature's head turned a millimetre and it seemed to lower itself down further. Three quick breaths, a strange flick of its tongue and it seemed to grow more excitable. The fingers twitched and the eyes blinked rapidly.

There was a bleep-bleep and a brief flash of orange light as a car unlocked, and the footsteps suddenly grew closer, mere metres away now. A mobile phone ring tone shattered the silence.

"Jonas, here… yes, Sophia?" A pause. "Shit I forgot about that! Leave it on my, desk; I'll take care of it in the morning, right now I'm going home to get seriously and pathetically pissed!" Detective Jonas chatted into the phone as he walked. "I've literally had a few days right out of hell, I…" he paused as a sound intruded, it seemed to be coming from the bins. "Yeah, I'm here; just thought I heard something, I…" he paused again. Was there something there, looking at him?

"I'll call you back," he hung up the phone and peered into the gloom.

It was then the creature screamed and pounced.

Home Truths

Jacobson walked back from the kitchen carrying two cups of strong coffee. I accepted the one he held out to me. I could not help but notice the way he gripped the mugs instead of the handles. I expected to see burns on his hand when I took the mug from him, but there were none

"The ceremony itself is dependent upon certain circumstances. For example, it must take place during the vernal equinox when it is moving through the sidereal zodiac." Jacobson took a drink from the mug, "the exact details are unimportant, but suffice to say that there are very few set times and dates when the ceremony is possible, and often centuries can go past before another one can be attempted. During the last attempt, the creature, as you call him, his real name is unimportant, and I will not speak it!" he said with more venom than I had seen in him so far. "He had researched and worked for many centuries upon an old myth, very old even back then – you know of it as The Thirteenth Parable. To be brief, it involves twelve Noble Born from certain families. These twelve must possess certain abilities which, when drawn from their blood and properly aligned and ingested directly by the Thirteenth, will create from the thirteen, a new being - one who cannot be stopped and who will have more power than can be imagined, changing matter, altering time – these things would be easy for such a one.

"Clearly, there were those amongst us who did not want this to happen and so opposed it. We prefer to live in the shadows alongside humanity we do not wish to rule or control you, although some do on occasion do just that- I am sure there are many politicians, company executives, and such like whom you would quite righty suspect of being one of us."

I sat there in silence, taking this all in – and he was right, a few names did spring to mind.

"We heard, back in seventeen twenty-five, that he was to attempt the ceremony again. I followed the progression of the ecliptic and knew when he would make his attempt. There were those among The Twelve who were willing to help him; others were not. Those who weren't, he killed and kidnapped what he needed. Some of us banded together and attacked the castle in the Braničevo district. We were able to cause the landslide that buried the castle and sealed him in forever, or so we thought." Jacobson covered his eyes with his head. "What I have not told you, is that I am of one of the twelve families that he needed. For the ceremony to work, it cannot be just anyone from the family, it has to be one whose blood is most pure and thus as close to the original bloodline as possible."

I watched as tears formed in Jacobson's eyes. My… my daughter was the closest in my family. When she disappeared, I immediately knew he had taken her. I knew there was no hope of rescue and I left her to die in the castle, it was either that or let him defile her and give her a slow death to satiate his plan – and I only hope the death I gave her was the lesser evil of the two." He wiped his eyes and cleared his throat in an attempt to regain his composure.

"For many years I led a lonely existence with but one aim – to watch over and protect my family. I knew he would still live in that castle, and I wanted to make sure he remained buried. I worked feverishly to cover up stories; to hide the truth and to belittle and discredit anyone who tried to look into the story of the buried castle. For years and years, I worked and slowly the knowledge was lost, until you humans came up with something that made it impossible…" He waited for me to realise what he meant.

"The internet," I said softly.

He nodded. "Exactly. With the information flying freely across the globe my task became impossible and I could no longer stop the rumours resurfacing and popping up everywhere, and by then I had virtually given up and would've perhaps lived in peace but for one stupid mistake. I was the last of my line, following the death of my daughter, and I felt sure that unless he could find another Noble Born family with the qualities he needed, then the Thirteenth Parable was over.

"One year, in eighteen ninety-six, I met a young woman. She was the kind of person with whom falling in love with was easy and I had not been with anyone since the death of my wife a century or so before. We became close and soon she loved me in a way I could never reciprocate. I knew she wanted children and yet I was fearful of what that could mean and so I knew what I had to do.

"Several of the villagers had gone missing over the years, some by blood-eaters feeding, some by other wild animals. Using this as my means, I left, making sure to leave behind enough of my own blood and tissue to convince anyone that I had been taken by a wild animal and had died," He paused then, I guess the memories were still painful to him after all this time.

I began to feel something then, something akin to déjà vu, like I had heard this before. I felt on the verge of a sudden realisation.

"For many years I lived as best I could, jealous of the finite time you humans have and wishing I could just die, and then something happened. I was sitting in a café in Italy, enjoying an espresso, when I saw something on a newspaper which a man at the next table was reading. 'Molti morti sulla scena degli scavi del castello!'

"Many dead at scene of ancient castle excavation," I said absently.

He nodded. "Immediately, I knew what it meant. The woman whom I had abandoned had been with child – my child! I hadn't stopped the nightmare, my bloodline continued; I had brought it all back!"

That sudden realisation hit me. "That child was my grandfather!"

Jacobson nodded. "Somehow, in his weakened state, the creature had been able to reach your uncle in some empathic way. He helped to push and mould him into becoming an archaeologist and in seeking him out. I can imagine his elation as your uncle actually fell into his hands at the castle. I can imagine his annoyance when he realised the blood carried in your uncle's veins was of no use to him. He needed another." He paused then and stared at me.

I felt suddenly sick, I groaned and fell back into the chair. "You mean me!"

Jacobson sighed and closed his eyes. "That is why I sought you out. That is why I have tried to protect you, I met with your mother and father and warned them when you were born, I tested their blood and knew they weren't strong enough. I warned them about the dangers of having a child."

As soon as he said it, a lifetime's worth of understanding hit me hard. This was why my father was so angry all the time, why he fought with my mother, why he drank and drank and eventually succumbed to a failed liver and all the horrors that represents.

"So, I am strong enough for this psycho mad hatter's tea party?"

"A crude allusion, but yes – you are. This is why we need to get you away from here." He jumped to his feet. "You must flee, son." For the first time I saw real fear in his eyes, it was then I realised it was not a fear for me, or rather not just for me.

As I pondered what to say, there came a stern knock at the door. Much to my surprise, Jacobson uttered a noise akin to that of an animal and he took what looked like a fighting stance.

I looked through the spy hole in my door and frowned. It was Detective Jonas.

"It's ok," I said, as I unlocked the door. "He's a police officer."

I opened the door and Jonas stepped inside. "Mr Anderson," he said politely. He stopped and stared, much surprised, at Jacobson.

I shrugged pitifully. "I guess you didn't expect to see him here."

Jonas frowned and rubbed his chin. "Well, I'll be damned."

Jacobson clung to the shadows and shied back. He seemed to be staring intently at Jonas and didn't take his eyes off him. "Neat trick, Mr Jacobson," he said. "Mind explaining it?"

"I see no need, Detective," he said as he sniffed the air. His voice was strangely clipped and formal. "What is the reason for your visit?"

Jonas smiled. "Should that not be Mr Anderson's question?" He stared back hard at Jacobson. "I am here to discuss my case privately, if you would care to leave?"

"I would not," said Jacobson abruptly. His sniffing became more prominent, and I swear his tongue shot in and out a few times and then up into the roof his mouth.

I looked back and forth between them. Something was not right. "It's kinda' late, Detective," I said, "could we take this up in the morning?"

"I'm afraid it's pretty urgent, Don," he said.

Don? When did we get so familiar? I thought to myself.

The detective smiled. "Mind if I come in?"

He took a step forward. Jacobson's reaction was fascinating. "No," he said, "you may not. I invite you to leave!"

The Detective shot him a sideways look through strange eyes, his lip curled into a sneer.

Jacobson drew himself up to his full height and, for a second, I thought I saw what looked like a faint pulse or shockwave move from his clenched fists, the dining chair to the left of him actually fell over. "Donald," he said softly. "Run!" As he did so his hands shot forward with such a speed as I have never seen before. As quick as he was, the detective was faster. He flung his left hand out toward Jacobson's face. I heard, or father felt, a whooshing sound. Jacobson uttered a strange guttural choke. I spun to look at him, and as I did so I saw his piercing blue eyes fill violently with blood. He coughed and hiccupped as though trying to breathe. As I stood there in shock, blood dripped from his nostrils, and dripped from his eyes like bloody tears, he blinked a few times and his head jerked in some kind of spasm. With an effort, he tried to turn his head toward me, then suddenly, rigid like some solid oak, he fell face first onto the carpet and lay still, blood pouring from between his open lips.

My mouth fell open in a gasp, and I turned just in time to see the detective seemingly melt before me into a tall, completely bald man with a white and sallow complexion. He was thin, very thin, with eyes tinged with bright orange. His blood-red lips parted in a death's-head grin showing very white and very sharp teeth.

"Well, Mr Anderson," he said in a strange eastern accent, which I assumed was his natural one. "I have been waiting a long, long time to see you."

I stood there, frozen in terror and unable to move as he moved ever closer towards me.

To Be Continued...

Sands of Time

He awoke to immediate chaos — blinding lights, disembodied voices all yelling incoherently, his head swam, so much so that he almost fell into unconsciousness again as the multitude of feelings and memories all cried out for attention at once. He grappled with his mind for control, fighting constantly with the darkness that hung on the very edge of his awareness and threatened to engulf him. It took several minutes for his mind to calm slightly and allow him the elation to focus on the unbelievable: I am alive!

"I'm dead! I'm dead!" His brain yelled incessantly.

He fought harder and harder and eventually the chaotic musings subsided leaving him to his own semi-rational thoughts.

Cautiously he opened one eye, then the other; saw to his relief that he was lying in his own bed. The same as last time, he thought to himself. The way it's meant to happen!

He tried to recall what the next event would be. He relaxed slightly as he remembered. Okay, my wife won't be beside me. She'll have gone to work. He turned to his left and saw that he was alone in the bed.

So far so good!

How do I know all of this? He cautiously sat upright, fell against the bed's headboard as his sight began to swirl around him.

"You're bound to experience slight dizziness, don't worry, it's to be expected." The old man's words burned in his mind. "Just sit for a while, remember, your brain's got to come round again, catch up if you like, don't expect wonders immediately. It'll take time."

He lay with his back against the cold wood surface of the headboard concentrating on the coldness against his skin. It felt distant, as though his back was touching the board through a shirt or the like. It's a real feeling. Just let it remain for a while longer. He concentrated on the cold feeling, moved his back further along the board as it became warm with his body-heat. The slight, split-second shock of the cold against his back each time he moved became more real to him.

"Concentrate on the feelings. They're the key!" The old man's voice rang in his mind once again. "Don't think about who you are or any other memories, they'll overwhelm you and this will all be for nothing!"

Gradually his sight became less blurred, and he was able to move his eyes across the room, his gaze falling on his belongings as he did so.

There's the wardrobe with my suits. He moved his sight further and came to rest on the chest of drawers, on them, lay several photographs. As he tried to focus on the individual photos his sight began to fade, and the memories threatened to engulf him. Immediately he closed his eyes.

"If the disorientation comes back, shut your eyes and concentrate on something that didn't screw you up."

He thought back to the cold feelings of the headboard. He remembered the harsh nip from its cold surface; the shock it caused when he touched it.

Once more he felt his mind clear and steady itself. He risked opening his eyes and to his relief saw that everything was stationary again. Slowly — very slowly — he allowed his eyes to roam the bedroom.

He saw a freshly laundered shirt hanging from the handle on the wardrobe. A clean pair of trousers were draped over a chair, clean underwear lay on the chair beside the trousers, polished shoes lay on the floor next to the chair. A briefcase stood on the top of the small table beside his bed. He risked a look at the clock. It said nine-fifteen.

As soon as he read the digital display of the clock, his mind threatened to overwhelm him again. He heard fragments of a conversation echoing far back in his skull "…move! We got to get out of here! Come on – he's gonna kill us! We…"

He threw his hands to his face and clutched his head, but the voices and pictures wouldn't go away.

He saw a man run towards him and fall as a bullet hit him in the back of the head. He fell silently and dropped a briefcase. He then saw his own hand move out and pick up the fallen briefcase, he felt himself run away as bullets whistled past him.

"No!" he yelled as he opened his eyes to find himself lying in his bed.

He breathed heavily as he tried to make sense of the imagery his mind threw at him, but each time he found one, it twisted and disappeared, leaving him with nothing to hold on to. Eventually he gave up as more of the visions faded.

Dave. Is that my name? He risked stepping out of bed and to his surprise found that his legs held him. Holding onto the bed for support, he moved over to the chest of drawers and picked up a picture; it showed a man cuddling a woman in some sort of classy holiday resort. That's my wife!

He turned the photograph over and saw a narrative explanation of the photograph. It read:

"Dave and Sarah - Puerto Rico '88."

So, my name is Dave, he thought as he looked into the mirror and saw the unshaven, ruffled face; the same face as was on the photo. Dave who?

He moved around the room trying to find out more of what he should know. He stopped at the sport's jacket hanging on a peg on the door. He put his hand into the inside pocket and grasped a wallet. He took it out and opened it. It had a photograph on the inside cover and a name. it read: Dave Carlson. It went on to give an address and telephone number.

Dave Carlson looked inside the wallet and gasped as he pulled out several fifty-pound notes.

"Holy shit!" he exclaimed and replaced the wallet inside the jacket.

He jumped in shock as the telephone rang. "Hell!" he cursed and crossed over to the phone.

As he went to pick up the receiver, he felt panic invade his mind; a voice telling him not to answer it.

The phone's ringing burned in his ears and eventually he picked it up.

"Hello?" Dave answered.

"What kept you?" demanded a gruff, male voice. "I've been ringing for ages!"

Dave paused a moment, he felt he should know the voice, but the name and face were buried under several lairs of annoyance and near-anger. "I'm dead" his mind said.

"Hello! Are you there? For Christ's sakes!"

"I'm here," Dave said shakily.

"Look, if you can't handle this yourself then I suggest you give me someone else who can! I ain't gonna risk all this!"

Dave recoiled in fright. He felt anger and wanted desperately to shout at the person on the phone. "I'll take care of it! Trust me!" The words blurted out of him before he could think about it.

The voice snorted.

"Where will the meeting take place?"

"Go to the mall, He'll be waiting, Jack's got the mug-shot, be careful and for God sakes, make sure you're not being tailed!" He hung up.

Dave was left holding the receiver. He absently replaced the phone as the pips rang.

Dave walked uncertainly into the living room. There he felt reassurance once again as his mind recognised certain objects. The clock, the suite, the table; they were all familiar to him.

As he moved to sit in what he believed to be his favourite chair, an envelope caught his eye. It was addressed to him. He opened it and began to read:

> If you are reading this, then I assume it has happened. I was told that you would have no recollection of practically any events. I must therefore put down my thoughts and purposes onto paper for you/ me to read later.
>
> My name is Dave Carlson — yes, you! We're an undercover detective working for the L.A.P.D. We were sent to infiltrate a notorious drug ring and try and locate their leaders.
>
> I really don't know if what I am about to tell you will make any sense to you (or me when I become you!). But I feel it is necessary.
>
> As I proceeded to go to the rendezvous to meet the drug dealer who would take me to the drug-lord, I encountered a strange old man. He told me he was what he called a 'Truth-Seer' — a kind of clairvoyant. He told me that if I went to this meeting I would be killed. I told him I didn't have any choice and wanted to go on my way, but there was something magnetic and strange about him, I felt compelled to listen to him, unable to walk away. There was this strange feeling — a compulsion almost that made me want to stay and hang on his every word. You know the feeling when you're with a

beloved old relative from your childhood? That was how he affected me.

Normally I don't listen to such crap (Since you're now me, you'll know what I mean!) but this time I couldn't help but listen. He told me that he knew who I was, who I am, and knew all about me. He told me he understood that I had to go but said I musn't die; that I was vital to something that must happen in years to come and that dying now would precipitate a cause and effect that must not happen. He gave me some sort of liquid he had in a small metal flask and made me drink it. I must confess it was the most vile substance I have ever tasted and words are useless to describe it.

Soon after I began to feel some strange effects. The old man told me that I would die this time whilst confronting the drug-lord — nothing could prevent it, but that shortly after I had been killed, I would awaken once more at the beginning of the day that I died. (I know this sounds like a load of crap, but please try and understand! —it's very important)

This note is to let you know what's happening, to try and prepare yourself for it. If you make the same mistakes as I will make, then we both will go on living this same day over and over, we'll never escape this trap I've put us in, and believe me, it is a trap.

I don't know if I did the right thing, maybe I should have let well enough alone and accepted death, but I had to try. I can't tell you what choices I will make as knowing will only make your life — and job — harder, ignorance is the best way.

The only help I can offer you is to go against what you believe — work the opposite way you normally would. I will do things the way I normally would. If you indulge in a paradox of your beliefs, then perhaps that's the right way. Hopefully we will both be allowed to live again, and remember our lives from this point on are in your hands!

Good luck.
Dave.

He replaced the letter in the envelope and pondered its meaning. Was it all some kind of stupid joke? How could two people be the same? The more he thought about it, the more confused he became.

Eventually he returned to the bedroom and after a shower, got dressed in the clothes that were apparently waiting for him. He moved to the briefcase and opened it; inside he found standard police equipment and another note.

The note told him where to go, who to meet, and what he was to do upon arriving. He was relieved to read that it wasn't signed by himself this time, instead it was from a Sergeant Willis.

He dropped the pistol into a holster in his jacket and buttoned it up.

Dave found that the more he worked, the more he could remember. He remembered a vicious looking thug by the name of 'Cat' Michaels — apparently the drug-lord of the South Side.

As he prepared himself for the meeting with 'Cat' Michaels, he felt himself becoming determined to catch this guy and bring him to jail.

Dave checked his watch and saw that it was still half an hour until he met his partner — Jack Brent. He poured himself a cup of coffee and made some toast. Soon he was enjoying his breakfast as he read the newspaper.

Once he was finished, he walked out of the house and into his new Mercedes Benz. He felt familiar with the car's controls as he gunned the engine and drove to the mall. He was amazed to find that he knew exactly where to go.

As he pulled into the street where the multi-storey car park was situated, he noticed Jack leaning casually on the wall. He flagged Dave down. When he pulled over, Dave felt a momentary pang of grief as he saw his partner climb into the passenger seat.

"Rough night was it?" Jack asked as Dave drove up the long road to the car park.

"Sorry?"

Jack winked. "Well, the Sarge said you were kinda weird on the phone, I figured that maybe Sarah was eh, working on you."

"And you're a detective? Jesus!" Dave said with a laugh. He felt comfortable sitting with Jack, he didn't yet know why but knew this was a good man, apparently his best friend.

"Huh, what do you mean by that, smart ass?"

Dave laughed. "You're the smart one, figure it out."

Jack appeared hurt. He shook his head and took out a packet of sandwiches from his pocket. "I must have really screwed up in my last life to end up with you as my partner!" He bit deep into the sandwich.

"Just for once, do you think you could bring something other than egg?" Dave asked, screwing his face up.

"I love egg!"

"I know," sighed Dave, "I smell it every morning."

Jack smiled once again and grew serious. "So, do you think we'll nail this son of a bitch then?"

Dave shrugged. "I really don't know, but I'm sure as hell not leaving without a fight." His mind wandered back to the letter: He said I would die this time whilst confronting the drug-lord!

Dave chewed his lip. Does that mean I'll die today?

He thought about the imagery he had witnessed when looking at the clock, remembered his friend being killed. Was that Jack? But the picture was gone, and he couldn't remember the image clearly. Maybe I'm just tired.

"Hello? Are you with me?" Jack asked waving his hands in front of Dave's face.

"What? Oh, yeah, sorry," Dave muttered. "What did you say?"

"I said that you just shot past the parking lot."

"Shit!" Dave brought the vehicle to a halt. He spun the wheel and headed back the way.

Within a few minutes he had entered the park and stopped in an empty lot. He climbed out of the car and walked towards the lift, with Jack beside him.

"So what's the plan?"

Dave shrugged his shoulders. He was starting to feel a strong sense of De-ja-vu; certain things he was in the process of doing felt very well-known to him. As he walked along the bays, he felt that every car he looked at, he had seen before, but could not place what the next car would be.

As Jack spoke, Dave could almost think the words before Jack said them.

"I think we should check the mall out first. I don't like the idea of walking straight into a trap."

Dave spoke the words that he was so sure he had said before. "No, if we go snooping it'll only make our contact suspicious; we'll have to play it by ear."

Then he thought of Jack's almost certain reply: Okay, but I don't like it!

Jack sighed. "Okay, but I don't like it!"

What the hell is happening to me? Am I going crazy?

"Hey, here he comes!" Jack hissed.

Dave looked up to see a tall, stocky man walk towards him. His jet-black hair hung loosely around his shoulders and his unshaven face contrasted with the hawk-like eyes that lay between the small mouth. A large leather biker-jacket hung casually over his arm, a rock music T-shirt hung over his tattered jeans. The right breast pocket bulged noticeably with a weapon concealed there. Overall his appearance suggested a laid-back appearance, but his walk and posture said otherwise. This was a man to be avoided!

Dave felt rising panic as he saw the man approach, he had to resist from turning and running. He firmly held his ground and looked to Jack. His partner apparently didn't notice the threat from the villain, but Dave knew that Jack would be alert.

As Dave made a visual sweep of the area his heart missed a beat. Standing beside the lift was an old man who Dave felt he knew; felt he had to know!

The old man looked at Dave with such sadness that he feared the old man would break down and cry. The old man looked once more, shook his head slowly and entered the lift.

The note he had found came to Dave's mind in a sudden constriction of fear: The only help I can offer you, is to go against what you believe — work the opposite way you normally would. I will do things the way I normally would. If you indulge in a paradox of your beliefs, then perhaps that's the right way. Hopefully we will both be allowed to live again, and remember our lives from this point on are in your hands!

Dave felt himself begin to panic, his heart pounded, blood thundered in his skull. What would I normally do? He felt his whole life hung in the balance. Should he fire on the approaching man? Or turn and run? He felt fear rise up and threaten to tear him apart. Perspiration stood out on his forehead as the man approached.

He came up beside Dave and smiled, revealing dirty, stained teeth.

"Hi! You're Ben and Jeff, right? The suppliers?"

Jack looked to Dave to let his partner to speak — just as they had agreed.

Dave stood there, unable to speak. He could not swallow pass a constriction in his throat. His heart pounded; his breath came out in short gasps. Past voices and thoughts poured into his mind. He suddenly saw his whole life fly past him at near-light speed.

"I'm Jeff, this is Ben," Jack said suddenly. He shot his friend a side-ways look, concerned by the fear he saw in Dave's eyes.

"What's up with your friend, been indulging on too much of his products?" laughed the dealer.

"Yeah, something like that," Jack said with a weak laugh.

The dealer turned to look at Dave. "That it? You been eating what you're selling?"

Dave looked at him in horror.

"Perhaps we ought to come back later, Ben's a little out of sorts at the moment. His brother was shot last night," Jack said with concern.

The dealer became suspicious. "Yeah, who's his brother? I might know him."

Dave felt panic engulf him, he grabbed Jack by the arm. "We've got to get out of here!"

"What's the matter?" Jack asked angrily. His partner was ruining a whole month's planning.

Dave began to back off. "Come on! He's gonna kill us!"

The dealer saw the panic in Dave's eyes — saw the set up. "Cops!" he spat.

Jack backed off. "Hey! What you talking about? We ain't no cops!"

Dave saw the hand reach for the gun, felt the voices cry out in his mind; saw the end result in his mind. He tried to run but found his legs would not work.

The dealer pulled a gun from his jacket.

"Run!" Jack yelled, he turned and ran, Dave ran also.

Dave heard the gun go off, turned, and saw the head of his best friend explode in a shower of blood. The briefcase fell to the ground.

Dave saw the briefcase fall, bent to pick it up. Wait! he thought. That's it! I picked up the briefcase last time.

Dave ran as fast as he could away from the gunman, leaving the briefcase. His laughter rang out in a frenzied mixture of laughs and whimpers.

He ran and ran, bullets whistled past him. As he rounded the corner he laughed in joy. "I'm free!" he yelled. "Free!"

He ran out onto the street, turned, and saw the gunman curse and turn away, replacing the gun in his jacket as he did so.

So preoccupied with his thoughts was Dave, that he failed to see a large pickup truck screech round the corner. He ran onto the road, only vaguely aware of a screech of brakes, he lowered his head and let out a faint gasp. The truck slammed into him, throwing him into the air, and across the street, he crashed through the glass front of a shop called Second chances. The irony was not lost on him as he saw his vision go dark.

The last thoughts he was aware of, were of many voices talking about him. The last picture he saw was that of a very familiar old man standing in front of him.

All the other sights and sounds fell away and he saw only the old man.

The old man did the sign of a cross over his chest and turned away. Dave felt all hope leave him as he heaved his final breath and the cold darkness of death embraced him...

He awoke to immediate chaos within his mind, so much that he almost fell into unconsciousness again as the multitude of feelings and memories all cried out for attention at once. He grappled with his mind for control, fighting constantly with the darkness that hung on the very edge of his awareness. It took several minutes for his mind to accept the fact that he concentrated on above all others: He was alive!

The Ugly Little Statue

I have been asked by so many during the course of the last three weeks to recount what happened. So for those who want to know, for those who have to know and for those who really don't care but might read on anyway then here is my story.

It all started the day I took possession of the artefact in question. Though at the time considering it a somewhat strange gift that was the only thought I gave to it. Looking back now I can honestly say had I known the true extent and truth I have no doubt I would have destroyed the accursed thing on the spot. Though all I can say now is that it was ignorance and a little bit of pride that made me keep it, after all, it is a rare occurrence in itself that my Great Uncle Matthew should contact me, let alone send me a gift.

My mother had often expressed her disgust at my Great Uncle, though I'm not sure disgust would be the right word. Less than hatred and a little more than simple annoyance. "Keep away from that old trouble-maker!" she would often say. There were pictures of all my relatives on the huge mantelpiece in my mother's house, all except Great Uncle Matthew, I only heard of him through my grandmother who took great delight in telling me all about how Uncle Matthew got into trouble when he was little. Although after the Great Scandal even she made no further reference to him beyond that point. I was not even privy to what the Great Scandal was, though judging from Grandmother's stories, this had to be an almighty one for eve her to stop talking of him.

So, as you can imagine it came as a considerable shock when, one winter's night there came a knock upon my door. Upon answering, I discovered, upon the step, a small gift. Accompanying the gift was a short note. It read:

> Well my boy,
>
> It saddens me greatly to think that we have never met, and wounds me further to realise that we shall never cross paths, because by the time you receive this letter I shall be dead. My final instructions - to deliver this letter and gift to you upon my death.

I have no doubt in my mind that you will have heard terrible stories regarding me, the black monster of the family (I would use the term sheep, though your mother would insist upon calling me "Monster" so I save her a little time in christening myself).

Please take this small gift and accept my sincere apologies for a life time's absence.

Yours,

M.

And that was all I ever heard from him, a quick call to London verified that he had indeed passed away and was already buried as was his request.

Which lead me to the gift he had bestowed upon me. Unwrapping the unbelievably heavy object, I was astonished to discover that it was a solid iron statue bearing resemblance to the most repulsive looking little man I have ever laid my eyes upon. A trip to the library bore fruit when after much research I discovered that it was in fact a little hob-goblin.

I had thought of discarding the ugly thing as to be honest the beady eyes; the eerie grin and the downright ugliness of the thing continued to repulse me, though the pride I mentioned earlier took me - I had received a gift from Uncle Matthew, and to my knowledge no other ever had. So, I kept it. It took pride of place upon my fire place. I kept an open fire and placed the thing next to it, near the grate. The flickering fire gave it an almost life-like appearance, and he seemed to dance and move in the glow of the flames.

The first night nothing at all happened. I went to bed at ten thirty sharp. I believe I read until around eleven before drifting off to sleep. Upon waking the next morning everything was as I had left it the night before. The little statue still stood guard over my fire place, staring and grinning at me as before.

The second night, however, I was not as fortunate. I was awakened around three am by the smashing of a window. Pulling my robe over me and taking a heavy ornament for protection and use as a possible weapon, I descended the stairs to the sitting room. There, I saw the curtains billowing around the shattered window frame. I cursed loudly and quickly covered the offending hole with a large piece of wood located in my shed. I was on my way back to bed when something drew my attention to the fire place; there lay an empty space, previously occupied by my Uncle Matthew's statue. I recalled that I had not closed the curtains on account of it having been a pleasant enough evening and, as the fire was still glowing, the statue would have been visible to any one passing by my window, it had not even occurred to me to have the thing valued. Cursing my misfortune I returned to my bed, fully believing that someone was now much better off. Imagine my surprise when I awoke the next morning to find the statue once more sitting on my fire place. I recounted my story to my dear friend Walter Bingley whom I met in our usual haunt for morning coffee. Upon the climax of my story he laughed.

"Old boy, I do believe you ought to lay off the whisky!"

"Walter, I'm telling you, it happened!" I insisted. The thought that I had dreamed the whole thing was simply not possible. Besides, there was still the broken window to support my claim.

"Some drunkard smashed the window on his way past. You came down to investigate and simply did not see your horrible, little statue," offered my friend.

I considered his suggestion carefully and eventually concluded he must be correct.

"Besides," he said, "If I were you, and it is indeed as ugly a little statue as you suggest, I'd place it outside with a 'Please take away' sign upon the wretched thing."

Laughing in return, placed the whole thing into memory and tried to forget all about it. That is, until the next night it was once again gone. I heard a noise from downstairs and went to investigate, seeing nothing untoward, I cast my wary eye to the fire place and saw once more the statue missing!

"This is getting beyond the joke!" I believe I said at the time. Then, suddenly I heard a loud bang coming from the door; I turned sharply and let out a startled gasp. There, by the door, was my statue, full as life and moving! Moving of its own accord. The up until now cast iron limbs had now become fully articulate, and the small figure was for all intents and purposes now trying to reach for the handle, upon hearing my startled cry it scurried under the settee.

Ridiculous as it may seem, the only thing I could possibly think to do was to call out, "Hello?"

The statue stopped and there followed a moment of silence.

"Come out, please," I called, scarcely able to believe that I was trying to communicate with my little statue.

There was then a little scurrying of small feet and the statue appeared from under the settee. It raised its small hand to its mouth and let out a tiny high pitched hiccough.

Smiling at the absurdity of the situation, I knelt down beside it. "Hello," I ventured.

The little man smiled, the iron of his face simply rippling from stern conservation to a toothy little grin, quite a strange sight to witness. "Hello," he replied in a peculiar, high pitched voice.

I pondered my next statement for a few moments, unable to think of anything to say, I only managed, "What exactly are you?"

The little statue threw its head back and laughed, a quiet high little squeak, not dissimilar to that of a mouse. "What do you think I am?" it asked.

Over the course of my strange conversation it transpired that my statue was, for want of a better word, a little pixie. I decided then that I would not reveal this little man to any one, not even my best friend Walter. The pixie and I agreed that if any one came to my home then he would act only as a statue. We shook on it, his little hand managing only to grip the end of my thumb.

So, for several days I enjoyed playing and talking with my little Pinocchio. I even recounted the tale of the wooden puppet who became a boy, my new found friend howled with laughter, though he refused to answer any questions regarding his origins or his life, insisting at all times that "men are not yet ready".

My life, though now a little stranger, began to return to normal. Or so I thought. Late on Friday evening I received a call from the local constable. He looked troubled and so I invited him in, gave him a hot cup of Earl Grey, for it was bitterly cold outside. Once suitably thawed, I enquired what I could do for him.

"Do you know this man?" he asked me, showing me a picture.

I recognised the face at once as belonging to our convenience shop owner, "Why, yes. It's Donald MacPherson. Is he in trouble?" I asked.

"I'm afraid, sir, he's dead," replied the constable.

"Dead?" I asked in horror. Donald and I were quite friendly, he would often visit me after work or we'd meet up in Maggie's bar on occasional weekends.

"How?" I asked.

"He was found dead outside his shop," replied the constable, "it appears as though he was murdered."

"Murdered?" I whispered. "He had not an enemy in the world! Who would do such a thing to the poor old gentleman?"

"I was hoping you would be able to shed some light upon the matter, sir. So far everyone I've talked to says you were his closest friend. Do you know of any reason someone may have wished him harm?"

I shook my head. "I wouldn't say we were friends, Officer, true enough we'd share a word or maybe a drink or two. Donald was really a private man; ever since his dear wife passed away we began to see very little of him." I sighed then. "As to your question regarding wishing him harm – No, Donald was well liked, did right by everyone he knew. Why, that fellow didn't have a bad word to say about any one."

"I was told that a Mr Mike Garvey had a little run in with him just the other day," said the constable. "Are you familiar with this gentleman?"

"Mr Garvey? Yes, Donald told me about that only yesterday; it was just a little argument over credit. Apparently Mr Garvey requested an extension to his already mounting bill. I do believe that Donald flatly refused, and rightfully so, Mr Garvey is a gentleman well known for his penury, and his reluctance to settle a bill. Though that was typical of Donald and he would help men all he could, I believe that he had finally reached his limit with Mr Garvey. I would not have considered that sufficient grounds for violence."

My answers appeared to satisfy the good constable for he left shortly thereafter, thanking me for the tea and for my help. I attended poor Donald's funeral two days past his unfortunate demise.

That was not to be my last funeral, however. Over the course of the next several weeks there followed a spate of unsolved murders, mostly against the older members of my little town. Each time I was called upon to answer various questions. Almost overnight I had become the town's authority on local history. It became clear over the course of these quite bloody weeks that young Mr Garvey was not in fact the culprit for he was under firm lock and key during the time the last three murders were committed.

It was upon the Tuesday of the third week that I received a letter from my Grandmother. Now I feel it important to mention that the dear old soul had been admitted to the town's sanatorium some years earlier and as a result was not considered a source of reliable information. The letter read:

> My dearest child,
>
> News has reached me of the hideous murders now taking place. Get out of there at once! I implore you, child! You are not safe there! It's his curse, you hear! You must take what family you have and flee! Do not look back! I can only believe that I too shall suffer the same fate as dear old Donald! For come for me he must!
>
> Go, now. I implore you to abandon me and this town. Talk to no one lest he find you and kill you too.
>
> With hope,
>
> Grandma.

Convinced that the poor old dear was under the spell of some delusional state I am sorry to say I paid no heed whatsoever to the letter, though I did make a few enquiries as to who "He" was. To my knowledge no one in my family had ever been spoken off as having laid a curse.

My life carried on as normal for much of the week. I went off to work, went to the local bar with what friends remained and answered the questions the constable asked. Although we were still no closer to finding who the murderer was. Or indeed what his motives were.

The big break so to speak occurred on Thursday evening. I was in bed once again curled up with a cup of tea and a good book when my little statue friend appeared, as he had been doing for a while, on the end of my bed.

"What are you reading?" he asked in his tiny voice.

I held up the hard-backed book and let him read it.

"Treasure Island." He chuckled. "I once read that too," he said.

I laughed. "You can read?"

"Oh, very well, my friend," he said cheerfully, "there are a great many things I can do. A great many, why I bet there are things I can do that even you cannot."

"Like become a statue," I said, mockingly. He looked at me then, a strange way which seemed to convey malice. His eyes narrowed to mere slits and he flashed a toothy grin. The experience was none too pleasant.

"I'm talking human things, my friend. Dark things you may not even think of in your darkest, most secretive of dreams."

I must admit that although his words and actions chilled me to my very bones he had piqued my curiosity, and I asked him to explain further, when all of a sudden there came a knock at my door. Pulling on my dressing gown I hurried to the door. There, stood the local constable whom I had befriended and two of his colleagues. Immediately I noticed a change in his manner. For one, the friendly smile had been replaced with a stern frown and distrustful gaze.

"You are under arrest," he said officially. I believe he then read me my rights.

"Under what charge, sir?" I cried.

"The charge of murder in the first degree," he replied without emotion, and out came the handcuffs

I cried my innocence. Here I was being accused of the very murders I had attempted to assist the police with!

I must admit I am sketchy as to what happened next, as in my panicked state I fell into brain fever. I do recall being allowed to dress myself where upon I was then escorted to the police station and bundled into a cell. I must have yelled my innocence a dozen times, while running a gauntlet of emotions from fear to confusion to near anger at this slur against me. So I sat down to await further answers.

I received none. In fact, all I received was a bowl of porridge, cold, and a cup of tepid water in the morning followed by several more questions. It transpired that I had been under suspicion for quite a long time. Evidently the officers, after conducting a thorough search of my home had uncovered several letters supposedly by all the murder victims begging for a variety of favours. They ranged from asking me not to hurt them to cries for help and asking me for forgiveness.

I heartily claim to having never laid eyes upon any of the letters, however my cries fell upon deaf ears for no one chose to believe me. I was led off to court the following morning. (Since there was very little crime in my quaint little town the Assizes were seldom busy).

The outcome of my trial was: Guilty of murder in the first degree. Thirteen counts. I was to be taken back to my cell, fed and prepared for a public execution to be carried out the following Monday morning at eleven am.

Desperate, I acquired some paper and a pen and wrote to whomever I could think of; fathers, wives, friends of my so-called victims begging them to help me. Imagine my surprise when a few of them turned up. Instead of assisting me they either spat at me or yelled at me, I was even given a few letters that I was accused of having written. The contents of many of them promised dire retribution against them for crimes against my family.

I was horrified! Never in my whole life have I ever written so uncouth and vicious letters like the ones I was seeing, signed with perfect clarity in my signature, even down to the way I always cross sign my letter T's.

It was on Sunday night that I was to finally solve the murders; the answer came to me while I slept.

Hearing a metallic noise I looked down. There upon the floor, by the bars stood my little statue friend. He was smiling at me.

"Well, well, about to be punished, are we?" he asked.

I nodded dumbly. "They think I committed the murders," I said. "They honestly believe I killed all those people! It is entirely egregious!"

The statue nodded. "I know, I'm sorry about that."

I thanked him for his altruistic concern.

He laughed then, a cold, calculating laugh that once again chilled me.

"You have no idea who I am, do you?"

I shook my head, becoming more and more fearful.

"How sad I am, how sad it is that my Great nephew should grow up to become such a dullard!"

Realisation hit me painfully in the chest, almost knocking the wind out of me. Before I could respond he nodded. "That's right, son. I am your Great Uncle Matthew!"

"But... but...How?" I stammered.

"A long time ago, son, I was tried and convicted for my so-called crimes. Donald MacPherson and several others formed a lynch mob, they attacked my home, burned down my study and destroyed all my work and research! And they beat me. Oh how they beat me!"

"Why?" I managed.

"Why? They believed me to be conspiring with the very devil himself. They could not see my research for what it was - a brilliant feat of evolution!" The upraised arms of the small statue looked almost ridiculous. "I was working on a way to prolong life! To beat death! Yet those fools could not see past the sacrifices that were necessary. In order to save all a few must perish!"

He talked then about how he was going to save the human race from death; to banish ageing.

Then, he turned and stared at me with those metal eyes. "They left me for dead. Thanks to their wretched beating I lost my right arm- hacked off in a savage attack!

"I lost my speech when they stabbed me through the throat, severing my vocal chords. My sight left me where they tore my eye out!

"I was horrifically burned when they set fire to my study before running off to leave me in the midst of that terrific fire! But I escaped! Oh the pain; the agony!"

He paused and shook his little head. "I left this little town, sending them all a message, a curse! Telling them that one-day I would return to wreak my revenge and look at how I got that revenge!"

I sat there, totally stunned by what he was telling me. It transpired then that he had abandoned all research into his anti-ageing process and instead turned his remarkable mind to planning his revenge. Apparently it took him the remainder of his life.

Turning then, he locked those cold, metal eyes on me with such intensity I thought I may fall into them he smiled, a cold and weak smile. "I took up reading the dark chapters themselves. I learned all there is to know of the occult and dark rituals. I transformed my very existence!" He smiled then and I believe I witnessed a look of fear in those iron eyes. His next words were barely audible and I had to strain myself to hear. "I made a pact, Great Nephew, with the darkest, most evil of them all! I was given this body in return for my eternal soul. It was the only way I could complete my life's task!"

"Why me?" I demanded then, I felt as though I were on the edge of insanity. Each word he spoke drove me ever closer to that deep chasm. Down and down into darkness my mind fell, as he spoke his blasphemous words.

"I needed one more sacrifice," he said sadly. "I was refused the right to keep this all to myself. I tried to save you, my dear boy, but The Devil himself laid down the rules."

I shook my head in horror, unable to speak, so my demonic friend continued unabated: "He returned me to this realm as this!" He indicated himself, "as this statue. I had to present it to someone, and that someone had to accept it into their home, and then had to accept me, then and only then could I carry out my fiendish raison d'être." He then climbed up and laid his tiny metal hand on my larger fleshy one. "You lose only your life, my nephew. I lose my very soul. When you die this morn, I shall complete my long journey. I shall descend to the pits of hell where there I shall forever stay, slave to the very embodiment of Evil."

That was the point I believe I actually lost my mind. Screaming with rage I took up the statue and hurled it with all my might against the stone wall. As it left my hand it once more became a solid statue. It struck the wall with an almighty force and fell to the ground. The right arm broke away, the neck split slightly and one of the inset metal eyes rolled free."

The guard suddenly appeared and yelled: "Hey! Quiet I'm there! Others are trying to sleep!"

I sobbed and pointed at the statue. "Officer, get that out of here! Please!"

He turned to where my statue lay. Then looked at me with a quizzical look. "Get what out of here?"

"That!" I yelled, pointing, "the statue! Please get it out of here!"

The guard looked once more to where I pointed, shot me a very strange look before shaking his head and walking away. What was wrong with him; could he not see it lying there as dead as stone? I believe I cried long into what remained of my last night. I never went near that statue again. I lay there, I stood, I fell, I prayed, replaying the event over and over in my shattered mind.

Did I make the whole thing up? Did I create this fantastic tale in order to plead sanity and perhaps escape death that way?

That is up to you to judge, for as I write these final words that represent my epitaph, I can hear the lock turning and the murmured voices of a priest and guard in muted conversation on their way to lead me out to my gallows…

Other Works By This Author

For The Latest Information On

New Releases

&

Coming Soon

Please Visit

JasamiPublishingLtd.com

Poetry

Following are
two poems from Andrew's collection

My Villanelle

What a terrible thing, is insight.
What would happen if you only knew
Now I'm losing this fight!

I've tried and tried, and still it's not right
But more than anything, I want a life with you
What a terrible thing, is insight.

It's getting harder now, try as I might
To accept what I must just to stay true
Now I'm losing this fight!

I scream and I cry and I hold on tight!
I don't know what else I can possibly do
What a terrible thing, is insight.

I thought about talking and telling tonight
But it's better I don't, for me and for you
Now I'm losing this fight.

Maybe I'll just shut up and act all polite.
For if I got it wrong, perhaps you did too!
What a terrible thing, is insight
Now I'm losing this fight.

Andy 06.08.21

Lockdown Two

I am no longer the same
Changed, deranged.
Altered
Covid 19
We changed.

What happened when the world stopped?
Everyone, everything disappeared
The silence from venues, from clubs, from pubs, from people.
Played far louder than any music ever did
And we live lives vicariously, while social media makes cyranoids of us all.

Mum!

I need a cuddle
But fears of matricide cloud my Stockholm.
So this time I hide away through love and not through regurgitated teenage angst.

We sit indoors and watch empty streets dream
Of rolling tyres and of socially boiling kettles, of footballs bounding over dividing walls.

Four months in and I don't want to go back
I have become chelonian, and now I hide.
Out there - too full of people.
And they all demand an interaction I no longer want.
So I parade mysophobia as my excuse.

Coronavirus, Covid 19 - our pandemic.
Generations will talk of the time we stopped
We shut down the world to save the world.
People died, politicians lied, and nature took a moment.
But soon, all too soon, we'll forget what we saw.

And walk blindfolded and dazed into a past-oriented future; to chase the money and to forget those we missed and yearned for as we stand shoulder to shoulder and neck deep in twenty first century myths.

Tom? Tom who?

Exactly!

Candles and claps - all forgotten
As we are lured by summer sun and fleeting fads
And dreams of far away beaches bury our fears in their sand.

Can we forget?

I don't want to go back.
Do you?

Andy 01.04.21

About the Author

In addition to his poetry, Andy has always been a voracious reader and keen storyteller, and as this anthology shows, has never been confined to one genre, and cites Horror, Sci-fi, Crime & Thriller as being among his favourites.

Andy lives in Moodiesburn with his wife and family and when not reading or writing can be heard often playing guitar and bass guitar and when alone describes himself as "the best singer in the room!"

Words of wisdom from the author...

"I love how a good book, or tale can lift you right out of your seat and take you to an infinite number of other fantastically wonderful worlds."

Printed in Great Britain
by Amazon

11645470R00119